IRON BALLOONS

IRON BALLOONS

*Hit Fiction from Jamaica's
Calabash Writer's Workshop*

EDITED BY

COLIN CHANNER

AKASHIC BOOKS
NEW YORK

Published by Akashic Books
©2006 Colin Channer/Calabash International Literary Festival

ISBN-13: 978-1-933354-05-7
ISBN-10: 1-933354-05-4
Library of Congress Control Number: 2005934824

First printing

Grateful acknowledgment is made to Peepal Tree Press for permission to reprint "Marley's Ghost" by Kwame Dawes, which first appeared in *A Place to Hide* by Kwame Dawes (Peepal Tree Press, 2002); "Sugar" by Sharon Leach originally appeared in *Stories from Blue Latitudes: Caribbean Women Writers at Home and Abroad*, edited by Elizabeth Nunez and Jennifer Sparrow (Seal Press, 2006).

Photograph of Colin Channer by Joan Chan.

Akashic Books
PO Box 1456
New York, NY 10009
Akashic7@aol.com
www.akashicbooks.com

To youuuuuuuu . . . dis one dedicated to youuuuuuuu . . .

Editor's Acknowledgments

One day, when I'm really rich, I'll give each of the following people a 60GB iPod fully programmed with their favorite music: Kwame Dawes, Justine Henzell, Roger Brown, Mervyn Morris, Geoffrey Philp, Kaylie Jones, Johnny Temple, the forty writing fellows who entered the first Calabash Writer's Workshop in 2003, Russell Banks, David Winn, Chris Abani, Marie Brown, Junot Díaz, Dr. Edison O. Jackson—President of Medgar Evers College, Dr. Elizabeth Nunez—Chairperson of the college's English Department, and Professors Gregory Pardlo, Linda Jackson, Nellie Rosario, and Tom Bradshaw—the creative writing team.

Addis and Makonnen, my American children, oonoo yardie faada love oonoo. Eternal Father bless our land.

Thanks be to Jah.

Table of Contents

Introduction
THE KINGSTON 12 OVERTURE
by Colin Channer

If I wanted to be safe, dear reader, I'd begin by sharing lovely and interesting facts about the stories in this book. After that, I'd become quite grave and academic when I talked about the book itself—about what gap it fills, what discourse it furthers, what development it traces, call it a radical . . . *something*, and hang it on a branch of a thematic tree.

In short, dear reader, I'd try to justify why you should be holding this book so closely, close enough to read. *Iron Balloons* is an anthology. Compared to novels and memoirs and collections of verse, anthologies are the ugly sisters of the literary world.

But I won't speak for *Iron Balloons*. It's a collection of outstanding fiction, and good fiction speaks for itself. The writing in this book knows how to grab and hold attention, how to keep it going once your interest has been lit. In short, it knows how to seduce, so it doesn't need an editor to play the spinster aunt, to speak on its behalf and set it up.

It has charisma, depth, and character. A voice that keeps you listening. An intellect that shines. A shape that you can sense beneath its clothes.

Set mostly on the island of Jamaica, but narrated in a continental range of moods and tones, the stories in *Iron Balloons* are unified by setting, but also by their connection to the Calabash Writer's Workshop, where many of them were born. Some were born to students; some were born to tutors; and some, through close editing, were born to both.

The name "Calabash Writer's Workshop" has a fancy ring, which might give you the impression that we spent our days in alternating modes of lounging and carousing at a nicely renovated farmhouse with its own organic garden and a pond—what some city people in America think of when you say "upstate." I say *some* because the word also refers to jail.

The truth is, we had our workshops in a house without a roof in Kingston; not the one beside the Hudson River in New York, but the oddly scary and alluring one that keeps on spreading in defiance of its geographic borders—tall green mountains in the back, and in front a big polluted harbor, the water macho gray in blunt refusal to assume the sissy turquoise of the tourist traps that dot the Caribbean Sea. The one where I (and I) was born.

However, things were not as bad as I just made them seem. We held the workshops in what today is quite a spiffy mansion right behind Vale Royal, the Prime Minister's official home, a gabled eighteenth-century house. When we first saw the place that would become our home, we were struck by its landscape of wise old trees that seemed to stand in judgment, the gracious dip of its sunken lawn the size and shape of an Olympic pool, and the practical potential of its side cottage with two bathrooms, a full kitchen, and a tiled veranda decorated with potted plants and rough-hewn chairs from Mexico with puffy leather seats.

But the cottage also had a tenant. On top of this, the mansion was undergoing tedious renovation. It was a husk. A shell with no windows, roof, nor doors. But it was big and beautiful, and was easy for all forty students and four teachers to reach. And if we played our cards correctly, we knew, it would be free. In the end, it was. And for this we're grateful to its owner, Roger Brown, who instructed his workers to make sure that we'd have at least a temporary floor.

When I say *we,* I mean the Calabash International Literary Festival Trust, a not-for-profit organization founded in Jamaica in 2001 "to transform the literary arts in the Caribbean by being the region's best-managed producer of workshops, seminars, and performances."

Our producer, Justine Henzell, was the person who got the house and supervised the team of volunteers who set up rented tables and chairs. The twenty fiction writers worked inside the house. An equal complement of poets worked outside in pools of lignum vitae shade. The tenant? Justine spoke to him as well, and he was kind enough to go away for weekends whenever we were there.

If you somehow got through Mr. Brown's big gate, especially if you did so at lunchtime, and, more importantly, if you were someone who had no idea how writing workshops operate or, on the contrary, someone with a tightly fixed idea of how they should, you might have gotten the impression that you'd stumbled on a group of idle people who were simply hanging out—and you would have been half right. *Half* right, because we were hanging out, yes, but in productive ways.

First off, we were the *right* mix of people hanging out, students with the desire to learn, and teachers with the understanding that only a part of what it takes to be a fiction writer can be transmitted through instruction—mainly the mechanics; the other part, what one could call the feel, or instinct, is learned by catching on.

Hanging out creates the context and the opportunity for catching on. The best writers are unbelted martial artists who've served a long apprenticeship in verbal jabbing, sly exaggeration, and the scrappy but effective sparring known as "talking shit," all of which are well-established story-telling forms with native modes of dialogue, narrative voice, character, characterization, plot, and point of view. Although their value may be hard for outsiders to discern, these styles of mental *capoeira* develop and in turn depend on high levels of agility, strength, and grace in a range of vital skills, including pacing, rhythm, pitch, description, and painting with symbolic language. When you combine these skills with magic, good luck, and in-born gifts, you get stories that people want to experience over and over again. You get hits— hits like Marlon James's *John Crow's Devil* (Akashic Books, 2005).

Marlon was admitted to our basic fiction writing work-shop in 2003. Two years later he would publish a debut novel that went on to be a finalist for both a *Los Angeles Times* Book Award and the Commonwealth Writers' Prize (Caribbean Region). Does it get much better than that?

The Jamaican music industry was built on hits. It was also built on hanging out. We knew this. So can you imagine our pride when a musician friend of ours came to visit and remarked that the workshop had "the magic vibe of Studio One, Joe Gibbs, or Federal," the Jamaican equals of Motown, Stax, and Mussel Shoals?

The workshop had the feeling of an old Jamaican studio by accident as much as by design. Like me, festival programmer Kwame Dawes, who taught poetry to the senior group, knows and respects Jamaican music and the folks who've worked to make it a global success. Among Kwame's many published works are *Natural Mysticism: Towards a New Reggae Aesthetic* (Peepal Tree Press, 1999), which makes a compelling case for reggae as a literary model, and spotlights my first novel *Waiting in Vain* (One World/Ballantine Books, 1998) as a refined example; and *Bob Marley: Lyrical Genius* (Sanctuary Books, 2002), the first major critical study of the songwriter's work.

But on top of this, we had a lot of common sense. As such, we didn't feel the need to be obedient to conventional models when we conceptualized a workshop for our literary trust. There was very little searching, really, or long debates. The choices were instinctive. They were also pragmatic. In Jamaica, the music model has worked—has managed to develop from fragile beginnings to become a biosphere with a continuous cycle that allows new talent in the hundreds to sprout up each year and grow—and the literary model has failed.

The Jamaican literary establishment—despite the fact that its members have traditionally come from the educated middle class, and despite the fact that it has produced some solid writers, including John Hearne, Roger Mais, Vic Reid,

Erna Brodber, Velma Pollard, Andrew Salkey, Louise Bennett, Olive Senior, and Neville Dawes—has never been able to truly establish itself with relevance outside the academic world, guarantee its survival by creating either a devoted local readership or a mechanism to nurture new talent and future growth, or create an industry in anything more than name.

The very fact that one can now speak of a Jamaican music establishment speaks to the success of its membership, whose origins are almost exclusively poor and working class. What makes its success all the more stunning is that a musical establishment—in the sense of an identifiable set of working artists with the economic power and social influence to shape what people think about, read about, and imitate—did not exist before the mid 1970s.

From the beginning of the local industry in the 1950s till then, the standard of living of the most skilled and highly paid Jamaican singers and musicians barely measured up to that of a civil servant, teacher, or nurse.

A great leap in earnings would be triggered in the early 1970s, when Chris Blackwell's London-based Island Records re-entered the Jamaican market, where it had been founded in 1959.

There are many interesting facts about the label's re-entry, but what is most fascinating to me in the moment of this writing is how much the industry had changed in the intervening years, how much it had developed with almost no investment from overseas in barely more than ten years. Jamaican businesspeople, many of them owners of bars and liquor stores, had invested their own time and money to build retail outlets, wholesale distributors, pressing plants, mastering labs, and recording studios (often in the very same location); but almost none of this investment would have come—it would not have been justified—if the talent pool to produce a vast amount of good music wasn't there.

By the time Island Records signed the Wailers in 1972, the Jamaican industry had produced the likes of Bob Andy, The Heptones, Delroy Wilson, Ken Boothe, and The Paragons, and it kept on producing acts of international note, some of whom joined Island Records as well. These include Third World, Inner Circle, Black Uhuru, Burning Spear, and Gregory Isaacs. In the early '80s, Herb Alpert's A&M Records signed perhaps the most influential reggae singer to date, Dennis Brown. The momentum has continued to the present day, as evidenced by the careers of home-based performers with international careers, such as Bounty Killer, Beenie Man, Junior Gong, Morgan Heritage, Elephant Man, and Sean Paul.

In contrast, there is almost no book publishing industry to speak of in Jamaica today, outside the specialized areas of education and law. Today, I cannot think of ten established, active, home-based novelists, memoirists, or poets below the age of sixty-five. Those who I can identify are the remnants of a small group that came of age before independence in 1962—more than forty years ago—yet Jamaican music is increasing its local and global relevance every single day. Dancehall reggae is hiphop's only bona fide competition for the hearts and minds of urban youth around the world, and its global march seems to have increased its local pull.

What explains the difference in fates? There are several

obvious reasons, most significantly the island's history of illiteracy and poverty. This has limited the amount of people who can actually read, the popularity of reading for leisure, and the habit of reading beyond the world of the essentials (like newspapers).

But one of the key reasons for the differing fortunes of the two industries is fundamentally related to the architectural structures and related social models that defined the mode of development that each one pursued. Jamaican literature followed the structural model of the university, the salon, and the club, which worked very well in Britain—and is continuing to work for Jamaican writers living in the U.K., Canada, and the United States—while Jamaican music developed along the lines of the tenement yard. The more inclusive model won.

Most of the great Jamaican recording studios were based in converted houses with concrete or dirt yards where the lawns used to be, and although their gates were guarded by what are now legendary roughneck men, their owners understood that there was something to be gained by having lots of people with a love of music hanging out and milling round—that a vital energy could be created from the chemistry of a well-selected crowd.

The Jamaican industry exploded in the 1960s in part because the early studios allowed a lot of people with extraordinary talent to serve apprenticeships with established artists. Most of this apprenticeship took place out in the yard.

The yard was the garden where the talent grew. In one corner, you'd see some talent learning how to sing in three-part harmony. In another, some were learning how to play guitar. Underneath a guinep tree, dance moves were being rehearsed. Inside, another set were watching a session going down, wondering when they'd get their turn. But everyday, while all of this was going on, there'd be some *lyming* (hanging out)—and this is how the spirit of the music was absorbed, how apprentices both learned and caught on.

At Studio One, the most famous of them all, you never got a chance to cut a tune until a veteran said to owner and producer Clement Dodd, "Ah t'ink 'im ready, y' know."

When a veteran at Studio One declared that you were ready, it meant that you were in possession of a song worth singing, that you'd found and polished your voice, that enough people in the yard had heard you singing and thought you were good, and that people where you lived and in the yard had begun to greet you with the title "Singer" instead of your regular name. All of this together meant that you were ready to break out, or, as Jamaicans say, ready "fo' bus'." And things are pretty much the same today.

So, the last thing you want to be as a Jamaican singer is an *iron balloon*. Why? Because "iron balloon cyaah [can't] bus'."

If you've been going to the studio for a very long time without earning the chance fo' bus', or if you've gotten chance after chance but you just can't bus', then you're a certified iron balloon.

The student writers in this book have all been working hard in relative isolation for a number of years without getting the chance fo' bus'. But see—dem bus' now. They've been published by one of planet's most well-regarded independent publishers, and, on top of this, in the company of prize-winning authors like Elizabeth Nunez, Kwame Dawes, and Kaylie Jones.

I can't prevent myself from wondering how the students' lives would have been different if Jamaica were a different place, one where writing talent had the chance to prosper in a vital world of opportunity, like the one inherited by singers and musicians from their industrious, forward-thinking peers.

If this had happened, the world of literature would be a different place. According to the *Guinness Book of World Records,* the island of Jamaica produces the most records per capita in the world, a fact that isn't contradicted by anything I've ever heard or seen.

This is fantastic. It says a lot about the lyrical ingenuity, entrepreneurial drive, and technical know-how of the island's people. But it's also tragic. For it means that hundreds, even thousands of Jamaican novels, plays, and poems have been kidnapped in the mind over the last forty-something years and pressed into service as three-minute songs.

It's especially tragic when you consider that Jamaicans are the most gifted storytellers in the world.

Sure, people talk about the literary genius of the Irish. Their legacy is great. I'll give them that. But I don't think the Irish are as *naturally* gifted as Jamaicans. What the Irish have in addition to their talent is a longer history—specifically, a longer history of literacy, access to publishing, and freedom to express themselves with the printed word. So frankly speaking, if you're going to judge both countries on achievement, the Irish win hands down. Joyce alone could take our crew with *Ulysses* alone. Just one lick—*boof*—and we all fall down.

But Joyce was not just gifted. He was born in a place

where being a writer was not merely possible; it was valued. He was born into the kind of world that Jamaican singers and musicians have made for themselves. For Joyce, the possibility of becoming a successful, published writer was concrete. So the meaningful comparison isn't between Vic Reid and James Joyce. If you want a meaningful comparison, you'd need to sit in at a whiskey bar in Ireland then come and visit a Jamaican ghetto "corner" when a yout' with a name like Deebo or Drop Kick is about to "give a drama" . . . or simply drop by an East Kingston rum shop.

We established the Calabash Writer's Workshop for a single reason: to help more Jamaican writers get published— by more presses, in more countries, more often. We also wanted them to be published in more forms and genres, from more points of view. We still do.

As such, to get into our workshops you must compete. You must send in a manuscript. It's the only thing that counts. If your writing gets you in, you pay nothing. If it doesn't get you in, we're sorry—you can't just buy your way.

The teachers lead the workshops for the love of it. None of us get paid. This point is even more remarkable when you consider that all but one of us come from overseas. When we come to Jamaica for our three-day intensives, we don't stay in hotels. Calabash can't afford it. We stay with family and friends and put the savings to good use. What would go to accommodation goes to things like putting out a daily spread in case we have some students with a lot of talent but not enough to eat. It's a form of dignity insurance. Having food for everyone allows those in need to benefit in a self-respecting way.

But another rationale is simple joy—the joy of working with the knowledge that a mango slice or melon wedge is just a step or two away, along with hot Blue Mountain coffee, frosty orange juice, and sticky almond buns; the joy of knowing that the cooler has a Red Stripe *and* a Heineken that bear your middle name.

We don't have a lot of money. We don't even have a proper office. But as an organization we believe in certain things. Although all our offerings are free and open to the public, we believe in affirming the personal dignity of everybody we serve. Although we operate in a Third World country, we believe in reaching for the highest global standards. We believe in truth and beauty, in having fun, in breaking rules, in taking chances . . . doing things with style.

The work in *Iron Balloons* and the art direction of the book itself are illustrations of the things that we believe. They also illustrate our commitment to going beyond developing more Jamaican writing talent, to actually getting more Jamaican writers into print.

Iron Balloons is not the debut publication of the Calabash International Literary Festival Trust. In 2005, with the support of the Reed Foundation, we inaugurated the Calabash Chapbook Series, six volumes by student poets: Mbala, Nikki Johnson, Andrew Stone, Saffron, Ishion Hutchinson, and Blakka Ellis. The series editor was Kwame Dawes.

In 2005, we also worked with Peepal Tree Press to co-publish a special Calabash fiftieth-anniversary edition of John Hearne's novel, *Voices under the Window*. And in 2004, we worked with Macmillan Publishing to bring out a fiftieth-anniversary edition of Roger Mais's *Brotherman*. Like *Voices*, *Brotherman* is one of the most important novels in the Jamaican (and wider Caribbean) literary canon, and had fallen out of print. Yet even though *Iron Balloons* is not our first publication, it still holds a special place for us, for many reasons; but the one I'd like to talk about is our collective admiration for its publisher, Akashic Books.

Our emotional involvement with Akashic began in 2002, when I read an article on Cuban writer Daniel Chavarría in the *New York Times*. He sounded really interesting—and believe me, he is. But what really got me hooked was that his publisher was based in Brooklyn.

I'd never heard of Chavarría's publisher although I'd lived in Brooklyn for ten years. So I googled it—Akashic—found it online, tried to call the office just to talk, but there was no phone number on its website.

To me the name *Akashic* sounded slightly cultish, conjured mental images of Satanists who liked to dress up like Hasidic Jews and publish clever books encoded with demonic messages that only showed themselves beneath a special purple light.

So time passed, a year. I forgot about Chavarría and Akashic and went on tour to promote my second novel, *Satisfy My Soul*. Then, in 2003, I met the man I'd thought of as the King of Brooklyn Satanists at Medgar Evers College on a balmy Brooklyn afternoon.

I'd just finished listening to a panel discussion at the National Black Writers Conference and was walking down a crowded passage when I saw a table full of books that had the most compelling titles and designs I'd ever seen. I stopped to look and saw copies of Chavarría's *Adios Muchachos* and *The Eye of Cybele*. I began talking to the guy selling the books and the story in the *New York Times* came up. I mentioned the freaky business about the website with no phone number, and during a casual conversation it came out somehow that the guy was not who I'd suspected—a clerk or intern sent to babysit the books—but Father Akashic Himself.

"What's your name?" I asked.

"Oh. Johnny."

He had one leg crossed over the other and he was smiling, both to me and to himself.

"Johnny what?"

"Johnny Temple."

My first thoughts, in order, were:

1. That's the coolest *effing* name I've heard in a very long time.
2. Why is this white man selling books by mostly non-black writers at the National Black Writers Conference? Doesn't he believe in profits?
3. If what I see here on this table is any indication of what this guy thinks about and champions and values, then the soul of Island Records lives on in Akashic Books.

So we got to talking. He lived in Brooklyn, and I lived in Brooklyn too. He lived in Fort Greene, and I lived in Fort Greene too. He lived on South Oxford Street, and I lived on South Oxford too. Between Atlantic and Hanson Place . . . and I did too.

Oh yes, he lived across the street from me. I know a good thing when I see it, so I made him an offer he couldn't refuse.

"I run this little literary festival in Jamaica by the name of Calabash. Little thing. I think you and Akashic should come next year. Here's what I want you to do. Choose four authors—you don't have to do it now—and tell me who they are and which airport they'd fly out of, and Calabash will pay the bill . . . airfare, accommodation, transfers, a little per diem for expenses."

He said, "You're kidding me."

I said, "No. It's like how we do it in the recording studios down in Jamaica. When you ask a guitarist that you have a feel fo' to come in and give you some licks, what the man does is his t'ing. But that's why you ask him. You want his t'ing."

With animation now, we began to bat ideas back and forth, and somehow it came out that he was into music. Well, more than that. He was a musician in the rock band Girls Against Boys. What instrument? Bass.

"Oh, I play bass too."

Akashic made its first appearance on our program in 2004, with not four, but five authors—Nina Revoyr, Sean Keith Henry, Kaylie Jones, Arnaldo Correa, and Yongsoo Park. Akashic has had a presence on our program every year since.

Like many Calabash-Akashic ventures, *Iron Balloons* began as a telephone call. It happened in the weeks after the festival in 2005. The poets from the workshop had already been published in the Chapbook Series, but we hadn't found a way to get the fiction writers into print. They were disappointed. So was I.

I kept assuring them that something big was going to happen, although I wasn't sure what. I did know that I wasn't going to get them into print in any "mom & pop" way. I also knew that I wouldn't bring them certain opportunities until I was confident that they were really ready fo' bus'.

The decision to get the poets into print before the fiction writers had come after weeks of long discussions by phone with Kwame, who lives in Columbia, South Carolina. It was a conscious decision to bus' the poets first. There were several factors, but in the end it came down to this: They had come into the workshop at a higher level than the fiction writers for reasons that would take too long to explain . . . Okay, I'll explain one of them. An unskilled writer can learn the rudiments of poetry from listening to music. Poems are also, generally speaking, short. As such, more people attempt to write poetry than fiction anywhere you go. In Jamaica, the near complete absence of mechanisms to produce fiction writers further skewed what is a naturally occurring imbalance. It's a numbers game. It's easier to find twenty good poets out of 2,000 than to find ten good fiction writers out of twenty. I'm not saying these are the actual numbers. But I'm sure you get the point.

After working with the fiction writers on developing their stories, I called Johnny Temple when the time was right.

"Hey, Johnny T.," I said, "I have this great idea."

"Oh cool," he said. "What is it?" I told him. He mused, "Oh yeah. I think that could work."

But I didn't understand how much work *I'd* have to do.

I'd never edited an anthology before. They're much more complicated and involved than one would ever think, which is why I have to thank my friend and guide and close collaborator, Kwame "The Godfather" Dawes, who gave me crash courses by phone and e-mail according to my need.

Despite Kwame's guidance, I still lost control of the project at some point because of my obsessive streak. I wasted months just weighing options, slowly chewing every choice until it turned to mush . . . criteria for selection . . . gender balance . . . organizing principle. Blah, blah, blah, blah.

Johnny began to worry. But even when he was worried he was always patient, always understanding, always nice.

When my breakthrough came, it happened the way many of them have come over the last ten years—from something Kwame said. He was talking about a reading he'd done and how well some of his reggae poems had gone over, and he said, "Boy, Channer, you cyaah lose if you trust the reggae every time."

And so I asked myself, what would a great producer do? How would Duke Reid or Coxsone Dodd choose material for a great LP? What would King Tubby, Lee Perry, Mikie Bennett, or Prince Jammy do? Jack Ruby? Steelie and Clevie? Niney the Observer? Digital B? This is it.

They'd select the best combination of known and new voices from their stable, consider each work in terms of pace, subject, style, and mood, then put them in the sequence that would have the best effect.

They'd ask some trusted people for their points of view,

but they'd leave the ultimate decisions to themselves. They'd trust their own experience, their knowledge, their instincts, and their taste. They'd imagine how they want the person who experiences the material to be moved, then sleep on it . . . and wake up with a little doubt, but doubt illuminated by something else—an awareness that on some level, all they'd really done was make an educated guess, that they'd done all they could and that now the work would have to go into the world and speak for itself . . . grab and hold attention . . . spark interest . . . keep it going . . . seduce.

In short, they'd trust the reggae, and this, dear reader, is what I've done. I hope that all is well with you. One world. One love.

Smiling as I write this,

Colin Channer
Founder & Artistic Director
The Calabash International Literary Festival Trust
March 7, 2006 (10:59 p.m.)
Brooklyn, New York
(A dub version of "Answer," mixed by Scientist at King Tubby's studio, throbbing through iTunes)

THE LAST JAMAICAN LION
by Marlon James

Ché Guevara, fat, dead, and shirtless, appeared on the front page of the evening paper. Surrounding him were several other men, all in uniform, none dead and none really men, just boys with automatic rifles that they clutched like phalluses. No boy in the photo could prove he had fired the fatal bullet, but all claimed to. Some of the claimers weren't in the photo, or the barracks, or even the region, but claimed it nonetheless. With his trousers on and his boots off, with his dazed eyes open and his mouth in the crooked tilt of a half laugh, Ché looked not dead but aroused from sweet sleep. Beside that story was another: *Boy Last Seen on Aloysius Dawkins Street Has Not Been Seen Since.*

"Blackheart man did catch him, you know, Mr. Minister, Blackheart man did catch him."

Morrison had left public office almost seven years before, but his maid Clemencia still called him Mr. Minister. It took him years to relieve the suspicion of mockery in her voice and accept that she was being genuinely obsequious. He even married her for it, though she continued to act as maid and call him Mr. Minister. He called her Mrs. Minister, partly in affection, partly in mockery, but affection and mockery were two things lost on his wife. A perfect wife for the likes of Morrison.

He studied Clemencia from the ridge of his nose. She waved her feather duster all over the veranda, stirring up more dust than she was getting rid of. The veranda was sealed off with a wall of louver windows, through which a chilly wind shook him. Mosquitoes sometimes. She would have closed them had he not raised a fuss, something about meeting the evening, the only visitor who always kept her word. Behind him was a gray wall, cut in the middle by a dark hallway that led to the kitchen. *This country prefers windows to mirrors,* he heard a voice say, but shook it out.

"Stop chatting donkey shit in me ears, you old bat," he scowled.

She continued dusting with no change in speed or countenance. He wondered if it was not all an act; if she knew full well that he often degraded her and was planning something slow, sweet, and vengeful, like a pinch of arsenic in every cup of evening tea. He concluded that this was mere paranoia, a consequence of old age as regrettable as it was inevitable. He was seventy-five years old and had no children.

Morrison became the first Prime Minister of the country in 1965. He was an impossibly tall man, lanky and white, with wild sideburns that seemed to have sprouted from the century previous. His thin hair went white from thirty and it would have given him dignity were it not for his notoriously foul mouth. Born white in one of the northern parishes, he grew up poor. But within a few years after his fifteenth birthday, he became an expert horseman and owner of his own filly.

Morrison had a way of making something out of nothing that mystified people. Sly and smart, he used his inferior birth to his advantage, manipulating his richer cousins who felt sorry for him. He would beat well-bred gentlemen at poker and horse races, worm his way into richer white society, and fuck the wayward girls of the gentry, the ones who tired of white flesh but could never stomach black. His wealthy uncle in the city took him in at seventeen to teach him manners and broughtupsy, but that succeeded only in teaching Morrison the difference between women who wouldn't and women who would.

Being tall and white, people looked up to him in mind and manner. Moreover, he loved people genuinely, Negroes in particular. Negro women, to be specific. He prevented three scandals with his own concoction, passed down, he would say, from an Obeah woman on the northwest coast, and guaranteed to "finally solute the problem." The simple thing, chunks of green papaya laced with pepper, force-fed to the Negro girls who had other plans, could abort even the most stubborn fetus. Thinking about those days caused a twitch in his crotch, a feeling he welcomed but never trusted, something like the phantom itch of an amputated leg, the lost leg he remembered his mother asking him to scratch. His own legs were useless. Morrison could stand, but diabetes and sin had caught up with him and he could never walk very far. In that way, he was finally like his hero, Franklin Delano Roosevelt.

In just three days there was to be a huge ceremony. So important he was that his enemies were putting on the most important, grand, expensive ceremony of the year. In three days, Maximilian Morrison was to be given the nation's highest order. He was to be declared The Most Honorable, Right Excellent, National Hero.

But the newspaper made no mention of it. 1967. They always hated him, the press. They hated his bluntness and brusqueness and his failure to get a degree. They hated that he never read *Silas Marner*, never climbed up through the civil service, never went to Munro Boy's School. They hated how he made the Queen laugh in a most unqueenly fashion during her last visit. They hated that he always seemed to have red dirt under his fingernails. "A rascal, that Prime Minister," the Queen was heard to have said as she covered her smile.

Many men, upon realizing that they will never win love, choose to wreak fear. Maximilian rose to the top of his party by sheer dint of bad will. Sometimes, usually before an election, a dead rumor would awaken like the stirring of old dust. Rumors of how his two rivals came to meet their untimely deaths within five years: one by fire, with his corpse so gruesomely burned that proper identification was impossible, the other by a sleepwalking leap from a balcony, despite no history of sleepwalking.

Maximilian would hear an invading whisper. He would listen for the tinkle of chimes behind him, the hurried wind through louver windows, or the loose strand of a wandering conversation from the house next door, and think that they have come back to warn him, a Jacob Marley to his Scrooge, that reckoning was upon him. It wouldn't be the first time. They had told him only three nights ago to expect a return on Wednesday. Today.

But he was ready.

Maximilian Morrison looked at himself. His hands and feet were covered in red spots like tiny islands. *Now is the winter of our discontent*, said a voice he did not recognize, from a book he had never read. Reading was for a specific Jamaican, the type that gathered with other specific Jamaicans on manicured lawns to argue about what was wrong with the country. Maximilian never trusted talkers. He was a doer. He solved problems, sorted out people and knew what they wanted, something that came from having the color of privilege but no wealth to go along with it.

"I said if you want something to eat?" she shouted from the hollow corridor.

"Is you goin cook it?" Maximilian replied.

"Then who else, Mr. Minister?"

"Me no know. I was considering starvation, with all the tripe you giving me lately."

"Suit yourself," she said.

She did it again. Spoiling for a fight, he had not realized her masterstroke until too late. She had left him hanging on the cusp of cussing, shot him with apathy while he stood waiting for a fuse so that his mouth could explode. He had to swallow his own malice back down. Maybe she was getting smarter in her old age, a sort of sage foolishness that was better than sense. He had underestimated her again.

Maximilian was bored. His neighbors, men missing hair and mind, and women who now wore stockings rolled up to the knee, all seemed to be at peace, with boredom being the last rung before heaven. Not Maximilian. He felt cursed for having an alert mind but a lost body.

On the table were beetles and butterflies, all dead, but

whose wings sparkled with a luminescence. He thought to collect them; he had the pins ready, but never really started.

Evening was threatening to come. The two men had said three days hence. Maximilian told himself he was ready for the visit. And should they come to take him to hell, they would just have to fucking wait. Not even the devil was going to have him before he became a National Hero. This was what balanced his life's great imbalance, something that made a life of no children worth something. Not that he ever wanted children. But the two men in a dream, or a vision, warned him of a visit today. Maybe not a warning, he thought, but a promise.

Maximilian did not tell his wife of the dream. Sleep was always a shifty thing, even when he was younger. In dreams he would travel to new lands and dark women, but would hear the bark of a dog in the next yard, or the hum of distant trucks, or the hushed call of a woman asking if he was awake.

So when Aloysius Dawkins and Teddy James told him to expect a visit, he couldn't remember if he was asleep or awake. There was a blur of words and he was lost as to whether he had heard or felt them, but there was also his wife's snore right beside him, though he did not look at her to make sure. Maximilian remembered the men's shapes but could not recall seeing their faces in the dark. Nor could he remember who spoke first or what he sounded like. They had been dead so long that he had forgotten their voices, what their breaths smelled like after four beers. *Coming back on Wednesday*, one or both said. Today.

Maximilian watched evening dye the green grass silver.

Soon it would be night, then midnight, then day, and his fear would pass in a haze. He had thought that a man would age beyond fear, but that had not happened.

"What you say?" he asked his wife. She did not answer.

He looked at the newspaper again, at Ché laughing at him. Was it really Ché or was it an imposter, an unlucky son of a bitch in the wrong place at the wrong time, with nothing left to show but a bloody cavity? Did he escape, as he had several times before? Wasn't he dead already? Was he still there? Here? Did he finally betray the cause and flee to America, where he was busy fucking the bourgeoisie's finest white women with his liberator?

The article quoted Fidel Castro himself, demanding Ché's body. Maximilian had wanted to meet him. He had met Fidel, of course, and no amount of facial hair and green uniforms could erase the Catholic schoolboy in Commandante. *General Elections a Surety in 1970*, read a headline beneath the fold of the newspaper.

He had won a few elections but lost more. His cousin became his rival and won the last. The leadership of Jamaica was up for grabs; all she needed was a man with a strong enough grip. Maximilian wrapped his fingers around the country and made a fist. How she had slipped out, he didn't know. Slippery thoughts made him think of milk and the way he always kept the carton up to a week after the expiration date. *It still good*, he would say, cussing his wife when she went to throw it out. Now it rested on the table beside Ché.

Maximilian wondered how long Ché had been dead when they took that photo. Smiling to the last. The photo could not have been more than two weeks old. Things moved much faster these days. Faster than even telex. Maximilian remembered his first horse and last, his first automobile and last, totaled in a collision with a steel suspension bridge. Maximilian had such promise then, he and Ché. And now Ché was dead. 1967 would move on without him.

Was he not a liberator as well? In his own way? A truck passed by but refused to answer. Instead, from the windows pulsed a sound that the poor people called reggae, with a man riding the rhythm and wailing that *The gal Caroline say she live cross the line/The gal Caroline say she live cross the line/Some of them say she a thirty-nine/Some of them say she a forty-nine/She just a walk from Pegasus to Skyline.*

He wondered if Ché 's body would be sent back to Cuba for an official funeral. People had to be called, ministers rounded up. The Cubans would expect if not the Prime Minister then certainly the Deputy Prime Minister and the Minister of Foreign Affairs. Fidel would insist, even though the Jamaican government did not officially recognize any Communist republic. He wondered who would be there. Perhaps a Beatle or a Rolling Stone or Michael Caine, such a rascal in *Alfie*.

He tried to get up but his legs would not allow it. He wondered why old age had snuck up like a whispered promise. Or warning. Night waited outside. Surely they would not be coming again. He was relieved. No entertaining the company of dead men tonight. Maximilian could not have his wife thinking he was senile. Cantankerous bitch was probably arranging for him to live at the old folks home, where rats chewed off people's toes at night.

"Are you okay, Excellency?"

"What? Is mock you mocking me, woman?"

"Just want to know if you're alright, sir."

"Leave me alone," he said. He thought to add, *I'm expecting company*, but left that sentence on his tongue. The room had the sweet stink of antiseptic. He wondered why he hadn't noticed before. He noticed other things as well: how the smell seemed to come from both the floor and his clothes, how the floor even in the coming dark bounced gray light from outside, and how his wife had taken to wearing white all the time as if she planned on getting married again. There were rumors about her and Teddy James, the one who sleepwalked off the balcony despite no history of sleepwalking. That was in January 1960.

1960? Maximilian looked at the date on the newspaper and it said 1967. A song came back to him. *Engine, engine number nine/Engine, engine number nine,* it said. Damn this chair, he was going to stand. Like Franklin Roosevelt in 1945. Like Nelson. He gripped the chair and pushed himself up. His mind made the first step long before he did. But then the left foot moved, then the right, then left again, and he thought of perhaps running away from the house and the wife with her white dresses, as if she was a cute nurse, and the antiseptic. His left leg strayed and struck a chair.

"Fuckin bomboclaat!" he said.

"What goin on in there?"

"Nothing!"

"Your nothing always sound like you up to something."

"A chair turn over."

"Don't make me come in there."

Maximilian was furious. Who did she think she was, talking to him as if he still shat his drawers? Did she remember that not long ago he was famous for sitting down with the baddest of people, spreading his arms wide behind him so that everybody could see two holsters peaking from his jacket, one for each shoulder, stuffed with ivory-handled revolvers given from the Prime Minister of the Congo himself? Did she remember that certain men were ready to unleash hell in the ghetto on just his say so? Did she remember that after Teddy James sleepwalked over the balcony, no fucking motherfucker had dared to fuck with him since then? Did she want him to get all country in this raasclaat? Did she, bitch?

Power felt like an itch. He made another step and caught someone fleeing, just a blip, and grabbed for the holster that was not there. He cursed again and stepped back. There was a person off in the deep dark of the left corner of the room, white as he was and shifting in some sort of mockery. A mirror.

Engine, engine number nine/Engine, engine number nine/Going cross Chicago line, the song said. Maximilian lumbered over to the mirror. A white man looked back at him. With white hair and sideburns that exploded in fright, as if running away from his face. His face seemed gray but that could have been the evening moon. His hair looked like a mane and he thought of growling but that would raise his wife. National Hero indeed. When did his eyebrows go white? He knew it was 1967, he knew that the election was three years away. He thought of the idle girl he'd had sex with only four weeks before, a juicy black girl with honey-dew breasts from the Back o' Wall ghetto. Honeydew was a word his cousin used. They only shared a girl once, five years ago—or was it five girls one year ago? Ché could have told him, but the newspaper was on the table along with dead bugs and spoiled milk.

He sniffed ash and sour flesh and jumped, thinking the room was on fire. There behind him in the mirror was Aloysius Dawkins, blacker than usual, dark as night, with smoke twirling from his head. His eye a glowing white to his skin's burnt black. Aloysius raised a hand but a finger fell off. *Never a man for words, that Aloysius*, said another voice, in perfect Oxford-degreed English.

"Teddy," Maximilian said.

Cousin.

Teddy stood behind as well; beside Aloysius, his white skin seemed to pop. His smile was as bright as ever, yet as his grin grew wider, teeth appeared missing. Suddenly half of his face went crimson from a flush of blood flow.

Heavens, I think I've popped my top, Teddy said.

"What you want, eh? What the bloodclaat you want?"

Maxy, Maxy, is that any way to treat your cous—

"What you want? Is pound of flesh you come for?"

The Merchant of Venice? *And they said I was the well-read one.*

"Why you coming here? Why the raas you come now, don't they make you National Hero already? What about me? Why you come now?"

"Who you talking to in there?" Her voice came from another room.

"Bloodclaat! Can't a man think out loud in peace?" Maximilian stepped away from the mirror.

Why do we come now? Old chap, we never left.

"In the course, in the necessary . . . in the course of, of events, sometimes the practical becomes the necessary for the greater good of—"

Good, good. I remember when I wrote that. Powerful stuff, all that sturm and drang nonsense. Have to say, though, you delivered it way better than I ever could. You had just that, that . . . uncouthness? Is that the word? Let's use that, uncouthness. Yes, you had the uncouthness that it needed. I left it out for you, you know.

"No, you didn't, I take the thing from your, from your room, when you . . ." Maximilian covered his mouth.

Cock mouth catch cock, said ashen Aloysius. But it cost him a lip, which fell.

Who'd guess that it would take just one fire and one push to turn number three into number one? Teddy added.

Maximilian left the mirror. He hopped and dragged himself back to the chair. The room smelled of ash and old blood.

"Everything in this life me want, me have to snatch it like greedy baby. Nobody give me a fuckin thing."

True, true.

"What the fuck God think him was making? Joke? Give me white man skin but black man poverty? But I show him, though, I show the fucker."

You show everybody, Maxy.

"Bloodclaat right. Show you too."

Well . . . technically, you know what that word means, don't you? Well, technically, you didn't 'show' me anything. See, you were behind me, so I couldn't see you.

"Shut up! You always talk too fuckin pretty and too fuckin much!"

Aloysius seemed to hiss, but it was just the sizzle of his burned flesh.

"The two of you get out and don't come back."

The hero can't talk to we no more, said Aloysius.

"Leave!"

But we never left, Maxy. What do you think has been tickling the back of your head since 1960?

"What? We in 1967 now. Ché Guevara just dead. It in the paper. Damn fool you is to—"

Aloysius giggled in a high pitch that sounded like a wheeze. Teddy James's laugh barreled through the room like thunder. They sounded like a harmonized, mocking chorus. Maximilian grabbed a plate and flung it into the dark corner where the mirror was. The crash woke up the room to light.

"What the hell is going on here?" she demanded, her hand still at the light switch.

"Nothing. Nothing at all. Go back to spoiling dinner."

She sighed. "Why don't you sit down and behave yourself?"

"Why don't you sit down and behave *your*self. I look like pickney to you? Me is a National Hero."

"Yes, Mr. Minister. Is me push you in you wheelchair to collect you medal two year ago, remember?"

"And another thing. I don't like when you talk to me like that. I don't like it at all."

"How you want me to talk to you?"

"I don't . . . I don't know . . . Not like that is all me saying."

"You hiding your pills again?"

"I don't know what fart you chatting now, and—hold on, what you just say?"

"Me say if you hiding your pills."

"No, before that."

"Me not cassette tape, you know, Mr. Minister. You can't press rewind."

"Don't get fresh."

"Mr. Minister, you promised me you would take them. I trusted you. You want them to come force it down you throat again?"

Maximilian shook. He sat down. The woman moved over to the table and took up his newspaper. She rolled it up to squash a beetle on the chair.

"Him dead already," Maximilian said. He bowed his head.

"Every day you take out this newspaper. Is what so special 'bout it so?"

"I . . . I need to remind myself of the funeral. Ché's funeral. Goin be big."

"Well, if it in this newspaper then it gone already."

Engine, engine number nine, a song went.

Damn wife. Taking revenge now in her little wifely ways. "You just don't want me to go," he said.

"Then go. Me look like me care?"

"Why you stay so, Clemencia? What me do that make you cantankerous so?"

"Who name Clemencia?"

Maximilian Morrison looked at the woman and closed his eyes. His jaw fell open as if the breath was too much to hold. There was no ash, no sulfur, no flesh, and no blood. Only antiseptic, and it came from the woman. He looked at her as she scratched her temple. Her cap jerked up and down.

"Don't think that because night coming you not still getting a sponge bath."

Maximilian looked in her face but saw nothing.

"I just want to know one thing. One thing. How much more month leave in 1967?" he said.

The nurse peered at him and laughed. As she left the room, promising to come back with the basin and sponge, she was still laughing. Maximilian picked up the newspaper and it fell limp in his hands. The paper was brown, not white. 1967 was a year of promise. 1967 gave him Jamaica in the palm of his hands, and he was about to make a fist. 1976? The paper fell to the floor. Evening was leaving and night made his eyes clearer. For a minute.

Engine, engine number nine/Engine, engine number nine/Running cross Chicago line/Next year a 1979/Next year a 1979/Hey!

PARTING
by Alwin Bully

I've always known this, but I know it better now—parties are a place to meet interesting people. Even when it ain't carnival, parties are a kind of masquerade.

A few months ago, in Trinidad, a man from Dominica went to stay with friends who took him to a party on a hill because they thought he needed cheering up. He was a tall man, with short hair along his graying temples, and his white shirt, which was open at the collar, had pajama cuffs, which stated softly that perhaps he was an artist who'd known some success.

The drive was long, and on the way he smoked in silence in the back of the dark car, compulsively adjusting rimless glasses, which were tucked high on his nose. Every now and then he'd hunch with his elbows on his knees, remain so for a while, then fall back into a slouch with his arms stretched out along the leather top of the wide backseat, a Newport twitching in a corner of his mouth.

He was new to smoking and he didn't quite know how to hold a cigarette, and with unmoving brows he tried to recollect how he'd directed actors to puff with confidence on stage, trying different grips as he thought.

Every grip was followed by a drag and every drag was followed by a cough. Every now and then he'd nod toward the eyes that watched him in the rearview mirror. Sometimes he'd hold them in a stare, sometimes he'd drop his head in his hands or raise it up and keep it there like he could see right through the roof.

The smoke had caused the coughing, he was willing to accept. But not the smoke just by itself. The air-conditioning. Pelham's sport cologne. The musk oil streaked on Tina's neck. The showroom odor of the new Accord.

At the sprawling house, which was perched on a ridge near the foot of Fort George, he quickly took the owner's invitation for a tour. The owner was a middle-aged Indian who'd made his fortune selling textbooks, and he gestured broadly as he spoke above the volume of the music, which vibrated through the walls.

"So how you know Pelham and Tina?" the owner asked, while the coughing smoker gazed blankly at the front of the house, which was three stories tall and made of concrete and cut stone. They were standing on the lawn, and the owner was again relating that the stained-glass trim on the windows and doors had come from an old train station in Leeds. When the station was razed, his son who worked there as an architect had bought the precious glass "cheap, cheap, cheap" and shipped it to him in a thirty-foot container, each piece carefully wrapped and tucked in among the various household things.

"So how I know Pelham and Tina?" the coughing smoker paraphrased. He rocked back and forth in the damp grass, looked up at the star-spangled sky, and paused to watch the gyrating mass of bodies on the deck of a projecting section of the second floor.

"They said you were staying with them," said the owner, whose name was Anil.

The coughing smoker grunted, "Through work," but stopped short of explaining that he was a banker like Pelham though he'd worked in theater since he was a child.

What would have been the point? Anil was a bookseller whose big new house had only one shelf of books. On another evening, at another time, he would have said something snide. But to be snide you have to feel superior, and in this case he did not. The man had things he didn't have.

The man had his son.

"I got the glass because I wanted to give the house a spiritual feel," said Anil. "Like a temple or a church, you know. The way they kidnapping people in Trinidad these days, in all you do, you better keep God close by."

"God does whatever he wants to do," the coughing smoker said, taking a pull and coughing through the menthol-scented smoke. Under his breath, he said, "If he exists at all."

He glanced up out of habit when he said this and shifted to the side. His reaction made him feel stupid. His shift had been reflexive, but in any case too slow, nothing you could say was lightning quick, nothing that could beat a thunderbolt. So what had been the point? There was no point. Which was the point. Which was why he felt stupid. Stupid in the presence of Anil, whom he thought of as a stupid man.

Self-conscious now, he began to see himself the way that others saw him, and saw himself the way he was—terse in speech, erect in posture, shoulders square, gaze slanted—and he made a show of moving like the music moved him.

It was a fast, percussive soca tune, repetitive and simple as rain, but he moved slowly, torso bouncing on the bass line, head nodding off the beat.

"This is a good fête you have here, my friend . . . nice house too . . . but by the way, you heard anybody say if they found a chain?"

"No. You lose one?"

"I think so. The clasp was giving trouble and I forgot to fix it." He slipped his hand inside his shirt and made quick searching moves along his neck. "Listen. I catch you later. I going and retrace my steps."

He lied. He hadn't worn a chain in his life. Yes, he lied. And so have I . . . but not directly . . . in a way. You could call it acting. I'm the coughing smoker. This is all about me.

Tina met me in the living room, which was overdone with stuffed chairs in frames of dark wood. In another house, mahogany is the wood you'd assume, but Anil is the kind of guy who'd import dark wood from Botswana at four times the cost, who'd make a point to buy things that allow him to say, "Is one in the island. Only one in the place."

Tina sat across from me beneath a heavy chandelier. There was a glass table between us and we made small talk. She used to be a flight attendant in the air hostess days and she'd read some news in the *Guardian* that morning about BWIA that made her think for sure that by year-end the airline would be closing down.

She asked about Anil and I answered while imagining

whole scenes in which he appeared with his son, the son telling him that it was insensitive and plain stupid to have a contractor redo the plans he took the time to draw, and him telling the son that he think he know every damn thing because he go to big school in England. Line by line, beat by beat, scene by scene, I built it up, while Tina, in a low red top and tight black pants, hair pulled back into a frizzy bun, watched me through the mentholated haze, bemused.

In another country, Tina would have been mistaken for a trophy wife. She was thin with high cheekbones and breasts that were pertish even though they'd nursed four children. With a shade seen only on brass instruments and certain roasted nuts, her skin was a lust-arousing bronze; but here in Trinidad she was less a trophy than a nice enamel mug.

"There's a fellow been asking for you," she said. "Say he want to meet you but he kinda shy. Say he writes plays and he did you in CXC. You want me bring him to meet you?" Before I could reply, she added, "I going to find him and two glass o' rum."

I was expecting a boy of eighteen or so, but instead I met a man. He was dark with a nose that looked like a frog about to jump; and without looking, I could tell his skin was rolly-rolly where his head met his neck.

"Roger John," he said to introduce himself, while swiftly executing several moves—taking my hand, lighting a cigar, sitting down, and shaking his head as he cleared his throat.

"Lemme tell you something," he began, in a voice whose loudness I was sure would get no less if the music was turned down. "You change my life and you don't even know. If it wasn't for you, I would still be doing what I was doing before. But because o' you I leave that one time. I was a police. From I leave secondary school I gone in the force. And I moving up and moving up and moving up and t'ing, getting promote and promote and promote, but I never feel no satisfaction. And I keep saying, 'Is what so? Is why I ain't satisfy?' Same time, all my friends and them was telling me I had a flair. Cause I is a man could take off anybody from I was a small, small child. Any little t'ing you could say or do, I could do it just so."

He held out the cigar to me as if it was a ganja spliff. I reached for it and then declined, remembering that when he spoke he made a kind of squashing sound as if his mouth had extra spit.

"So anyway," he continued, "I say maybe is because I never pass no subjects in school. And I start to study that, and when they kick me off the force cause they say I taking bribe and all kinda mix-up, Anil hire me as a bodyguard, cause you know dem fellas and dem like to kidnap dem Indians cause they have the money to pay. So one day, he ask me where I get my flair and I say I have that flair from I born and he now tell me that I belong in show business. And you know what? Is like God was talking to me. And I say I going and develop my talent. But I say at my age now I ain't want to start at the bottom, so I say lemme take some evening classes and do some subjects. And when I doing English literature I come across your play, *Uncle Tony Never Come Back,* and I say, 'You know what, boy, you should stop this foolishness 'bout show business and all that, but you should still use your natural flair—cause I'm a people person—and write some plays.' So

I start to write some skits. Well, as you know, Anil is a businessman, and when I show him what I doing and tell him that I ain't bothering with the classes again, he say this t'ing could make some money, and he lend me some and I put on the play and it was a hit. And the rest, as they say, is luxury. You ever hear 'bout we? Crack Up & Company."

The look on my face must have told him that I hadn't, so he went on talking and I leaned forward with my elbows on my knees as if in deep interest, but the truth was that I'd seen a woman who even in this country could have been a trophy wife, and leaning forward offered me a better look.

She'd come around and down the spiral stairs behind and to the right of him, paused to look into her bag, then moved toward my right, his left, drawing my eyes but not my head, in sly pursuit.

When she disappeared out of the living room into the passageway, I felt compelled to cast my mind around the corner, to pursue a glimpse of her through concrete walls.

In those days, I was no longer what you'd call a believer. I'd already lost religious faith; but I still had trust in certain instincts, still believed I had the knack for telling when a special thing would come my way. My wife, Maria, used to call my instincts *animalistic*, used to cuss and say I was a ruthless predator who needed flesh to stay alive, that my instincts had one purpose, finding women dumb enough to stray 'way from their herd.

Yes, I've failed Maria. But she's not the only one. I've failed more important people in more fundamental ways.

"Roger," I muttered, as I thought of one of them, "can

you bring another rum?" He'd begun to talk about collaborating on "a modern type o' version" of *The Joker of Seville*.

He continued slinging words across his shoulder as he walked away. When he reached the landing of the spiral stairs, I turned my head to watch the wall.

My palms began to itch and I rubbed them as I talked to Maria in my mind—I've never found seduction easy. It's never really simple. At first. There's a part in the beginning when the glands are warming up and the old fears about yourself are hard and cold. When the glands are warm and the fears heat up, the fears will melt. But till then they're hard. Like rock. And you think you'll never be able to lift them up or roll them back or mash them down.

If you back out soon, you can be safe. But if you stick it out, man, if you stick it out, and the glands warm up and their heat begins to cause the fears to melt, you'll get a high, a real high, and you'll feel like you can play any role you want, that you can play the man you used to be, the one with the prospects, the good playwright, the good husband, the great father—no, the great dad—and you'll feel a jet of coolness just below the surface of your boiling blood.

I was in the middle of these thoughts when I sensed the woman coming down the hall. The music was too loud for me to hear her steps along the marble floor, so I stood and looked at Anil's art collection, which was not as bad as one would be inclined to think. With my back toward her when she came into the room, I thought, I'd sweep around and catch her from a turn. But as I timed her, voices shot above the music like a flock of startled birds.

"Come here, girl, and meet me father." I heard the

woman laugh and suck her teeth, then Roger asking, "You deaf or you dotish or what?"

The woman sucked her teeth again.

"Come," he said, laughing. "Come. This man is me father right here."

He caught me by the arm and turned me, used his other hand, the one with the rum, to fan the woman over, then he gave me the glass. He was standing to the side. She and I were face to face. She was as dark as dried blood, with a plump upper lip, and she wore a floral dress with darts that made it fit. Above her low neckline there was a heavy line of shadow where her bosom pressed together, and a fading scar beneath her right collarbone.

The first words I heard from her were: "Lord, Roger, why you like to misbehave so?" The second set of words were: "Nice to meet you, Daddy, but I really have to run."

I was out in the backyard when I saw her again. Two hours or so had passed. There were three retaining walls that kept the house from sliding off the ridge into flickering Port of Spain, and I was sitting on the highest one.

Light was spilling from the house and draining down toward me, streaming in between the trees, beading on the blades of shaggy grass.

My mind was heavy and the weight of all my thoughts had drawn my chin toward my chest. My eyes were closed. I felt sleepy. Five rums had passed and I was trailing off.

I was halfway gone when my nerves began to buzz. There was a drone inside my head—a slur of heartbeat, music, tree frogs, crickets, wind, and distant human voices, plus the intermittent murmur of an engine woken up to take some people home—and something had disturbed it. Before I looked, I caught her smell. It was musk so I expected Tina. I don't remember how I felt when I saw her.

"Is okay for me to pass?" she asked from twenty feet away. She had the wariness of someone speaking to the owner of a cranky-looking dog. "You okay?"

"Yes," I said, still sitting. "Yes. What about you?"

"I didn't mean to dis you like that before, but I had to take care of a little thing."

"Oh. Don't worry. I didn't take it too badly."

She crossed her arms and moved toward me. In her heels she was a little tentative, and every time she lost her balance she would make a squeaky sound. But soon she was in front of me, so close that touching her would not involve the full extension of my arm.

"You not from Trinidad . . ." she began.

Now my senses were fully aroused.

"Dominica," I said coolly. "But I live in Jamaica . . . Kingston . . . Kingston, Jamaica . . . where the bad-johns live."

"I couldn't quite catch the accent. But anyway . . ." She began to say something, then changed her mind and tried to make a clever observation: "Everybody nowadays is a mix-up, they say."

"So they say."

"I gone for a smoke."

She picked her way along the wall some twenty yards away and lit up. "Don't mind me," she said when I caught the early whiffs of ganja. "I could move further down."

She was making a bit of a fuss about bothering me, but

it was clear that she wanted to talk. When she's good and ready, she'll come, I thought. She's what? Forty? Forty-five? A little younger than me. We ain't no students. Either of us could teach this class.

Up the slope in a diagonal, two shadows came from opposite directions, looked around, then lay down quickly in a chaise beside the pool.

"The smoke is okay?" she asked after being silent for a while.

"Come here often?" I replied without looking.

I lit a cigarette. But before I could insert it, I began to cough.

"Not really," she said, coming over. "But I had to come. You know how sometimes you run from something, but as time goes on you realize you can't run anymore? How sometimes you try and resist something and you try and try until you give in because you face the fact that you can't resist anymore? Well, is like that. I had to come out here. I have a thing to do."

"Anil is your boss too?" I said, pretending to be naïve. "Not just Roger John's? Big party going on and the man giving you things to do?"

"I never said anything about anybody," she said, shifting her weight from one leg to the next. "Is more like I'm on a sort of mission."

"Oh, excuse me," I said in Roger's voice. "Lemme turn my back. Imagine, such a big house with so much space but not enough bathrooms to handle a normal fête crowd. Dem people is crosses in truth."

"With such a serious face, who woulda think you was so

dotish?" she said through a chuckle, as she put one foot up on the wall right next to me.

"If you're on a mission," I said, "who send you?"

I was thinking that I knew these kinds of games enough to know that all we had to do was keep it going till one person dropped the subtext and came out straight. Directness would be the cue to act surprised, then flattered, then confused.

"Who sent me?" she asked, slowly bending and straightening her leg, like she was warming up.

I brushed imaginary dust from her pumps.

"Yeah. Who sent you out here at this time of night, in a place where it have bad-johns who live in Jamaica . . . where they ain't no decent men? Only rogues."

"Your son."

"Roger is a fella full o' jokes, eh? You know he's not my son, right?" I began to explain, then changed my mind. What would have been the point? The whole thing was too silly. Too complicated. She must have known his introduction was a joke.

She began to answer, then cut herself off. Fell silent. It was an active silence, one that kept demanding that we talk. I wanted to talk—for there to be talking. Talking had lifted my mood. But I didn't quite know what to say. I was in that stage before the glands had fully warmed, and the old fears were still looking heavy and tough. I began to smoke again.

If either of us had walked away at this point, there'd be no story to tell. But maybe it wasn't just the staying. Maybe it was the staying plus the cough. Because it was the cough that made her touch me. It was a simple pat on the back, then a resting palm, fingers kneading knots from my shoulder.

Without asking, I laid my face on her raised leg. The skin was warm and damp with perspiration and must have been smooth. I don't know. I'd planned to wait awhile before I rubbed.

"You know, I'm not here to talk about Roger," she said, holding the weight of my head with the muscles of her thigh.

"I know," I said, my mind advancing to the moment when she'd let me touch her in more daring ways.

I wrapped one arm around her calf and drew it closer. She pulled away, dropped her foot, and took some hasty backward steps.

"I was sent here by your son."

I picked up my rum glass, which had been sitting on the wall. I shook my head and drained the glass. "You wouldn't understand."

"How you so sure?"

I passed the glass from hand to hand. "Because . . . because . . . because there are a lot of things you don't understand."

"I might surprise you."

I wheeled around and threw the glass away. "My blasted son is dead."

There's a story that my older brother Kenny likes to tell. Many years ago, at a party in Dominica, a woman walked up to him and said, "You know, every time I look at you I have to shake my head."

"Yeah? And why's that?"

"Because when you were twelve, you died—for a good few minutes—and came back to life again."

She told Kenny that our father had brought him to the hospital to have his tonsils taken out and that during the operation he'd died. His eyes had rolled over and he'd lost his pulse.

They tried to revive him. CPR. Other things I have forgotten now. Perhaps electric shock. Then, as the doctor moved to drape him and pronounce the time of death, my brother moved his hand, flexed his wrist, I think—there've been many versions of the story, so it's hard to say which one is true—breathed deeply, and began to live again.

Kenny claims to have a memory of another life. But in truth, he's claimed a lot of things, among them that I'm going to go to hell because I'm an unbeliever, that I have a sly vindictive side, and that I did everything possible to save Pierre, my son.

Whenever he tells the story of his crossing—the words are his, not mine—he always says it had the feeling of a dream. And whenever I ask him how he knows it wasn't just a dream, he tells me that he simply knows, that it didn't look like a dream, that the best way he can explain it is by saying he knows it in the way he knows when a movie was shot on video or film, that it's a deepness thing, a texture thing, a feel thing, a mood.

When he makes this point, which he always does, his voice gets a little spacey and drops a bit in pitch, and he speaks of floating somewhere above the operating theater, looking down at his body, the table being cold, the doctor and his nurses frenzied, at first frightened, then excited, their faces asking, "The boy came back to life but what the hell did we do?"

Before he'd met the woman at the party and she'd bamboozled her way into his life (he'd leave his wife of eighteen years for her and move with her to Barbados), he'd had no recollection of dying and coming back. Today he has a dream life in a beach house and his ex-wife does her best with my help to raise his kids.

But I must admit that Kenny has always had a certain gift. It's not so much that he can see things. He gets premonitions. He gets the feeling that there might be things to watch for, good things or bad.

The day our mother had a fatal heart attack, he'd spent the morning calling round to see if everybody was okay. The week before I got the call that four of my plays were going to be made into CXC texts, he called to tell me it was time I word-processed my scripts. And he'd been suddenly obsessed with weeding out the family plot in the weeks before Pierre shed his bag of burdens and walked on air in a subway station in Toronto only to be grounded by a train.

"My blasted son is dead."

I'd never said it that way before. I'd said that he'd passed on, or made his transition, or gone to a better place, but I'd never said that he was dead. Death is something for old people, something appropriately final for people who've gotten to a certain age, something as wide and deep as the sea at the end of a long highway. Young people aren't made for death. Death doesn't suit them. Doesn't fit them right. They haven't lived enough to earn their eulogies. They haven't paid the price.

Since Pierre's death six months before, I'd been trying to pay his debt, been trying to lead a better life. Trying to make it so that when my time came I'd earn the eulogy for both of us, trying to make it so that when they spoke of me they'd talk about how much I'd changed because of him, how much I'd used my life to live his dreams. Pierre was a dreamer. He wanted to do everything . . . make music, make movies, make art . . . make me understand that he was not going to be a replica of me . . . make peace with me, make peace with himself, with his sexuality, make sense of what it meant to have ADD . . . make sense of a world that refused to remain in one spot so he could focus. Could take his time and look.

When he said he thought he'd do better in college some-where else, was I too glad to pay the fare? Should I have kept him there in Kingston, the place that my career had made my home, and watch him suffer, watch him lock himself inside his room, watch his pants drip down when he didn't eat for days? Should I have encouraged him to try another treatment, get other drugs prescribed? Was it too easy to say yes when he said he'd like to go? Was I really trying to help him or help myself? Was I right or wrong?

"My blasted son is dead," I said again.

"I know," she said, and crossed her arms. "I know."

I needed comfort. Badly.

I asked, "What's your name, by the way?"

"Chloe."

She came forward once again.

"How are you, Chloe?"

"I'm okay."

"I'm Irving, by the way."

"Nice to meet you."

"So," I said, "how do you know about my son?"

His death was small news even in Toronto, so I figured she'd heard about it from Pelham or Tina. People see. People ask. People talk. Chloe could have asked them what was wrong with me, why I seemed so down, and they could have said, *Poor thing, he's lost his son.*

But instead of being reassuring, her *IknowIknow* felt glib. Pretentious. Airy-fairy cryptic. Which made me feel toyed with. Irritated. Annoyed.

"I know things," she said.

I shoved a cigarette in my mouth. My hand was trembling. I couldn't light it. She reached to help me and I slapped her hand away. The cigarette fell. I stomped it. Kicked what was left of it. Raised grass and dirt in the air.

"When I was fifteen," she said, while backing off, "I was living in Blanchichessue and I caught a fever and started to burn. It took three days before my mother realized that I was really sick, that this was no ordinary thing like she was telling the neighbors for two days. By the time she could get some men to put me in a van and carry me to the clinic, they said I was dead. No pulse. No breath. When they got to the clinic, they put me in a room to wait for the doctor to come and pronounce me. But everybody knew I was dead. When the doctor came, he gave me a shot and told the nurse to give me some chicken soup when I woke. She looked at him like he was crazy and he said a single word—'typhoid'—before explaining that although my vital signs were very weak, I wasn't gone. That is one death. My second death was fifteen years ago. I was working as a junior secretary in the Red

House when Abu Bakr and the Jamaat stormed the place and held the government hostage. That was 1990 during the coup. They shot several people. You remember that? Well, I was one of them."

She moved toward me now with her arms crossed and went to sit again where she'd sat when she'd begun to smoke her spliff, and I walked over. She wiped her face and said, "No," as I approached, and it was only then that I saw her tears.

"Both times," she said softly, as her shoulders squeezed up, "my soul looked down on my body from above. I saw it all. The nurse in the country clinic. The surgeon in the theater down at General, searching for the bullets in my chest."

Lightning looks for water. Men are drawn to women's tears. If I dig deep enough to analyze it, I might find out why. Maybe it's because experience teaches that a love-up is the hero's just reward. Maybe it's because the tears provide us with a chance to catch up on the moments we missed with our children. Maybe it's because a breakdown is exactly what we want them to feel when we're inside them, turning like tornados, collapsing them with overwhelming force.

But I've never analyzed it—even now—which means I didn't analyze it that night. In the moment I just knew I wanted to hold her close and tell her what she needed to hear to make the crying stop, whatever that might have been . . . to make her pull herself together, to make her feel the world was alright, to hold her, perhaps, as I wished I'd held Pierre the last time he cried before he made that leap of faith, chancing that there had to be a better place on the other side of life.

"It's going to be okay," I whispered, in the way I should

have whispered to my own sweet boy. And before I knew it, I'd held my arms toward her and she'd stood and come to me and I'd held her close. She was heavy in my arms, as if her legs had lost their strength to fully hold her up, and her body shook and trembled like there wasn't just a single Chloe in her floral dress but several Chloes rolling round and crawling round, scrounging for a place where they could rest, could fit, be safe, find home.

"Your boy wants to talk to you," she said through tears. "He wants me to connect you. He trusts me cause I've been to the other side. He sent me here to you."

By then she was no longer Chloe to me. The more I held her and thought of Pierre, the more I felt her changing, the more I felt her changing into him, the more I needed her to be him, for my sake, just so I could tell him that I loved him, that I loved him so, and that it was my fault, my fault, my frigging fault for not trying harder to know, to feel, to understand, to accept, to protect, to soothe, to query, to challenge, to fight, to encourage, to permit.

"Oh my boy," I whispered. "Oh my sweet boy. It's okay. You can tell me anything. Anything. You have my ear. My ear and my heart belong to you."

"First of all," she said, "your son wants you to know that he is in a place of incredible beauty. So beautiful that he finds it hard to describe. You would never believe it. More than that, he is surrounded by a group of loving, intelligent souls who are taking care of him, so you should not be worrying about where he is or what is happening to him. He's fine. He's more than fine. He's happy."

I wanted to let her go. Her words felt inauthentic. She

was struggling with the role. But I held her still. She was all I had. My blasted son was dead.

"Thank you," I told her. "Thank you. Thank you, darling. Thank you."

"Next, he wants you to stop beating up yourself with guilt. What happened was meant to happen."

I eased my hold on her. Fear rushed in between us, and I squeezed her tightly once again.

"No. No. No," I said. "Don't say that. Don't say that. No, son. It was not supposed to happen. That's not how it's supposed to be at all. You were supposed to grow old and carry my casket to my grave and cry for me, my love, then smile as you claimed your inheritance, all the things I left for you—the shoes in which I married your mother, the life insurance payback, the playbills signed by Derek Walcott, the house on the hillside in Dominica, all my artwork, the steel penknife which my father said had cut the tangled ropes on one of the *Titanic's* lifeboats, all the old kaiso LPs, my personally autographed copy of *Giovanni's Room.*

I began to find it hard to breathe. Like I was holding her too hard. It was fear. Fear like a blade trying to get between us. Like wind prying shingles from a roof.

A car had backfired on the plain and I'd been yanked out of the movie I was making in my mind, the one in which I was the loving father cradling his son, and the sounds of the world rushed inside my head . . . a mix of heartbeat, music, tree frogs, crickets, wind, and distant human voices . . . and I became aware of myself as I was, a desperate man holding a broken woman whom he wanted to die and come back as his son.

I saw myself like I was not myself, but another Irving

watching from above. Or so I wanted to think. So I wanted to believe. And I willed myself to believe it, and as soon as I did this, I could ask her to speak to him.

"Pierre," I whispered, "if you're here, let me know. Are you here?"

A hand slipped up my back and cupped my head. A voice said, "Yes."

"How do I know?"

"It's me. Yes, it's me."

"Me who?"

"Daddy?"

"Yes, son?"

"No. It's not Daddy. It's not Daddy."

"Yes, it's me. Yes it's me."

"No. It's not Daddy."

"Yes, Pierre. It's me. Please believe me. It's me."

"It's not Daddy. It's not Daddy. It's Dad."

"God bless you. God bless you. God bless you, my son. Yes. God bless you. Yes. It's Dad."

"Dad? Dad?"

"Yes, Pierre."

"I love you, Dad. Stop worrying. It's over. Don't bother to try and live for me. You can't live for me. Move on with your life. It's over, Dad. It's finished. It's done."

I stood there holding Chloe for a very long time. How long, I'm not sure. But long enough for Pelham and Tina to feel they had to come and find me.

It was an awkward scene: Chloe and I were hugging each other in silence with our eyes closed, rubbing each other's backs, crying when the crying would come, quiet when the quiet brought relief, but not talking, not talking. Then, in the middle of this search for peace, I heard Tina calling from a distance and Pelham coughing to warn me.

"I think we getting ready," Tina shot from thirty yards away. She was angry for sure. When I looked, she was already tramping up the grade. Pelham was squatting with his elbows on this thighs and moving his head from side to side as if he had to double-check what he'd seen. Before he left, he clapped his hands and laughed.

"So you're gone?" Chloe said, composing herself.

I began to do the same. "Yes. I gone."

"Thanks for holding me."

In a mutter, I said, "No. Thank you."

And somehow I knew, perhaps in the way my brother knew he wasn't dreaming that time, that I'd return to Kingston as a slightly different man. Different how and to what degree, I didn't know. But I knew.

"Be good," Chloe said, and kissed her palm. She placed it on my cheek.

"I will," I mumbled. "I hope to see you again."

"Some things you should leave in their time," she said.

"You're right, you know. That's true."

"You're not coughing anymore," she said brightly.

I touched my throat. "I only cough when I smoke," I said, and smiled.

"But you don't do that anymore."

"How you know that?"

"I know a lot of things," she said, and shooed me off. I realized then that she was wearing bangles. They clattered when they shook.

As I walked up the grade toward the house, I turned to look at her again. She was lighting up a spliff.

"He never used to call me *Daddy*, you know," I shouted. "He only used to call me *Dad*."

"I know."

"I was going to ask you how you know, but I think I know. Or at least I know what I want to know."

"You know," she said, "you're just putting up a fight."

"How you know?"

"Because," she said, "I know."

She was veiled in smoke. I could see the glow and smell the spliff burning fierce and new. My last impression was a shadow in a swirl of smoke dissolving in the glimmer of the city's lights.

SOMEONE TO TELL
by A-dZiko Simba

I t's the most incredible thing you've seen in your whole life. You can't move because of the incredibleness. It has stuck you right to the spot, so all you can do is stay there not moving. It has opened up your eyes wide, wide, so all you can do is look, and you can't even make a sound because it have yuh mouth seal up and lock down.

The only thing you can do is look and think. And the only thing you can think is "incredible."

Incredible. And you're so glad that last term Mr. Swaby gave you new words to learn every week, because without that, without that, you wouldn't even know what to think, but you do know . . . incredible.

But now the night is starting to come down and the trees are starting to turn into people with long arms and too many fingers and the Christmas breeze is starting to blow. It has a coldness in it, and when it passes, the tree people begin to moan and crack their bones like old people. Like tired old people grumbling up stairs. You run out of the bush and onto the road. It is not that you are frightened. Of course you are not frightened, but you just think you have seen enough incredibleness for one day, and anyway, you are hungry and now is a good time, a very good time, for you to go home. You run all the way. Not because the old tree people are after you, not because Delroy once told you that on certain nights, in certain places, dead people come alive in trees and take up stray children. You just run because you like to run and home is a good place to run too. That is all.

Mary Janga is on the porch. Mary Janga is always on the porch playing mummy with her dollies.

She talks to them like they're real people, like they can really hear her. Then she combs their hair and takes off their clothes and combs their hair and puts their clothes back on again. Then she gives them dirt and cut-up leaves to eat and you shake your head and you wonder about Mary Janga. Wonder if there is any hope. And when she stops talking and combing and feeding and bends her head to listen to what the dollies have to say, you realize there's no hope for Mary Janga at all.

But even so, you are happy to see her sitting on the porch because she is someone to tell.

Mary Janga says she will only listen if you tell her dollies too. You are too excited to care. You tell her, "Yes," and you wait for her to line them all up so they can all look in your face and hear what it is you are saying. Now they are ready. Mary Janga and her dollies are all lined up, all ready to listen, except for Floppy Florenzo the Rabbit, who keeps dropping over on his face.

Mary Janga listens with eyes open big and wide. When you get to the end she makes a face like she is trying to squash it up into a ball and stuff it through a little hole. And then she says, "Yuck!"

Mary Janga is not from planet Earth. An alien spaceship left Mary Janga in your yard one day. She has come from a place where they talk to plastic dollies and they say "Yuck" to incredible stories. One day her people will come back for her and you won't have to put up with this nonsense anymore.

You suck your teeth to let her know that you know the spaceship is coming any day now, and then you run inside to tell your mother.

She is in the kitchen. She is always in the kitchen. You wonder what it is about being a girl that always keeps them in places.

You just start to tell your mother the story. You don't even get anywhere yet, but she turns around and smiles and says, "That's nice."

Nice? Nice?

Nice bounces around in your head. You cannot believe she said, "Nice."

You feel like shouting, "NICE?" Like if you can make it big enough and make it have enough of a question in it, she will realize it's not the thing to say.

You have just seen the most incredible thing in the whole wide world and your sister says, "Yuck," and your mother says, "Nice."

You go outside to look for your father.

The truck's hood is wide open like a huge mouth. It has swallowed your father right up to his waist. Just as you reach him, the truck spits out his arm, and his hand searches around in the tool box, finds a spanner, and then disappears again.

The engine is roaring. The engine is louder than your voice.

You have to call him three times before he hears you.

He turns off the engine and stands up.

The light from the lamp stuck onto the battery puts shadows on his face. Where there are no shadows, you can see sweat and lines of black grease. He looks like he belongs to some tribe or some gang. In his hands are spanners and ratchets and screws and wires and chunks of metal that don't belong in his hands. He doesn't speak. Not with his mouth. He speaks with the look on his face. It says, *What happen?* like he doesn't want an answer, like he would rather listen to the engine. Like the engine has something more incredible to tell him than you do, like you don't have nothing incredible to tell him at all. But you do, so you open your mouth to tell him and he says, "Pass me the three-quarter socket."

And even though they're only words, it's like a needle jooking you. Jooking a hole in the incredible bubble of the story you have in your head, and so now you feel all the wanting-to-tell-it come hissing out, and you feel the story shrivelling up and folding away.

You pass him the stupid socket and then you run across the yard and jump on your bike and ride through the gate in so much vexation you don't tell anybody anything.

If it was daytime you would ride into town and ask the lady at the library who stamps books and knows everything if there isn't someplace you could go to complain about the family you are in.

You ride until you realize it's too dark to ride. This realizing it's too dark to ride occurs at the same time you feel yourself flying because the bike realized, before you did, that it's too dark to ride and it stopped this riding-in-the-dark stupidness before you did. So now you are flying, and flying would be okay if you didn't already know that at the end of flying is bush and macka and pain.

The bush comes with a *oorphrumph* sound. The macka comes with a *eeeyii* sound. And the pain—the pain calls down all kinda bad-word sound that you didn't even know you knew. But you do, and you holler them out like any old drunken man on a Friday night.

There is something about pain that makes you feel for home. Makes you forget how much complaints you have against your family and you just wish you were in the arms of your mother with her hands fixing up your broken body, with tenderness in her eyes and a worryness on her face. She can say, "Nice," now. She can say whatever she likes. You don't mind. Pain can make even "Nice" sound like something someone could say. Pain is like that. Pain is also like a worm chopped in two. It has a furious rolling and wriggling around in it and a crying for its mother in it.

You don't know about your father coming for you.

You don't know about him carrying you like you are two years old all the way back to the house or about your sister wailing when she sees you in his arms with your leg looking like it has been put on back to front, inside out, upside down.

You just know that this place, this bed, is not your place, not your bed. And when you try to move, you wonder if this is even your body. Your whole body feels mashed like pounded yam and your head is a fish swimming around and around and around in a bowl.

You try to sit up, and that is when you notice that you cannot sit up because of your leg. It feels like it is in concrete.

Your head is still spinning so you have to ease up carefully. Someone has put your leg in concrete, and around it is wire and pulleys like you are a machine. Slowly you begin to understand what has happened—*they're* turning you into a machine. Mary Janga's people have come for her and taken you instead, because they want to turn people into robots. And who with any sense in their head would take up Mary Janga when they could take you?

You have to escape. Just as soon as your head stop this spinning t'ing, you will escape, you tell youself. You tell yourself you will lie down for just a minute and then you will escape. You will lie down and close your eye for just one second and then . . . and then . . . and . . .

A big face is smiling down at you. It doesn't look like an alien face. It looks like a normal somebody's face. It is smiling but you don't smile back. You know you are in mortal danger of being turned into a RZ105 or something like that, with numbers and letters for a name. But the more you look, the more this face begins to look just like somebody you know. The face begins to be the face of Nurse Lawes.

The face says, "So how you feeling? You take a bad fall, y'know." (This is just the sort of thing Nurse Lawes would say.)

When you try to lift up, the Nurse Lawes face says, "A'right, take it easy. We have yuh leg in traction."

You wonder what your leg in concrete has to do with ploughing up land, but you figure tractors are big machines and your leg is like a machine, so maybe they correspond. You don't say anything. You just nod. Aliens can be funny, you tell yourself. Nodding is best.

Next thing you know, she's lifted you up with one hand, and with the other, she's organized the pillow into a back rest so you can sit up. You sit up and look around and realize that, guess what? Nurse Lawes is Nurse Lawes, because guess what? You are in the hospital. All around you are beds with children in them or not in them. Some children with bandages on their heads or around their arms are sitting in a corner watching TV and some are playing together with toys on the floor and some of them are reading books and some are just lying down still, but all of them have on pajamas.

Nurse Lawes tells you she is going to bring you a drink. You watch her walking to the end of the room. You want to call her back and tell her that you don't want a drink, you want to go home. You want your mother; you want your father. You even want Mary Janga. But you feel too shame to shout these things out and so you just think them to yourself. And while you are thinking these things to yourself, you start to think about what happened to put you in this bed that is not yours, in this place that is not yours. But all this thinking starts your head spinning again and you have to close your eyes.

In the darkness behind your eyes, you try to remember without thinking, but nothing happens. If your memory is a computer screen, it is blank. If it is a box, it is empty. If it is a sound, it is silent. You start to feel scared. You feel just like when you were seven and you went to cricket with your father and he told you not to let go of his hand, but instead of not letting go you let go because you were too big to be holding his hand. And so you let go, and in that second his hand, his arm, his whole body disappeared, and instead of it being you and your daddy at cricket, it was just you. You and millions and millions and millions of arms and legs and bodies you did not know. And you felt alone and scared, just like you feel now, because here you are in this strange place and the only person you know has gone to get a drink you don't want.

Your body is turning into a robot. Your head is a spinning top and your memory is an empty box, a blank screen, a silent sound. You feel all alone and . . . but wait! You *do* remember something. It's not the something you want to remember, but it is something. The cricket story is something. And your father and your mother and Mary Janga. They are somethings too. You don't feel so bad now. Not so, so bad, but there is still some feel-bad in you because yuh mash up and alone. The only thing you can think to do is pray and so you do.

Just as you finish praying you hear *swoosh . . . swoosh,* and you see Nurse Lawes coming back through the big plastic doors at the end of the room. The doors make that sound— *swoosh . . . swoosh*—when they open and close. Before she gets to your bed with the drink, you hear *swoosh . . . swoosh* again, and you think you see a little girl in a jeans skirt and a pink top come running in. Yes, it's a little Mary Janga girl in a pink top calling your name in a loud, screechy, excited voice that does not belong in a hospital.

Sometimes it takes a long time to get an answer to a prayer. Sometimes it can happen before you even finish praying and sometimes the answer comes and it makes you feel shame. Mary Janga calling out your name in that voice that belongs somewhere far away from here—somewhere where nobody can hear it—is an answer that makes you feel shame. But mix up with the shame is a smile and a gladness, and when the doors go *swoosh* . . . *swoosh* again, you know you don't even have to look up.

Your mother has brought you mangoes and bananas and June plums. Her eyes look like they want to cry and she keeps stroking your head. She tells your father to sit down instead of pacing backwards and forwards like that, but he doesn't. He keeps on pacing and shaking his head and saying, "Bwoy, me no know wha' 'appen to dis bwoy. Wha' de hell get into dis child? Eeh?" And you wish he would sit down because he is making your head spin again with all the up and down he's doing.

Mary Janga gives you something in a brown paper bag and then she drinks off all your drinks without asking, "PleasemayI?" and then some madness flies up into her head and she pounds on the concrete around your leg like she is pounding on a door.

Your crying-out-in-pain voice is even louder than Mary Janga's voice, and everyone in the room looks at you like you have something to tell them. Nurse Lawes comes for Mary Janga. You think, *Maybe they'll operate on her straight away and take out whatever it is that is in her that makes her so . . . so . . . Mary Janga.*

Then your father does sit down, and straightaway you wish he was standing up and pacing around, because as soon as he sits he has more questions—questions you cannot answer, like, "Bwoy, wha' 'appen to you?"

Questions like, "But whe' de hell you t'ink yuh was going dem kinda hours deh?" And, "So yuh never hear me a call to yuh? So yuh tu'n big man and cyan do wha' de hell yuh like now?" Questions that nobody in the world can answer like, "Eeh? Eeh? Eeh?"

And then your mother asks you the most difficult question of all: "So yuh 'member wha' happen to yuh?"

You shake your head and tell her that you don't remember one thing. And the moment you shake your head, it starts to spin faster and faster. It is spinning so fast it is ready to take off. It's on the runway. It has full throttle, you can hear the engines roaring, the engines roaring, the engines roaring . . .

Yes! Yes! You *do* remember. Your father with his head in the truck and the engine roaring and "Nice" and "Yuck" and ratchets and sockets and bubbles and . . . and how could you forget? The most incredible thing in the whole wide world. And the story bubble is big, big, big now, and it is so full of wanting-to-tell that it is ready to bus', and it does, and so you tell them about the sound that you heard and how you followed it into the bush and how you went softly, softly when you got near because you saw it was a goat. That big fat goat that belongs to Mas' Arnold in Spring Gully, and how the goat was lying down on her side and crying, "Mmeeeer-mmeeeer," and straining like she want to doo-doo but it wouldn't come out. Crying and straining and crying and straining and then, how, all of a sudden, this slimy thing like a big piece of Jell-O that someone forgot to color in just pop out, and how you could see something moving around in the Jell-O, and how it had you there like a piece o' rock just a stand up and a look and cyaah move. And how the mommy goat lick up the bag, lick it and eat it, and then how the thing that was inside come out, and how it was all wet and looking just like a real goat but small, small. And how the mummy goat start lick it now, and how it wobble around like it couldn't manage to stand up, and then it did and then it start to suck—just like Mary Janga when she was small and still like a human being.

And then you finish and you look up and you see your father, your mother, Nurse Lawes, and Mary Janga with a really-listening look on their face and all the pajama children are around your bed too and now one of them seh, "Fe real?" and another one seh, "Wow!" and then, for just one small moment, there is silence—your father has no more questions in him—not even Mary Janga is making a sound. Everyone has listened to your incredible story. Everyone. It's amazing. It's stupendous. It's . . . incredible.

It's night now.

All the parents have gone home and all the pajama children are in bed. You can hear the nurses talking softly and laughing at the end of the room. You can hear the trees moaning and creaking and tapping on the window behind you and you think of scary stories. You wonder how it is that scary stories always seem so stupid in the day but the moment night come down they don't seem stupid at all. You think they must have some magic in them, and if they have some magic, you think, then maybe they have some realness in them too.

You feel alone and scared.

You don't want to feel alone and scared. But you do.

You think maybe a mango will stop you feeling like this.

You switch on the lamp next to the bed and then you see the bag Mary Janga left for you.

You open it. Inside is Floppy Florenzo the Rabbit. Floppy Florenzo the Rabbit is lime-green with bright pink ears that glow in the dark. You quickly turn off the light and stuff Floppy Florenzo the Rabbit under the cover. You shake your head and think, *That little girl is something else.*

Floppy Florenzo the Rabbit smells of Mary Janga on the porch talking to her dollies, and your mother's tender hands and your father finding you at cricket and carrying you on his shoulders.

You yawn. You feel tired . . . well, well tired.

Just before you drop asleep, you hear Floppy Florenzo say, "So what? Yuh not telling me goodnight?"

SIBLINGS
by Rudolph Wallace

I t start off like a ordinary Saturday morning. Mr. Evans take time wheel him bicycle outta the front room from before 7 o'clock. If anybody ask him where him always go so early, him tell them him go look work. Him a plumber, and him nuh have no tools 'pon him, but nuh watch that. Him two pickney know better—say a more rum him gone drink.

Andre leave out little after 9, gone play football before sun get too hot. Him pass Annmarie inna the front room, a use a old towel sop up the piss 'pon the linoleum floor.

What is there inna this rum thing, my God, that turn big man inna little baby?

Donna come over around 11 fi give Annmarie a hand with the big bag o' peas she get in from country. Donna good with the gungo for she used to sell it too—though she nuh set foot inna Coronation Market from the day she meet this guy Tony two months ago, with the good U.S. dollar like it a come outta him ears. A pure Spanish that talk, y'know. Them coulda barely understand one another, but nuh ask if him never manhandle the body. Three weeks now Donna nuh see him and she still a walk funny . . . and still a lick out cash.

Donna did wa' set up Annmarie with one o' Tony friend, gi' her a chance fi eat a food. But Annmarie very partial when it come on to man—nobody nuh know wha' she a try prove. One thing Annmarie nuh like 'bout Donna—she chat sometime like them wind her up.

"So Annmarie"—she chaw the bubble gum and wait till Annmarie look 'pon her—"when you a go set me up with Andre?"

Annmarie cut her eye and kiss her teeth. "Me coulda say me love my little bredda and send him fi go deal with you, Donna?"

"Wha' wrong with me?"

"Me nuh wa' you inna mi family—that a the long and short. Fi one thing, you older than him . . . and fi a next thing, you a go keep man with him. Me know you too good."

"Suit youself. Is only help me a try help out a situation. You suppose to know say them have it outta street say him gone."

"You a chat shit."

"As God."

The two o' them position in front o' one another 'pon the veranda, 'pon either side o' the washpan with the bitch crocus bag o' green gungo a them foot—two hours work you a look 'pon at least. And with all o' that, whenever time Andre name come up, Donna can still find time fi drop her left wrist and flutter her finger them. God—He knows which part she get da move dey from—she mussie know one battyman pianist.

Annmarie nuh take her on more than so. "If any o' my

puppa pickney ever dare talk 'bout him a tun gay, that's the last word woulda come outta him mouth—me can tell you that fi a fact."

Donna don't out fi ease up. "Gi' me ten minutes with him and me can tell you if him a battyman, yes or no."

That blasted rumor. Every time Annmarie think it dead, it appear again—like herpes to rass.

"How come all of a sudden everybody a come to me with some little fuck-up remarks 'bout mi bredda? It look like oonu tired o' talk it behind mi back, so one by one oonu a test me. Me know what the problem is, y'know. A because him so cool and sexy, oonu vex say him nah look none o' oonu—that a the one and only problem."

"Cool and sexy, eh? A so them always cool with woman, but wait so till you see them 'mongst them one another."

Donna laugh—her loudest market woman laugh.

"Wha' you see wrong with him?" Is like Annmarie a count her word them. "Oonu can't say him effeminate nor nutten. A him captain Conscious Youth under-17 football team last year, right? And nobody nuh fight 'gainst battyman more than them dey young boy."

So she talk, she fling peas, trash, knife, everything inna the pan, then get up and shake out her skirt, make sure some o' the fine trash fly inna Donna eye. Donna make up her face but she nuh say nutten.

Annmarie go stand up beside the veranda railing where Donna can't see her face.

"You see why me hate Fletcher's Land people? Oonu brutalize oonu owna kind worse than any Saddam. A nuh no big thing when a seventeen-year-old uptown youth nuh have no girlfriend. But down ya? Unless him a go 'bout the place and boast 'bout how much baby mother him have, everybody start ask question. Oonu nuh business if him have a work or if him can support himself. So longst him a lay down with every frowsy-tail gal inna the community."

"Annmarie, you a take this thing too personal. A nuh your fault if you bredda touch. My mother have a cousin stay same way. Answer me this one question: If nutten nuh do him, how come him nuh have no girl? Fi him buddy join church?"

"Donna, don't you say you come over ya fi help me shell the peas? Then make you nuh bruk down the almshouse argument and shell the bumboclaat peas?"

Same time Andre come through the gate, soak with perspiration. Him T-shirt fling over him shoulder and all him have on is a shorts and him football boots. Him coulda never did pick a worse time.

Donna pounce right away. "Come ya little bit, young boy. Wha' you a do Friday night?"

"Friday night?"

"Yes. Them a keep a dance down a Nova and me have a nice girl fi you."

Andre, who-for spirit never too take Donna from morning, barely slow down fi answer her. "I mighta pass through if I have the time." Him fake fi throw a punch after Annmarie and she gwan like she duck it, then him skip go inna the house.

Annmarie make sure talk her piece loud so Andre hear her. "Nova dance them a foolishness. Andre nuh have no time fi waste."

"You see the problem?" Donna chip in. "Is like you a try

you best fi stop him from get involved with any Fletcher's Land girl. How the youth a go know pussy if you nuh 'low him?"

Da one dey jerk Annmarie. All of a sudden, outta the clear blue sky, a fi-her fault why her bredda nah go round and beg crotches. Without even say "skeffem" she march straight inside o' the house, lef' Donna same place. Eggs or young ones now to rahtid. She push Andre room door just as him a step outta him brief and she turn 'way her head.

"Hey . . . you a big man now, y'know. A high time you start to . . ." She make a circle with her finger. "You know wha' me a say?"

"No. Me nuh know wha' you a say."

"Cover up that dey big old ugly somep'n. Me nuh want it blind me."

"You see it every day from me born till now. Wha' the use hide it again?"

"Things change, Andre. Me a nineteen year old, soon twenty. You a seventeen. We a nuh little pickney again."

"That nuh say. Me and you ever bonafide, no matter we age. Wha' happen? Somep'n wrong? Me know you too good. Somep'n a bother you. Is wha'?"

Him move towards her but she back 'way.

"Nuh bother touch me with you sweaty self. Gwan go hold you shower."

Andre nuh bother close the bathroom door, for him well wa' hear wha' she have 'pon her mind. Him have fi shout over the noise o' the pipe. "I hope is not the gal dey Donna do you nutten, y'know, cause you know me will deal with her good and proper."

"Hold down you voice. She still dey 'pon the veranda.

No. This nuh have nutten fi do with she. You really out fi go this dance Friday night?"

"Go which part? You mad? You nuh know say me nuh inna dem somep'n dey?"

"Then why you tell her say you mighta go?"

"No special reason. Just a gi' her somep'n fi hold."

"You sure you nuh wa' meet her friend? Who to tell? You mighta like her."

"Uh-uh. Me can't see myself a knot up with any o' fi her friend them."

"You coarse, eh, man? Me is one o' her friend them, y'know. You couldn't knot up with me? I don't mean me personally, of course. Somebody like me."

Andre nuh say nutten more till him come outta the shower. Then, so him a dry off, a so him a go up towards her.

"Annmarie, how you a question me so? Everything a'right?"

Annmarie walk off. Them last few months ya she can't concentrate so good anytime the somep'n dey a dangle in front o' her—not like first time. "How come you nuh have no girlfriend, Andre? Is wha' you a defend?"

The question lick Andre. Is like him can't talk. Him only a stare 'pon her, and she only a look 'pon the last year almanac 'pon the wall. Nobody nah say shit.

Andre eventually find him voice. "Me nuh see *you* with no boyfriend. Wha' *you* a defend?"

"Me know who me like. Is just that him mightn't feel the same way 'bout me."

"Wha' him name?"

She nuh answer. Him go up to her again.

"Any man you want, you can get. You mightn't spend a whole heap o' money 'pon yuhself, but to how me see it, you look better than all o' them gal dey."

"You bias. And anyhow, a nuh me we a talk 'bout right ya so. A you . . . a you everybody a talk 'bout."

Him hold on 'pon her hand. "Me nuh expect you fi listen to dem dey careless people—"

All of a sudden, Donna shoob the door and come in. Annmarie so frighten she make haste draw back. Donna look like she frighten too when she see Andre, naked as the day him born, like him back up Annmarie between the bed and the dresser and the two o' them a look inna one another face. She give out, "A wha' this, mi Jesus?" Then the three o' them start fi stammer.

Donna ketch up herself and mumble. "Me just come fi tell you say me gone. Me cover up the peas inna the kitchen." Then she spin round and bolt outta the house.

Annmarie panic.

"Lawd, Andre, is wha' she think we did a do?"

Andre still a hang on to her hand. "Make her gwan."

Annmarie shake him off. "A because you nuh know Donna."

She run outside. Andre quick pull on a shorts and run back o' her, but Donna disappear long time. By the time them reach back inna the house, the most them can do is si' down 'pon Andre bed and reason it out.

Annmarie say, "You realize the trouble we into?"

"Me nuh see why. All happen, she see me and you stand up a talk. Wha'? You think say a through me naked with you inna the room? That nuh nutten."

"Donna can make gossip outta anything. You have fi admit you stand up so close to me it coulda look like you a rub up 'pon me."

"She fi learn fi knock, or she going get shock." Him jab the air with him finger—the good rapper style.

"You a treat this thing like is a joke."

"Wha' else me fi do?"

"The problem start from you come up inna mi face."

"Me come inna you face, nuh gi' you no space."

Andre that all over. Serious things a gwan and a now him choose fi form fucking fool. She bounce him with her elbow.

"Whether Donna did shoob the door yes or no, me and you was going have a problem this day ya."

Andre get serious. "Me nuh understand wha' you a say. We a brother and sister."

"Yeah. But sometime me feel say me and you too . . . close."

"Why?"

"Through we nuh really have nobody else, when you think 'bout it. Mamma dey States—she a try her best, yes, but we nuh know when we a go see her again. And Pappa only a drown inna the rum bottle. So a just you and me."

"Wha' me a ask is how that become a problem fi any-body—why you feel we not suppose to close."

"Me just nuh think we shoulda walk round the house naked in front o' one another. Me have fi take some o' the blame . . . me do it too."

"Which part it say inna the Bible we not suppose to?"

"Common sense, Andre. You nuh have no girl and me

nuh have no man. Next thing me a go start have feelings fi you."

"I woulda hope you have feelings fi me a'ready."

Annmarie let go him hand and stand up, nah look 'pon him.

"You know wha' me a talk 'bout, Andre. From now on, you keep you distance. Okay? And carry yuhself more decent round the house."

Andre roll over 'pon him belly.

"So like how me stay now, inna mi shorts alone, that alright?" Him voice kinda weak.

"Andre, I don't wa' you deliberately misunderstand me."

"Me understand you perfect."

"Simple as you take it, Donna probably have it all over the street by now, say she come in ya and ketch the two o' we a grind. That is wha' come from this—"

"Annmarie! Me nuh inna the ray-ray. Nuh tell me wha' Donna nor nobody else a say."

"Okay. Figet Donna. Me tell you wha' me feel. Right? This ya closeness . . . it nuh healthy."

"It nuh feel no way to me."

Annmarie look hard inna him eye. Them full up o' water. And him mouth set like how it used to stay just before him bus' out inna bawling. She si' down side o' him, so close them two leg a touch, then she drape her arm round him shoulder.

"You trying fi say this nuh feel no way to you?"

Andre shake him head hard but nuh take him eye off o' her. She take time bring her face closer to fi-him, till she can feel him breath. "And this nuh feel no way neither?"

Him nuh do nutten this time, except turn him head and

face forward. Annmarie take her finger tilt him chin, and bring it back round towards her. Him forehead damp like mango wha' just come outta fridge. Then she kiss him 'pon him mouth just so. The kiss nuh last more than 'bout one second. She surprise how him lip them cold. And before him even come to him senses, she get up, vex like hell.

"How that feel now?" she shout so loud him jump. "Answer me nuh! A that you want?"

Him nuh answer . . . is like the little choops have him giddy.

"Well, you can't say me never warn you!" she bawl out, then she stomp outta the room.

Fi the next five minutes, Andre stay same place like him balls a weigh him down. Then him get up and follow her. Her room door close. It nuh carry no lock, but him knock all the same. No answer. Him lean him ears 'gainst the door and pick up a little sniffling sound, like she a bawl. That a when him open the door.

Who tell him fi go do that? She lay down naked 'pon the bed, a face the wall. Him nuh sure which part her hand dey, and him nuh too wa' know.

"Excuse me."

Him start to back out, but she spin round 'pon him. "Andre . . . you can answer me one question?"

Him turn 'way him head. Right now, with wha' a gwan since morning, him dare not commit himself. Him just stand up dey like him stupid, nah go neither left nor right.

Annmarie go through and ask the question, though she done know the answer a'ready. "You is a virgin? Andre, talk to me. You a virgin?"

"Wha' kinda question that?"

"Me wa' know. Me have fi know if you nuh carry no feel-ings, none at all. Come here."

"Me a'right right ya so. You same one say we nuh fi get too close."

"I make a exception 'pon this occasion. Come here."

"Put on somep'n firs'."

"Nuh you say the nakedness nuh bother you?"

"A lie me did a tell."

She draw the sheet round her and him go si' down a' the foot o' the bed. "Rass, boy, you think me a go rape you?"

"Me nuh appreciate you behavior. Wha' make you a try fi embarrass me all of a sudden?"

"You think is that me a do?"

"Then wha' else it coulda be? You a come to me with all kinda slackness and nastiness, like a Donna them put you up to it. A nuh so me and you live, Annmarie, and me nuh appreciate it."

Annmarie make fi say somep'n else, but it come in like she swallow back the word them. She make haste cover up her mouth and flash her hand fi tell him mus' come outta her room. Still for all, before him coulda ketch the doorway, she bus' out inna one piece o' cow bawling. She bawl and bawl and nuh get up outta the bed till night come down. Andre reason say a so people bawl when them a repent o' them sins.

The next day, Annmarie put on her clothes and go church. That is a once-in-a-blue-moon thing fi her, so it look to Andre like him did guess right 'bout the repentance part. But a nuh that dey 'pon Annmarie mind at all. She only wa' go somewhere where nuff people dey, fi see if Donna start to spread the rumor yet. And the truth is, she never feel too comfortable inna the house, for the boy start to look 'pon her a way. By the time she reach back home, she little more confident. She cook a pot o' beef soup and she and her father sit down 'pon the sofa and eat and watch TV. She always like fi know say him have somep'n inna him stomach, for rum 'pon hungry belly can be a dangerous thing.

Later on, when Mr. Evans gone street and Andre a do him homework a the dining table, she draw up a chair side o' him.

She start off timid. "Andre . . . everybody . . . no matter who . . . have a certain amount o' sexual feelings, from them healthy any at all. Is a'right if you nuh wa' talk 'bout your own, but I hope you nuh mind if I talk to you 'bout mine's. You 'member yesterday me tell you say me in love with somebody but him nuh know? Well, me make up me mind fi tell him."

"That good, but . . . you wa' see . . . me a try do some work ya."

"Whether you wa' listen, yes or no, you going have fi hear. This a nuh somep'n me wa' happen. Trust me. People nuh have no control over who them love."

Andre shape fi get up, but she grab on 'pon him shoulder. Him shut the book wha' him a read, fold him hand, and look 'pon her vex.

She a talk fast now, like she 'fraid him run 'way before she done say wha' she have fi say, and like she know she won't have the courage fi say it a next time. "Me know say me crazy and me sick and everything that is bad. Me hear 'bout step-father. Me hear 'bout father. But from me born, me never hear 'bout no girl wha' fall in love with her little brother. Me nah ask you fi have sex with me . . . but if me nuh tell you, is like me going go outta me mind. Me know somep'n never right. You can't say me never warn you."

"Rass, Annmarie. Wha' you expect me fi say?"

"Tell me say you nuh hate me fi it."

"Wha' the blood . . . ? Cho! Is wha' a gwan? You a mi sister!"

"Tell me you nuh hate me, Andre. Tell me!"

"How me a go hate you?"

She get up and go her room like she satisfy with that. But it never done dey so.

The day she tell Andre was the first day she admit to herself say she have a serious problem. Is like from the moment she utter the word, a seed plant inna her chest, and the somep'n grow like national debt till it start fi take over her body, till she couldn't hold it in no longer.

One day she whisper tell Donna, who promise say she nah go tell a soul. Then she write and tell her mother, who cuss her dog rotten and threaten fi jump 'pon a plane and come fix her business. She smile when she read da part dey, because she know the mother nuh legal. After that, she work up the courage and tell her father—a that time dey Old Master take to the liquor!

Donna, with all the try she try seal her lip, couldn't hold in a news like that fi save her life.

When the story bus', Fletcher's Land people nuh talk 'bout nutten else fi two weeks . . . then somep'n else happen—two baby bun up inna a house and the mother run 'way and everybody forget Annmarie and Andre. Maybe a that Annmarie did want, because is like the rumor warn off all them gal wha' did wa' mess round Andre. Them gal dey can take 'way you husband or you boyfriend as you 'quint you eye, but them nuh know where fi start when it come on to brother.

One day car lick Mr. Evans off o' him bicycle, and him head bus' open 'pon the torris. From wha' the car man say, him dead 'pon the spot. That lef' Annmarie and Andre alone inna the house. And a so them live, them one, same place inna the little Fletcher's Land house. Andre never do so good inna school, but him manage fi hold a job with a printery, while Annmarie gwan ping-pong with the buying and selling. She done reason it out, say nutten couldn't gwan between them more than so. To how she see it, neither pumpum nor batty never interest him.

Sometime she think she shoulda did keep her feelings to herself instead o' frig with the innocent boy head, but then again, a Donna did force the issue. When she take a stock, her true feelings was going come out one way or the other, so might as cheap everybody just face up to the reality from early. One thing fi sure, she and Andre couldn't go back to how it was first time. From the day she expose her soul, right away she start to cover up her body. And she notice say little by little him a get more self-conscious too. If she come inna the room and him nuh have on nutten, him turn sideways or take time mask the tool with him hand—mussie think say she a go grab on 'pon it.

One Sunday morning before sun come up, Annmarie lay down inna her bed a sleep and she ongle hear when somebody shoob the door. It come in almost like part o' a dream. She open her eye and see Andre, stark born naked, stand up over her. None o' them nuh say a word. All she do a lift up the sheet and him come under it.

Fletcher's Land nuh know when him actually start fi cod her, but if you see them with them one another when them go out, you nuh have fi ask if little coddings nah gwan. Old people cover them grandpickney eye, or cross the road when them see the Evans them a come, but that nuh matter. The more people throw word 'pon them, the more them tight. Annmarie and Andre nuh know wha' a go happen next year, or even next week. But right now, them happy, you fart.

HOW TO BEAT A CHILD THE RIGHT AND PROPER WAY
by Colin Channer

G ood evening, fellow classmates. I'm very please to appear before you to present my five-minute "how to" speech in Speech 112 this evening.

I know many of you had a long day at work, so I'm going to be brief and to the point. I had a day off today, but that don't mean I should just go on and on because my energy is up.

By the way, professor, we could open the door? These trailers hot like jail. And while you doing that, can I ask you to give me a little break if I go over five minutes, please? I have a lot on my brain tonight. You're shaking your head. Consider it a graduation present. After this semester you won't have to see ol' Ciselyn again. You smiling now. You little devil you. You smile just like my youngest son.

So, fellow classmates, I need to explain something to you before I start. If you notice, I don't have any cue cards. What happen is that today I change what I had plan to talk about. So what I did the cue cards for don't really make any sense again. So, as the young people say, I'm going to do it on the fly.

So let me start over again. I'm very please to appear before you to present my five-minute "how to" speech in Speech 112 this evening. I know many of you had a long day at work today so I'm going to be brief and to the point.

My speech this evening is called "How to Beat a Child the Right and Proper Way," and the reason I decide to speak on this topic is based on the fact of something I saw today that remind me of something that took place on a Tuesday night in Jamaica thirty-four years ago, in 1972. Some of you never even born yet.

Anyway, today when I was in a Duane Reade on Broadway, over by Wall Street, buying some panty hose and some chocolate for my grandchildren, I saw this child of about seventeen back-answering her mother. Everything the mother say, the child back-answer. You know how these children nowadays can go on. Just rude. When the mother talking to her, you know what she was doing? Popping her bubble gum and rolling her eye. She fold her arms and shaking her leg, and sometimes when the mother say something serious to her, she look on her mother and laugh. The child just rude and out of order. Anything the mother say, she contradict her. If the mother say, "A," she say, "B."

But anyway, I wasn't really paying them any mind, you know, because I'm not a person that like to put myself in people's business. Plus, I was in a mood where not a thing was going to bother me, because I was coming from a luncheon for my daughter Karen. I can't really remember the place. Fancy place though. When you walk in there you see class. What it name again? It has a name like a person. But for the life of me I can't remember what. Fancy name though. French.

But anyway, a lovely place though, down Wall Street with plenty columns and chandeliers. Her office give her a big honor today, that's why you see me dress up like this, with my hat like I going to church. Cause you know me. I'm simple. I don't like fuss.

But anyway, when I reach the register now, the mother and the daughter come up behind me, and the arguing was still going on. Just *bloo-bloo-bloo-bloo* . . . *bloo-bloo-bloo-bloo* . . . mother and daughter back and forth, and my poor ears couldn't eat grass.

So when I sift through all the *bloo-bloo-bloo*, I pick out that the little girl get into bad company. She won't do her school work or go to school, and the mother went up to her school to talk to the guidance counselor, and the little girl tell her off. Tell her off in front o' the guidance counselor, the principal, and her English teacher. Denounce the mother and call her all kind o' names.

So this is what the mother was trying to talk to her about in the pharmacy now, when the argument start.

Some things the little girl tell her mother I couldn't even say in class. No child suppose to say those kinds of things to their mother. When you look at the little girl, you know, you can see that deep down she is a nice little child. But nothing more than she feel she big now because she turn seventeen, so her mother mustn't say nothing to her. When I tell you, nice looking girl too, you know. Small in body but you can see she have a nice shape. She have hips. And her hair is so tall and nice. Tall down almost to her bottom. And when you talk about wavy and thick. And don't talk about shine. And to top it off, she have a beauty spot on her cheek beside her nose. Have an Italian look. Pretty girl in her green plaid uniform, so you know the mother spending money to send her to the good Catholic school. But just out of order. Just out of order. Just out of order. And rude. Just calling her mother stupid and denouncing her how she don't know anything, and shouting after her how when anything happen she always take the guidance counselor and the teacher side.

When she say that, you know what happen? I feel like turn around to her and say, *Whose side she suppose to take? She's your mother.*

But I keep my mouth shut.

So anyway, I couldn't get the little girl and her mother out o' my mind even after I leave Duane Reade. But I had a lot o' time before class, so I went to get me exercise—you know, walk around.

That is how I keep myself fit, you know. I like to walk. That's how come I don't move from one thirty-five from I come to this country. I lose a little o' the height though. You know, the bones and age. But I born with height to give away.

By the way, when I say I like to walk, that don't mean I like to walk any and anywhere, you know. I don't like to walk in parks and all that kind o' thing. I like to walk in Manhattan. I like to walk in the city. While I walking, if I see anything for my children or grandchildren I can stop and pick it up. Or if I want some tea or something to eat, like for instance if I get some gas, I can stop and take my time, then start to walk again. Plus, when I watch New York 1 I hear 'bout too much women who get rape off while they exercising in the park in broad daylight. I don't know why they bother go and tempt fate for. You think is yesterday man like to rape woman in bush? So you know this now and going to go out and run beside the bushes with you leg expose in shorts? Listen to me, I never once hear 'bout a woman getting rape in front o' Rockefeller Center at half past 12. So what that tell you? Stay with the crowd!

So anyway, Wall Street is one o' the areas where I like to walk. Down there is like England to me. You have your little streets and your old white buildings. And almost anything you want to shop for you can get down there. Plus, is a orderly kind of place. Is a business place. Down there, you don't have nobody running up and down like they wild. Take for instance Times Square or further down where I work in Herald Square—too much wildness up there, man. Too much young people idling with no ambition or nothing to do. Just running 'bout the place and talking loud. If they bounce you by accident, they wouldn't even say, *Excuse me.* And when they ask you a question is like they don't know the word *please.* But sometimes you can't really blame them. When children come like that, is the parents' fault.

Speaking of fault, you know if they don't organize a luncheon for me at Macy's, is my fault. As I mention Herald Square I remember that this month make it thirty years since they took me on. If they know what I know, they better have a luncheon for me like my daughter office had for her this afternoon. Even if is just accounting alone. Or is hell to pay!

But anyway, when I say I couldn't get the girl and her mother out of my mind, it was the *mother* I couldn't forget, in truth. And when I walk about two blocks I start to hear a voice telling me to turn back. And I kept telling the voice that is not my business. But the voice wouldn't stop, and all the fight I keep fighting it, you know what I do? I spin round and turn back down to Duane Reade.

The way I was stepping down Broadway, people must be think I was mad. Because you know how down there stay— everybody moving like they have battery, or somebody wind them up. Just *voom-voom-voom-voom . . . voom-voom-voom-voom*. Worse, is summer, so all the tourists come and make the place more pack. And they don't know how to walk.

So imagine my dilemma now. You know how the side-walks down there stay. Hardly two people can pass. And is me going one way, and is them coming the other way. And is me boring through, and is them getting mad. But I don't care, because I had to talk to that mother. I had to talk to her. Because when I take a stock, I realize that her hands were so full and she don't know what to do.

And . . . hmm . . . let me tell you . . .

Hmm . . . *ahh bwoy* . . .

You see my daughter Karen, who I went to the luncheon for? She might be a Senior Vice President at JPMorgan Chase now, but don't think it did always look like she was going to turn out the right and proper way. At one time it look like she was heading for the gutter fast, fast. But you know what save her? I, as mother, did what I had to do. Because, le' me tell you something, you know: Once they go past a certain point—these children?—don't think it easy to bring them back. When certain kind o' rudeness come, you have to nip it in the bud. When they want to spring up like they fertilize themselves and act like they big, but you know for a fact that they small, don't wilt in front o' them. Stand up firm! Hold your ground! Push them back. Sink them down again below the grass, and stand up over them like you have a machete in your hand. If they push up they head again before they time, don't hesitate. Take one swing and chop it off.

So anyway, when I reach by this big store here . . . the one where you can buy everything from clothes to luggage but your mind always tell you to really look 'pon the label good—Century 21—I think I glimpse the two o' them, and I stop to focus. And you know what? It *was* the two o' them in truth.

When I almost reach them now, I call out to the mother.

I say, "Excuse me, miss. You were in Duane Reade?"

I could touch her on her shoulder, but I don't like to touch people in this place. Since 9/11—especially down that side—everybody get extra jumpy, m'dear. Next thing, you touch somebody and them turn round and think is terrorist and shoot you.

So, when I call her now, the mother stop and look at me and say, "Yes. Is something wrong?" She must be see a little thing in my face. Cause I'm a person like this, you know. I can't play hypocrite. And I can't take hypocritical people. I'm like Flip Wilson. What she name again? Geraldine. Don't you cry and don't you fret, cause what you see is what you get.

Anyway, the mother had on a tan coat that catch her to her knee. Not a dark tan, but more like . . . you know those Clarks shoes? Same color as these chairs here you sitting on. It was a spring coat with a belt round the waist, and from I see that I know her dress was not in good condition. Because now is May, and is just too hot for that. Plus, she didn't polish her shoes. Some twenty-dollar pumps. And the shoes itself was lean.

And when I see that now, I say to myself, *Dear God. Imagine, this woman sacrifice for this child so much and this child treat her like dog mess. The parents who do the most get the least thanks.*

Breeze was blowing. And like how they don't have the World Trade Center again, it was coming right through . . . *whih-whih-whih* . . . from over by the Westside Highway. I had to turn my back and take off my glasses before it blow off. For if it blow off, is me same one have run it down, and next thing dirt blow into my eye and blind me.

You're laughing. But is true. You can't take any chance again, you know. Not when you're old. I accept that fact. When the breeze start, I say to myself, *Glasses, hat, and frock.* You wondering why I say *frock?* Heh! People nowadays wi' scrutinize you same way. No matter how you're old.

So anyway, I ease over underneath one o' the awnings down by Century 21, and the mother and the daughter follow me. And when I straighten out myself now, I say to the little girl, "Sweetheart, I overheard you in the Duane Reade. Why you talk to your mother like that? I can see you're a nice girl, from a decent home. Look how your mother work and send you to school, eeh. And look how your uniform neat and nice. Why you speak to Mummy like that? You not to do that, sweetheart. When you talk to Mummy like that, you will make her feel embarrassed, like she don't train you at home."

That little wretch! You think she pay me any mind? No sir. She just take her mother hand and say, "Come on, Ma. Let's go."

But is like what I say gi' the mother a little *choops* o' strength, and she pull her hand away from the girl and wipe her face. But still yet, when she talk to me, her voice sound like she can't mash ants.

Hear her: "She's going through a very hard time."

So I say to her, "Ma'am, I understand. But you're her mother. No matter what she going through, she must know she can't talk to you like that."

When I say that now, you know what the little girl do? She fold her arms and whisper, "Mind your *effin'* business." And believe you me, she didn't say "effin'." She said the actual word. When she say this to me and done, she turn to her mother and say in a kind o' tired voice, like she's the one suppose to be frustrated, "Let's go." Then she swing herself and walk off.

And believe you me, the mother was going follow her.

When I see that, you see, I grab onto her hand and say, "Don't follow her up. Don't follow her up. Make her go on. Make her go on. If you follow her up, all you going do is make her think she can lead you. Don't make that child lead you like she have you on a chain. You're a woman. She's a child."

Now, you could see the mother know it was sense I was talking, you know, but she so accustom to making the child treat her like a little puppy, that she start to whimper now, "Jessica. Jessica. Jessie. Jessie. Come here. Come here."

And you know, the little demon never even look back at her mother and say, *Yes, dog?*

When the daughter pass and gone round the corner now, I take my other hand and turn the mother face to me. I look at her and say to her softly, cause I know she was feeling the pain, "Look here, miss. I know how you feel. But never mind. Never mind. I go through the same thing, a'ready. She has money to go home?"

She shake her head and say, "Yes."

"She normally go to school by herself?"

"Yes."

"And come home by herself?"

"Yes."

"So let her go on then. Let her go on. Don't follow her up."

She cover her face and start to bawl loud, loud now. You could stay across the street and hear. So, I put my arm around her like she's my friend long time and hush her. And as I hushing her now, she start to tell me how the girl was a nice, nice girl until she turn seventeen last year. After that, she don't know why, but the girl start to follow some friends into a bad crowd. And now she want everything to be her way. And she not studying her books.

She didn't exactly say "bad crowd," but that is what I pick from it. I know how to pick things out o' things, you know, and how to make sense out o' nonsense. If you ever hear how much money that mother spend on psychologist! And how she waste the guidance counselor time! When all she had to do was what she as a mother was suppose to do. But I know why she didn't do her duty. She 'fraid.

Anyway, as I'm listening to her now, I realize that when I thought she and her daughter was Italian, I was wrong. To tell you the truth, I can't tell you exactly what she was. But is not Italian. She look Italian*ish* though, and she had a funny accent. But Italians in they forties not coming to America again, like one time. And you could tell how her accent thick that she didn't live in America long. Plus, I know Italians. I live with them.

When I just come to America in 1976, is mostly Italian use to live near me, you know. That was up in the Bronx . . . up by Boston Road and Eastchester Road there—3678 Corsa Avenue, the first house I own in this place.

Serious as a judge. You might see mostly West Indians up there now—though I hear a lot o' Hispanics moving in— Lord Jesus. But it was pure Italian up there in my time. Even now, out in Long Island where I live now, guess what? I buck up on Italian again. Is like they love me. Perillo one side! Moretti next side! Polish in the back.

So when I say the woman wasn't Italian, I *know* what I talking about. But you could tell she was some kind o' cousin to them though . . . something from round that side. I'm not so good with the European setup, so I can't tell you where exact. But that don't mean I don't know the continent though, you know.

My son Andrew, the one who follow Karen—the bond lawyer—he must be send me over there about six or seven times a'ready. Everything first class! But I didn't go where use to be the Communist part though. And I think she's from over that. Listen to me, Communism come in like germs, you know. When you think it gone, it come right back and hold you. And when you think you have the medicine, it change on you. It evolve! Look at Russia. They say they free, but is Communism still. Can you imagine if I go make my son pay for me to go over there and something happen to make me can't come back? What I would tell Mr. Macy's Monday morning?

Thirty years at Herald Square, and never missed a day! Never been late! Perfect record. Thirty years! That's why I can do as I like up there. They don't bother with me. You know why? I'm a dedicated, disciplined worker. And these days especially, when workers like to jump from place to place, you can't beat that.

So anyway, as I said, they wasn't no Italian. But Italian was never the point. Here was a mother in distress. And this was a distress that touch something in my mind. As it touch me now, I told the woman that I went through the same thing with my daughter Karen, who is older than her. The woman, as I said, was in her forties. Karen must be fifty now. For I'm sixty-eight.

"You see, when they get like that and you try with them," I say to her, "and you keep on trying with them, and they still not hearing, is only one thing left to do. You have to beat they ass. Don't make America turn you into any fool. You don't come from here. As there is a God in heaven, when children—especially girls—start to act a certain way . . . like they is equal to you . . . you have to put them in they place. And don't make them or anybody else frighten you 'bout police and child welfare and all o' that. If you know *exactly* how to beat a child—call the police? You mad? After what they get from you?

Hmm . . . they wouldn't dare!

When the woman run off screaming down the street, a

voice say to me that maybe I didn't really bring my point across. Maybe I didn't fully explain the whole thing with the police. So I start to think how when you look at the state of young people in this country today, there's a lot of parents who could benefit from knowing how to grow their children right. What to do when they start to bend away from how they brought them up. How to grab ahold of them and straighten them out.

So it's this voice and this incident, my fellow classmates, that made me change my speech from "How to Make a Budget and Stick to It" to one more beneficial to the world these days: "How to Beat a Child the Right and Proper Way."

By the way, professor, I see you giving me the signal that I'm over my time, but I should point out to you that neither Singh nor Avila nor Cumberbatch are here this evening to give their presentation, so you might as well give me their time. And look. See, everyone agree. Why you think they clapping for?

So, Professor Hansen and considerate classmates, to understand why I behaved the way I did today you have to understand a little bit about my life.

I was born in Jamaica in 1938, and although you mightn't believe it, when I was coming up I was very poor.

My mother and father had eight of us. My father was a postman, and my mother use to work in a sweetie factory, making lollipops and bubble gum. When you have those kinds of work in Jamaica, especially in those days, things was very hard. It's not like up here, where if you are a postman you can live a decent life. Down there they use to pay the postman like he was a child riding a bicycle and all they had to do was give him pocket change. But he use to have to pedal round the city in the heat with pounds and pounds of mail.

So when you see me now, don't grudge me. I'm coming from very far.

Now, the house where I grow up was at 2a Saunders Lane in East Kingston. It was a board house, a rent house. It was smaller than this trailer here. By the way, professor, I can't take this room. It make me feel like I waiting for bail. Anyway, all of us live in that one-room house. But you know something? We keep it clean.

There was about six house in the yard and only one pipe outside by a mango tree, where everybody have to go and brush their teeth and bathe. And one kitchen too, where everybody go and cook, although sometime you use to just catch up a wood fire and cook your food on that.

I'm the last of all the eight, and I watch as all of my brothers and sisters turn twelve and my parents take them out of school and send them to a person in the area to learn a trade. But I didn't want a trade. I wanted a profession. From I was small I want to be something important in life. I don't know where the ambition come from, but that is what I have inside me from I born.

But anyway, it didn't look like life was going to work out like I want. Although teacher said I had the brain in primary school, my parents didn't have money to pay for the exam to pass and go to high school. And even if I did pass the exam, who was going pay for the uniform and the books?

Plus, you know something? My parents never think it

was important. None o' them never go to high school yet. And none o' them never know nobody that went to high school either. But for me to go and learn a trade like making hats or sewing clothes was a normal thing.

To cut a long story short, I got to go to high school, but not the whole entire time. My bigger brother, Ezroy, was twelve years older than me, and he use to be a mechanic for the railway until a diesel engine drop on him and crush him up in 1953. Well, he use to like to gamble a lot. But he use to lose all his money because he was dunce.

So when it was coming up to exam time, I went down to the train yard by West Street and tell him that I can help him to win. He ask me how, and I explain to him that Crown & Anchor and most of those games with dice use things from maths, and I knew my maths very well.

He didn't believe me at first, so I took him down to the market where some men had their boards set up. It was a Friday evening and everybody get them pay and the crowd was big. All the women had their baskets with their yam and banana and their fruits out on the sidewalk. And when you walk you have to make sure you watch where you put your foot—for if you step in somebody basket or knock over them things, is war.

So I tell Ezroy I need to watch how the dice playing for the first twenty throws, and when I finish now, I take him one side and tell him how to bet. But only in him head. I tell him not to put down any money. Afterward I take him one side and ask him how much money him bet in him mind and him tell me. Then I ask him how much money him make in him mind and him tell me too. Then I ask him if him ever win money like that before and him say no. Then I say to him is time to bet with the real live thing, but first, we have to make a deal. The first set o' winnings have to go to me because I need to pay for some exams.

So that is how I get to go to high school—Ezroy. He paid all my fees until he died. That school doesn't exist anymore. Salem College was the name. When Ezroy died I had to leave the school at fourteen, with no trade now, and go and look for work.

By the second week I get a job at National Tanning Industries, which make handbags and shoes.

But believe you me, I only spent five years on the factory floor before I got an office job. All the while I was stitching bags and shoes I use to put away a little money to take some correspondence course. In those days, high school exams in Jamaica use to come from England, from University of Cambridge. But if you didn't go to high school you could still study and pass, because they had schools up there that would stay from there and teach you, so long as you have the money and the time. So one day I see a advertisement for one o' them in the paper and I write to them, and going back and forth, and back and forth, is how I pass six subjects in Senior Cambridge by myself. To tell you the truth, I didn't pass English; but I get distinction for maths.

When I get my results, I go to work extra early the next morning and wait for Mr. Parnell—rest in peace—who use to own the place. Mr. Parnell was a Englishman. And you know how they strict a'ready. So I make sure put myself together spic-and-span, and when I see him step out o' him blue Cortina I go up to him and show him the paper with the passes I got.

He said, "Miss Thompson. Congratulations. I'm so proud of you. I hope you keep it up."

One thing I use to love about Mr. Parnell is that he knew every worker by face and name. And let me tell you, today I know every single person who work at Herald Square.

Anyway, I said, "I don't have anymore to keep up, sir. I pass my subjects now. What I want is to apply for a office job. But I know the people who work up there won't give me a chance because I work in the plant and I'm not fair skin. Not that I try, but they wouldn't even let me see a application if I ask them. I know how they stay. But I know you as a fair man, Mr. Parnell, so I come to talk to you."

Mr. Parnell face turn red and then him start to laugh. But him wasn't laughing at me. I just catch him by surprise.

He said to me, "Miss Thompson, we looking for somebody in bookkeeping. But we need experience, so we don't have anything for you up there right now. But keep up the good work, okay."

I said, "Mr. Parnell, as long as it have to do with maths, I can do it. Just let me watch somebody do it for a week. When that week done, I want you to give me a test. I don't want anybody else to gi' me the test—I want you—because they will sabotage me, because they don't want all like me to work up there because my skin too dark."

Mr. Parnell kind o' hold down him head and mumble. What I pick out of the mumbling was, "What you saying is true. It's not right. But I understand."

"But if I fail the test," I say to him, "then I don't want to work here anymore. Because I can't pass subjects like this and be sewing handbag and know that certain people working in the office and they only pass worm."

So that is how I end up doing accounts, until now.

By that time I was already married and Karen was already born. My husband was a solider man—Dalton was his name—and, basically, we get married because I got myself in trouble. Stupid, man. Stupid. Lose my focus. Get my priorities out o' line.

Marriage? I wasn't ready for that, but that became my lot in life because I made a bad mistake. And even though it was a big mistake, I wasn't going to add to it by disgracing myself and my family by bringing no bastard child. It was a stupid reason. I agree. But I was only eighteen, and that is how it went in those days. Plus, I had the example of my mother, who was a *Mrs*. She wasn't any common-law wife or concubine.

Suffice it to say, the marriage didn't work. My husband was an alcoholic, but I have to say he didn't use to womanize. And by the time I left him in 1968, I had three children to care for. Karen and Andrew were three years apart. Roger came four years behind.

When I left my husband, I didn't take anything. I just leave everything, because I couldn't stand the arguing anymore. Next thing, I say I want to take something, and him say it should stay, and it boil into a fuss and get loud like a market, and then is just a big disgrace. Plus, whoever leave a marriage should prepare to leave everything behind. Hopefully it won't come to that. Hopefully you can work it out. But if it not working out, make up your mind before that you won't make things like furniture and all o' that hold you back. When you got to go, you got to go.

When I was walking out o' that house, which was at 1c Deanery Road, I made three promises to God: one, I wasn't coming back; two, I was going to buy my own house very soon with only my name on it; and three, all o' my three children was going reach further than me in life. So it meant I had to take a second job.

By the time I had to beat my child the right and proper way, it was 1972, and I was heading up accounts at the plant, which was down on Foreshore Road—they rename it Marcus Garvey Drive later on—a hectic area near the wharf. In fact, the plant was in the same compound as the wharf, for most of those shoes we use to make was to export. A lot of other factories were around or nearby, down on Spanish Town Road. Beer. Rum. Tiles. Paper. Ice cream. Mattress. Cornmeal. Ice.

The plant was also near to a little airstrip. In fact, sometimes I use to look out my window and see eye-to-eye with some o' the guys who use to fly those little planes. No exaggeration. Wave to them sometimes. Sometimes when I feeling mischievous I use to even blow them a little kiss. And when I was bored or tired, sometimes, I use to stand up by the window and watch the harbor pilots use the tugboats to guide in those big cargo ships coming from all across the world.

If you doubt me, you have to remember that my office was third floor—upstairs—and most of the buildings around was lower than us, mostly one-story and two-story, so we in the office could see everything. Sometimes we use to watch the white sea birds them just glide in and perch on the big red cranes they use to use to take the cargo from the ship. And you know what we do sometimes? Gamble. In fact, we use to gamble nearly every day. Not for any big money or anything, but like for who going buy who lunch. Well, you know that as the boss I was the bookie. I use to give them the odds—how many birds was going to perch on a crane in a hour? If a crane was full o' birds, which bird was going be the next one to leave? Yes, man. I was the house. And you know why? The house always win. And I don't like lose. I was born to lose in life, but I find a way to win. So I not going go back to lose again.

We had moved up to Havendale by that time, far from where we use to live at Deanery Road. We lived in Range between Havendale and Deanery Road. Havendale and those places was like night and day. Only new-style house was up in Havendale, and the area was not like how I hear it turn now, a place where any and anybody can live. In those days, is only bank manager and people like that use to live up there. Lawyer, doctor, politician, businesspeople. Is only people like that could afford to buy the lot. If you have a teacher or a nurse up there, it was because their husband was something else. No sir. They couldn't afford to live up there without help.

How it went is that you had to buy the lot and get a contractor to build your house how you want it. But you had three or four that use to do most people house. You don't have those type o' house in New York, so I can't even give you a example for you to see what I talking 'bout. You have to go to the older parts o' Florida to see what I talking 'bout.

Solid, concrete house with steel bar inside. And even Florida not building house like that again. As soon as storm lick Florida—*boof*—all the new house blow down. Frame house. All they do is clap some piece o' cheap board together and disguise a pretty look around it. And people buy them, for they look nice. In Jamaica, frame house is what we make to keep chicken round the back. Fowl coop.

So anyway, we reach Havendale now, and everything is behind us. Progress time! Every time I think about that house is like water want to come to my eye. It was the first house I own. When you talk 'bout land space. My lot was a half-acre, and you still had some bigger than mine. And everybody use to keep up their lawn, and line it round with flower beds, and plant they croton or bougainvillea hedge beside their fence. To tell you how the land was big, when we moved there, Roger, my last boy was eleven years old, and he couldn't throw a tennis ball to reach his brother on the back porch from down by the back fence.

But to be honest, it was hard to keep up. We were the only house I knew that didn't have mother and father there, and I didn't want anybody to think of my children as less. Because, let's be frank, I was a divorcée—worse, without the schooling or the color like them. So although the two-job thing was tiring, I use to keep it up.

I use to drop the children to school every morning and pick them up every evening in the blue Cortina that I buy from Mr. Parnell for a very good price. I'll never forget the license plate, R 7255. Boy . . . that Mr. Parnell. When I was thinking how to buy the house, I went to him and he lend me five thousand dollars to put on what I had saved up myself, and we shake on it to say I'd pay him back little-little over time. No paperwork. You know why? I was a dedicated worker, and although I had the chance I never t'ief.

So anyway, when I picking up the children is really on my lunchtime, because schools use to over between 1 and 1:30. What I use to do is: pick them up, bring them home, and leave them with Miss Noddy, the helper, who use to live in, then go back to the plant. When I leave the plant at 5 o'clock, I use to batter with the traffic all the way from the waterfront to New Kingston, which was brand new those days, to my second job in the office at the Pegasus Hotel.

That hotel is still there. Still nice. Tall and broad like a big domino. Blue on the front and white on the sides. But it look a little different now, because the golf course across the street, they turn into a park. I don't know why that make it look different, but is true. You still have all the flags in front of it, so it still look official. But without the golf, a little bit o' something gone.

I use to work at the Pegasus till midnight every night, then drive home alone to 64 Border Avenue. When I reach, I barely had the strength to eat a little dinner. I use to heat it up myself. I never use to bother wake Miss Noddy. I wasn't like some people who use to bother their helper whatever hour they come in. Some people never have no conscience, you know.

After I eat and done now, I use to bathe off the day and go to sleep for a few hours to start all over again.

But in truth, the first thing I use to do when I go home wasn't eat. Every night I come home I use to make a beeline to the children's room to leave a Cadbury chocolate for them in their bed. Each one like a different kind. Roger like Dairy Milk. Andrew like Whole Nut. And Karen like Fruit & Nut. And if I ever mix them up, you see, they use to tease me and laugh and play all kind o' jokes like bring me a slice o' cheese if I ask for a slice o' bread. Then when they see the look on my face, they use to just bus' out in a laugh. In truth, we use to have a lot o' fun. Those were very good times.

On Saturdays now, I use to drop Karen down at the Singer store in Tropical Plaza for her sewing lessons, then take the boys to YMCA, because they use to like to swim.

Then while the children at their lessons, I use to go up to the Pegasus to do any work left over from the week. If I had the time or the feeling, I would go up to the doctor's compound at the university, where I had a doctor friend. This would only happen sometimes. I didn't want nobody spreading rumors. And rumors was easy to start, because in Jamaica those days you didn't have a lot of cars, so everybody know is whose car park up at your gate. And they use to watch and see for how long. Plus, that kind o' friendship wasn't very important to me. That kind of friendship will distract you. And next thing you know, you start to put man before your children.

Listen to me, when you decide to go it alone, you have to go it alone. When the children get big now and gone, you can think 'bout yourself. But when they small, you have to be responsible. Next thing you bring in a man on them and you think the man is the greatest thing on earth, and when you hear for the shout, as soon as you turn your back, the man taking all kind o' step with your girl child. Or next thing your son can't get on with him and that make the boy can't concentrate on schoolwork—and to get an escape, now, the boy go turn Rasta and start to smoke ganja and get worthless. I see it happen. Is not guess I guessing. I telling you from experience. I giving you facts.

Anyway, when I pick them up after they lessons now, I use to take them for lunch at the hotel. After all, children should be exposed. And when they finish with they lunch, they use to do their homework in the office with me, then all of us would go home. If not, we'd most times stop off for a movie at Premiere.

When you have to be moving like that everyday, everything has to be on time. So I trained the children a certain way. I made them understand certain things. And one of them is that when I'm ready to pick them up, they *must* be ready for me.

Every school in Jamaica has a big tree where children wait for their parents in the afternoon, and all three o' my children went to different schools. So if one of them late, it make the next one late, and so on down the line. When they're late then I'm late. And although Mr. Parnell liked me, he was an Englishman, and English people worship time.

Liver damage kill the children's father two years after I left the house at Deanery Road; so all I'm thinking every day is that there's no one to look after the children if I lose my little work. They had uncles and aunties, yes, but they couldn't do more than take care o' their children or themselves.

So anyway, this is how the story really start: One evening when Karen was about sixteen, I went to pick her up at school and she wasn't underneath her tree. I nearly went mad.

When I really look under the tree, I saw a girl that look like she could be in her class. And I say *could* because I was too busy working to go to any PTA. So in reality, I use to hear the children calling various names at home, but I didn't know who was who. Plus, when I use to pick up the kids in the evenings, I only use to have a little time. So it was open and shut. Open car door. Jump in fast. Shut car door. And drive.

So I clap and point to call the girl—none of the boys didn't know her name—and she told me that Karen was gone with Claudia deMercardo to Woolworth's in Mall Plaza to window shop, and walk up and down, and flirt with boys.

When I heard that, I thought I was going to go out o' my mind. Now, the girl didn't say exactly what they'd gone to Mall Plaza to do. But that is what I pick from it.

You see, although my mother wasn't a educated woman, she had a lot o' common sense. And from I was a little girl, I use to hear her say that you have certain signs that wi' tell you if a girl going grow up and behave like a prostitute. And is not just because she's my mother why I agree with her. I take my own two eyes and see it, so I take it as truth.

Take what I say and mark it. Write it down if you want. You ready? Here we go: Any girl that like to walk up and down from store to store after school instead of going home to study, because her eyes are in love with pretty things; and any girl who like to pluck her eyebrows so she can look like a big woman when she is still a child; and any girl who like to sing in the shower like she want the whole world to get excited that she naked in there—you take it from me,

Ciselyn Thompson, that girl is going to be a prostitute. She have a whoring nature. She have certain intentions in the back o' her mind.

Now you might say I'm being harsh or that a girl might have inclinations, but that don't mean they have to come to light. You listen to me right now. You have grown men who could see these things in young girls before the girls see it themselves. And these men use to make it a point o' duty to go up to the plazas and prey on aimless girls. Friend them up. Buy jumbo malt for them at Woolworth's. And soon after that now, they start to give them little things. Little earrings. Little chaparitas. And tell them to tell their mother and father lie that they school friend give them for they birthday. Then after that now, they start to give them car drive. Pocket money come later. Then when the child least expect it, they start to pressure her for sex; and nine times out o' ten, they give in.

Now, you use your own brain and sift what I just tell you before you answer. If a girl sleep with a man because him give her things and money, is not a prostitute that?

Yes, professor . . . I see you giving me the signal again, but I can't stop now. I have to go on. Bear with me. Bear with me. This thing is too important. Way beyond this class.

My fellow classmates, that girl that Karen went to the plazas with, Claudia deMercardo, use to pluck out her eyebrows till all she leave back was a line. At the age of sixteen that girl already had a dirty reputation. She was—excuse me—a damn mattress.

I use to say to Karen when she use to ask if she could

shave her eyebrow, "That look good to you? That look good? What sense they leave that line for? They no might as well just finish and done and just shave it off. What? They eye need a Parisian moustache?"

I use to talk to Karen about Claudia deMercardo all the time, because she was always asking Karen to ask me if she could spend the weekend at her house. Her people was real money people. They use to own in-bond stores and gas stations and a car distributorship. Where they use to live had everything, from pool to tennis court. And as far as I knew, people with that kind o' money never really like people who black like me, especially when they *think* they white.

So whenever Karen ask me if she could go up there, I use to tell her no. Any parent who allow their sixteen-year-old daughter to do her eyebrow like that is not responsible. They're slack! And slack parents make all kind o' slack things go on in their house. Next thing you know, they allowing Claudia to drink, and have boys coming there and all those kind o' things.

Listen, man. Let me tell you something. Boyfriend and that kind o' thing couldn't work in my house. Boyfriend? For a girl in school. University is a different thing. That time they're grown. But *high school?* You must be mad!

I use to instill it in Karen every day: "Don't put man on your head. Put your books." I use to remind her that Claudia deMercardo and those fair-skin girls she know from school don't have to pass no exam to get ahead in life. As soon as they finish school their parents giving them a job in a business. And even if they do start from the bottom, in two twos they reach the top, regardless of qualification. I told Karen,

"They not like me and you! People like me and you *must* have a profession."

But at the time she didn't want to listen to me. She wanted to follow fashion. She wanted to act like she was carefree, as if she didn't know is me alone she have to make everything work for her, and that if I slip, she slide. She wanted to rebel.

You know I had to wait for Karen for a hour? You hear me? A hour. I kept on saying, "Lord Jesus, I wonder if something happen to Claudia and Karen." Because I couldn't believe that Karen would do that to me, when she know I only have my lunchtime. And is not like now when you have cell phone and can call people and say you're running late. In those days, if you late you just late, and by the time you get to where you was suppose to be, everybody face done make up a'ready, and everybody jump to their own conclusion. So it don't even make no sense you try explain.

So in my distress now, I pu' down my forehead on the steering wheel, and my mind just drift away. Then all of a sudden, Roger touch me on my back and say, "Mummy, Mummy, Mummy, see Karen there."

When I look up I saw her running fast across the hockey field with her short plump self, her blue skirt and cream blouse dark with sweat. I don't know where the blue tie was. She must be take it off. Claudia was right behind.

When the deMercardo gal see me now, she slip off one side and leave her friend to come and talk to me alone. Now what kind o' true friend is that?

I said to Karen, "You don't consider me?"

I said it so softly I could hardly hear myself. The tree was next to some tennis court, which was right beside another court where some girls was playing netball. And anywhere you go netball girls always loud.

She didn't answer, so I asked her again, and raise my voice a bit. Same time now, the girl I ask for Karen when I just drive up, come up to my window and say, "Oh, you find her." Then, before I could answer, she ask a question. But it really was a comment: "You're Karen's mummy's friend?"

I say, "No. I'm Karen's mother."

She squint up her eye and look at me good, then she put her head into the car a little bit and take a look at the boys. "Oh."

Then she gone.

I knew what she was thinking—how I could be their mother and be dark like this? Well, the answer is that their father was a red man. He looked like a Puerto Rican in his features, but he had brown hair and hazel eyes. In just color alone, in certain light, you could make mistake and call him white. And you know something? That's the only thing he ever give those children—a fair complexion to make things a little easier for them in life.

Anyway, when the girl left, I say to Karen, "Missis, beg you just get in the car."

And you know what she said?

"When are you going to get off my back? Why're you always harassing me? I'm like a prisoner. I can't go anywhere. No matter what I do, no matter what I say, I can't be right. Just leave me alone, Mummy. Just leave me alone, man. Just lef' me, Mummy. Just lef' me. You think I don't know why you going on like this? Is because you see me with Claudia, and you don't like her. Why you always going on like she do you something? Is what she do you, Mummy? Is wha' she do you so? Well, you know what? I don't even care. Because Claudia is my friend. Right? Claudia is my friend. But you just don't want me to have any friends. I don't know why? I don't know why? Well, she's my *friend*, Mummy. She's my *friend*. See it there. She's my friend . . . and you better believe that dirts. And as a matter of fact, I don't care what you or anybody else have to say. Claudia is my friend. Claudia is my friend. And who don't like it, bite it."

I didn't say anything. I couldn't say anything. I don't even know if I did want to say anything. Perhaps if I did say anything, I would just sound like a fool.

She got in the car and slam the door. I had turn off the engine to save gas, so when the shame take me and I try to leave, the car couldn't move off. Pure confusion take me. I confuse so till I forget which way the key suppose to turn. You see my distress?

While I there fumbling with the key, every now and then I take a glimpse through the window at the girls under the tree, and I see them watching me with their fair-skin self. They acting like they not looking, you know. But every time they see me look, they cover their mouth like they eating banana chips, or act like they tired and cover their mouth like they going to yawn. But they never cover their eyes though, and when I look at them I see pure laughing. Some o' them was even running water.

So we on the way home now, and Karen is sitting in the front seat, and she just can't keep still. She have her school bag in her lap and she hugging it up like is her boyfriend, or like she have something in there to hide. And so she moving, so she snorting. You'd think she was a bull. Bouncing back against the seat. Bracing her shoulder on the car door to get away from me. Sweating. Trembling. Breathing hard.

To tell you the truth, that's normally the kind of thing I would just box her for. Before that she'd done one or two little rude things, back-answering and the like. And sometimes I use to have to give her a box for that. But this kind o' bad behavior she was showing now was just a different type.

I had to drive on Constant Spring Road by the plazas to get home—it wasn't a one-way then—and as I drove I heard a voice saying in my head, *You can't make children rule you, you know. If you don't control them they wi' break away. And when they break away, you can't always catch them back. That's when they end up worthless.*

Listen to me, when a boy end up worthless is bad and not too bad. But when a girl end up worthless is a different thing. You can talk what you want to talk about equality, but with some things you have to accept that is just so life go.

Let me ask you something: If a girl waste her time and end up leaving school without any skill or education, or any way of getting ahead—let's say a job with prospects, or acceptance to a college, and let's say all her friends from school move on—you think that girl can feel good about herself? She might seem happy-go-lucky, and her face might always have a smile, but something else is going on inside.

When a girl begin to feel worthless is a easy thing for her to start act like she worthless in truth. She start to lose her confidence. She start to need attention, especially from men. And this make her start to dress and act a certain way. And when that happen, men just start to take advantage, start to full up her head with lie, cause they know from experience what she want to hear. You see, when that happen, before you know it the girl start bouncing round the place, and she might even feel as if she having a lot o' fun. But to them she's just a mattress. A place where they lie down and get relief. And from that, is just a matter o' time before she breed and the bastard children start to come with more than one last name. Of course now, she can't mind them on her own, so she need the man them for support. And you think they going give her support unless she give them back something? And if you give your body for money, you is what?

So all along the way, Karen going on like how I tell you—with her bad bull self—and even with what the voice was saying I couldn't find the strength to discipline that child.

Because let me tell you, I'm the kind of mother who will discipline a child anywhere anytime. I don't like to do it. But if I have to, I will.

If I gi' you the look, and you act like you don't see it, then I sneak up on you and gi' you the pinch. And if the pinch can't stop you, you getting something hot on your behind. Who don't hear must *feel*.

But looking back at it now, I'm not even sure if is strength I didn't have. I think I was just confused. I was just in disbelief. I never thought my daughter had it in her heart to talk to me like that.

When we get home, she come out o' the car, and instead

o' opening the gate so I could drive in, she open it just enough so she could walk through by herself. So Roger jump out quick time and open out both sides.

To tell you the truth, until that happen I didn't even remember that the boys were in the car. They were so silent. I wasn't even sure who was driving home, who was really at the wheel. Because it wasn't me. If it was me then it was only partly me, because I didn't feel as if the whole o' me was there.

I left the children with the helper, Miss Noddy, and spin round same time to go back to work. When Miss Noddy was closing the gate, I saw Mrs. Lee Yew watering her lawn across the street, and I remembered to ask her to make an appointment with her husband about Roger's eyes.

I couldn't concentrate when I got back to work. Luckily for me, it was the middle o' the month, so the work wasn't heavy that day.

There were twenty-eight of us in the office. Most of the others use to work in a open area with nothing to part the desks. A smaller set use to work in twos and threes in some little office separate with glass sheets, but they didn't have a door. Only me and Mr. Parnell had a office with a door. He needed one because he didn't have a manager. He use to run the place himself.

At around 4 o'clock, the office maid came into my office and ask if everything was okay. Miss Minto was her name. From she see me lock the door, she know something wasn't right, cause I wasn't the sort o' person use to lock up myself. Anybody could come inside my office anytime. Same thing at Macy's today. Ciselyn? She's Miss Open Door.

So anyway, when Miss Minto ask me how I was, I told her everything was fine, but I was begging her a cup o' tea.

Although I can't take the smell o' cigarettes nowadays, I use to smoke a lot that time. It started when my husband use to come home drunk at Deanery Road and mess up himself—sometimes the soldier uniform too—and I use to have to strip him off and clean him like a baby. I use to smoke to kill the smell.

When Miss Minto bring the tea, I went and stand up by my window, which was right between two big bookcase. I had a ceiling fan in the office, but I couldn't turn it up because it would blow all the papers around the place, and I couldn't open the windows fully cause the sea breeze would be worse. So the office was hot and had a salt and dye and leather smell.

I start to daydream now. Is so long ago I can't remember what exactly was on my mind, and then my eyes drop on the parking lot below me, and I saw the spot where I approach Mr. Parnell years before. I see my car, which use to be his car. I had every reason to feel proud o' myself, but all I feel was shame.

After a while I put my forehead on the window, then ease round and lean up with my back against the bookcase. I use to like collecting pretty calendars, and I had one from China on the wall. It was one o' those that was a big poster with the months in a pad on the bottom, and when you finish a month you just tear it off. They had a pretty girl on the poster part, and she had a pretty fan. I use to always like to look at her. I don't know why. Maybe it was just because she use to look attractive. There are some people whose personality just shine in the way they smile, and even when you see them in a picture you can know they nice. And she was one of them. So sometimes when I was feeling down or something, I would smile and look at her. My little Chiney friend.

So anyway, I get tired o' looking at her, and to be frank, she wasn't doing anything to ease my mind, and I find myself looking through the window again, smoking up the glass. Every time I blow, everything get cloudy and I feel like I could hide away, then the smoke get thin again. And the ashes? I just kept dropping them on Miss Minto floor.

We use to say the floors belong to her cause it was she who use to go down on her knee and take the coc'nut brush and clean them once a week. All we use to do was tramp on them. They use to say the office people use to walk and stomp because we never use to have to buy no shoes, for Mr. Parnell use to give us half a dozen pair every year.

Anyway, as I was thinking of Miss Minto and her floor—is like something come to light—I realize what was bothering me. Yes, it had to do with Karen, of course, and her behavior. But the thing itself that was depressing me was how she talk to me—like how most people talk to their maid. Is like she feel like she could talk to me anyhow and nothing wouldn't come out of it cause I don't have any status in life. Like I'm just this little dark girl who is right where she start out, and don't reach nowhere, like I not good enough to be her mother.

As I start to think of this, I start to notice my reflection now. I could see it when I did a little thing with my eye.

In those days, I use to part my hair in the middle and flip it up like Doris Day. But it was hard to manage, you see. I had to press it every Friday evening. If I miss a Friday, it would get coarse and unruly, and all the straightening would come out. I look at my cheeks, and they look so hard, so— what's the word again?—*pronounced*, even though I dab a little rouge on them. They look so unladylike, so tough. Then I begin to examine my nose. For all the times I use to clamp it, it was still the same . . . spread out like a van run it over, or a big truck lick it down. And the blue eye shadow? It only advertise how I was black.

Jesus Christ, I thought, *you know you really, really black? Why you bother even try with makeup base? That kind o' black can't hide. You black like doctor never take you from your mother belly. Like him grab you from a clinic that was burning down . . .*

And when I take in all of this—you tell me, what I could do but cry? So that is what I did. I smoke my Benson in my brown skirt suit and think about my daughter, then I look at myself . . . and cry.

Later that evening, while I was working at the Pegasus, Roger called to sweet me up. Poor little heart. When the switchboard put him through, he told me that he need me to help him with some homework for his English class.

Now, Roger don't call me at work unless is something important, and him never need me to help him with his homework yet because Andrew was always there to help. Plus, on top of that, he was extremely bright—passed his exams for high school from grade four, when most kids took it in grade six. And in any case, most of them who take it didn't pass. Karen was one o' them. She take it three times in a row and fail.

So I ask him, "What's the composition about?"

"Well . . . Mummy . . . my teacher asked me to write a composition on a work of art."

"Lord. So now we have to go to National Gallery?"

"No, Mummy, because I selected you. You want to hear what I put in there already?"

I start to smile now.

"Yes."

And then my bubble burst.

He said, "*My mother is a most resplendent example of God's imagination. He made her more beautiful than all the creatures. My mother's beauty is special. Do you want to know why it is special? Most people's beauty is on the outside, but that kind of beauty is only skin deep and will not last forever. My mother's beauty is of the permanent type. Her beauty is on the inside, and that is the kind of beauty that will always last.* How does that sound so far?"

I said, "Oh, my little husband, that was so nice. You say all those nice things about me? You make me feel so good, Pops. Bye-bye."

"Bye-bye, Mummy."

I start to cry again.

When I left there, no one in that office knew that anything was wrong, for I'm a woman like this—I don't show weakness. Everything could be wrong with me, but you'd never know.

It was 9 o'clock when I get home. Roger was in his room finishing off his homework, lying 'cross the bed with a dozen model planes hanging from the ceiling like they going to bomb him.

Fright take him when he saw me, cause I usually come

home after midnight, and on top o' that he didn't hear me when I come in. What happen is that as I was driving up the road a voice just told me to leave the car outside and walk round the side to get a better understanding of what's really going on. So instead o' bringing the car into the carport and opening the front door from the veranda, I came in off the back porch, where we use to store old things, and Miss Noddy use to wash and press the clothes.

"How you come home so early, Mummy?"

I put my finger to my lips to make him quiet down himself.

"Where is Miss Noddy?" I asked.

"She gone to church. She soon come back."

"Where's Andrew?"

"Over by the Lee Yews. Bobby taking him up with econ."

"How come I don't hear your sister?"

Roger push up him glasses on him nose and say, "She's in the living room . . . I think."

I sat down on the bed beside him.

"Roger, beg you tell me. What she do since she come home?"

Him start to hem and haw.

"Well, I don't know, Mummy, because I was doing my homework in my room. I ate my dinner at the table, but I did my homework in my room. So maybe you have to go and see for yourself."

"I see." I kiss him on his cheek. "You finish your composition, Pops?"

"Oh . . . yes. Yes, Mummy. Thank you very much for the help."

"Ahh, Pops. Life is not a easy thing. You hear?"

So I'm walking down the corridor now. The house had three bedrooms on each side, with the living, dining, and kitchen in the middle going down, from front to back. When you come off the front veranda you're right in the living room.

Each side had its own bathroom. If you count Miss Noddy bathroom off the porch around the back, then call it three. My room was in the front, on the right-hand side. From the front door I had to pass through the living room and a heavy curtain to a passageway to reach it.

As I was going into my room, I glimpse Karen through a crack in the drapes. She was in the living room. Still in her uniform, playing the radio, the record changer, and the TV same time, like we have money to waste, like deMercardo is my last name.

Now, I don't know 'bout you, but there is certain things that can't happen in most West Indian house, and mine is one o' them.

1. You can't gallivant in your school uniform. As soon as you come home you suppose to take it off. That is something you suppose to respect and revere. That is not something you just wear round the place like that and disgrace. Plus, they are expensive. When you start to drudge them out, before you know it they start to rip up here and there, and things start to stain them up. So when that happen, how you going to go to school in the morning like you're suppose to be—neat and

clean? And you *better* go to school neat and clean in the morning. If you go to school untidy it mean neither you or your parents have any pride or ambition. And let me tell you, if you don't have pride or ambition, you ain't getting nowhere in this thing name life. You have to reach beyond the span o' your arm.

2. You can't watch TV before your homework done. School is your vocation as a child. So you can't put fun before your studies. I hear these children nowadays complaining that school ain't fun. Well, it ain't suppose to be fun. Is like medicine. It ain't suppose to taste nice. God gave man the brains to make medicine for cures, and education is a med-icine to counteract the idleness that grows like mold on top o' the brain. If you don't counteract it daily, you'll be sick with idleness and sloth all your life. When you finish your homework and your studies, you can do whatever you want to do—within reason. I like my little TV too. I like to watch this English fellow Simon on that show where the people try to sing and become a star. He's a man that don't put up with no foolishness. That's a man who tell you straight. Some new people in my department call me so behind my back, you know . . . Simon. But you think I care? Who you think decide they bonus every year?

3. You can't have on three big appliances at once,

especially when is things for enjoyment and not for work. Electric current isn't cheap. So when you're watching one show on the TV, and listening to another show on the radio, and playing music on the record changer same time, you're just being wasteful and greedy. You can't even enjoy the three o' them same time. And even if you could enjoy them, what you could absorb? To even think about that is idle, and as you know, the devil find work for idle hands.

I went into the bathroom to bathe but I change my mind. The water was running and everything, but I change my mind and turn it off. I just went into my room and lay down. I didn't even turn on the light. I just lay down in the dark. I start to roll from side to side to twist myself out o' my clothes. I was so down I couldn't bring myself to sit up. To tell you the truth, I never even care 'bout neatness. As I take off the clothes I just fling them down. When I scatter them now, I just lie down plain in my panty and brassiere, just listening to everything going on.

A little drizzle had come down earlier, and the rain smell was coming through the louvers from the flowerbeds. Every now and then a bus pass by. But what I mostly heard was cars. Somebody's dog just wouldn't stop barking. Just *arr-arr-arr-arr-arr*. The crickets were going and the tree frogs too. When they start, you know, is like a video game. But the loudest things to me were in the living room. I could also hear the shower crackling like fire. You'd think it was a flame.

The radio was playing reggae music. I never use to listen to it, so I couldn't tell you what group. To me, every song use to sound like *boogooo-doop-boogooo-doop-boogooo-doop*, so I couldn't bother with it. And I didn't like that radio announcer, a fellow by the name of Errol Thompson who use to make a lot of noise with this stupid rubber ducky. I hear he use to smoke a lot o' weed.

I could follow what was on the TV too. She was watching this Burt Reynolds show—*Dan August*. To me the show was stupid. Whenever Burt Reynolds chasing down a criminal, the same thing happen every time—him going to run upstairs or climb on something high, then dive on the criminal back like Tarzan.

But the worst thing though, was that she was using the record changer to play out my Al Green. Now, I don't know 'bout you, but my records is my records. I know is CD time now, but still. The children *know* I didn't like them to play my records, because just like how they didn't like to full back the ice tray, they didn't like to put back my LPs in their case.

Is either they don't put them back or they mix them up. But something always have to go on. One time I find a Curtis Mayfield and a Engelbert Humperdinck force up in a jacket for *The Student Prince*. What could Curtis Mayfield and Engelbert Humperdinck have to do with *The Student Prince?* And I won't even tell you what they did to my Mantovanis.

Let me tell you—to this day I love my Mantovani. If I don't play a Strauss waltz every couple o' days, is like I don't feel too good.

But anyway, I really wanted to say something to Karen when I was lying down. But I didn't know where to begin, because you know what? I began to feel a little rage. You know why? I stayed in the bed and hear Roger go to her and ask her if she did her homework. The way he was asking her, you could tell he was trying to warn her, or make her come to her senses . . . hint her a little bit, you know . . . give her some help. That is what I pick from it. And you know what she said to him? Ungrateful little wretch?

"You little informer, you. What? Your mother call you from work and send you to spy? Well, I don't do any homework. You hear? I don't do any. And you better move out o' my way before I t'ump you. Don't I told you and Andrew not to come out here?"

"But Mummy—"

"Roger. You must be think I 'fraid for Ciselyn Thompson. She like to go on like she bad, but I don't 'fraid for her."

"Karen—"

"What happen? You going wring out my name?"

"But, Karen, Mummy—"

"You don't hear I say must leave me alone? You want a t'ump?"

"I going tell Mummy."

"Yes, double-oh eight. Tell your *mooma* when she come home tonight."

I hear when Roger walk off and come like he was coming to my room door, but for some reason him turn back. And in my mind I see when Karen cut her hazel eyes and use her hand and flick back the light brown hair I use to wash and condition every week because it was too long for her to manage. Before I authorize her to cut it to her shoulder, it was tall, way down her back.

I stay in the room and call to her.

"Karen."

She didn't answer me. So I sat up in the bed and call her name again. This time with a question sign—"Karen?"—for I was trying to ask her if she forgetting herself.

At the same time, I was trying to ask myself if the person outside was really and truly the first child I bring into this world or a alien. Because the way the anger had me trembling, whatever it was out there, whether it come from my womb or not, I was ready to take its life.

A voice inside my head was telling me to take the bed-side lamp and go out there, that I shouldn't even bother to put on a robe, to just march out there in my panty and brassiere and take the lamp and bus' her head. Just kill it!

But thanks be to Jesus, God stayed in heaven and stretch forth His hand and take the thought away from me. That's all I can say—God stop me. Because I know my daughter heard me. Because I know my voice. And I know that house. And I know that child. So although the radio was playing, and the TV was on, and the record changer too, I know for sure that child heard my voice in that house.

But the damn gal was feeling so powerful after she put me down in front o' her friends that she thought she was on top o' the world. Like she was some kind o' . . . you know . . . royalty . . . like she could do anything she want without considering the price.

A piece o' heavy breathing take me in the bed, you see. And the room start to feel like it closing up. And my head start to beat like somebody put a speaker box inside it like a car. And I quick time put on a duster and run down to Roger room and ask him to go over next door to Mrs. James, who was a pharmacist, and get a Valium for me.

When Roger gone I went out on the back porch to get some fresh air. Karen heard me in my panic—she had to—but she didn't come to see what was wrong.

When Roger come back I told him to use a razor blade and cut the ten milligram in two and give me half, then I send him to make some green tea for me. After that I turn off the light and si' down in the dark.

When I take the pill and drink the tea now, I say to him, "Pops, I'm going to tell you something, and I hope you wi' remember it when you grow up . . . the parents who do the most get the least thanks. I've done everything a mother can do to make that girl happy, to make that girl's life a success. But she hate me like I do her something."

"Mummy, she don't hate you. That's not true."

I say, "When she took her exam to go to high school, she took it three times and never pass. Now, if I was like most other mothers, I would make her go to a junior secondary school or a technical school, which you know is where you go when you fail. But I couldn't make her feel shame like that. I know she had it hard when me and Daddy didn't work out. Then shortly after that, God took him away. She was the oldest and she remember him the most, and she was very close to him, so she feel it more than you and Andrew. You two were too small. I didn't want to give you children a broken home. Roger, I didn't want that at all. As there's a God, I didn't want to do that to you. But what I was suppose to do? Stay with the man and make him carry we down?"

"No, Mummy."

I say, "You know how many nights I clean piss and shit off the floor down at Deanery Road, Pops? You know is from cleaning shit and piss why I start to smoke? You know when Karen fail her last chance to pass her exams I drive around to every single high school in Kingston that take girls, and beg the principal to take her? You know I tell all those principals is my fault why she never pass her exams, because I was the one to leave the marriage and break up the home, and that is why she couldn't concentrate?"

"No, Mummy."

I say, "Pops, you know how many times I tell your father to come and look for you children, and him promise me him was coming, and never come? You know how many times, Pops? You know how many times? Pops, you think I like working two jobs?"

"No, Mummy."

"I hate it down to the ground. But is what I have to do to make life for you children . . . so you can come out better than me. I can't believe your sister denounce me like that in front o' her friends, Pops. After everything I've done. The parents who do the most get the least thanks. Pops, you love me?"

He said, "Yes, Mummy," and came and hug me up.

I said, "Pops, you think your mother pretty?"

He said, "Yes, Mummy. Of course."

I said, "Inside and out?"

He said, "And upstairs and downstairs too." But he didn't tell me, "Yes."

Years later, some time after his first book come out, Pops and I was talking 'bout what happen that night. By that time he was in this thirties and was teaching English at UCLA. I had gone to visit him just to see what was going on.

When I let him know how much I needed him to tell me I was pretty, Pops said he couldn't understand it at all, because he use to think I was a gorgeous girl, so gorgeous that he use to be in love with me when he was small.

Now, I could have said to him, *Well, how come none of your girlfriends ever look like me yet? How come is pure fair-skin girl with long hair you like?* But I didn't want to make him feel bad. What would be the point? He was doing his best to butter me up. So why try to catch him in a lie?

But that night, though, out on the back porch—let me tell you—that little darling really help to calm his mother nerves. Yes, I had my tea and Valium, but they were not enough.

Listen to me. Let me tell you something. Don't make ghost fool you. Nothing can lift you like the love of a child, any child, but especially a child who's yours. I had two in that house, but only one was showing me any kind o' love.

I'd be the first to tell you I was defeated, that I found myself in the situation where what Karen thought of me was the thing that mattered most in life. If at that moment she'd come to me and told me she wanted to spend the rest o' the month up at Claudia, and if I felt that it would make her come and tell me that she love me, and she not ashame o' me, I would drive her up to Claudia myself. And if she say she was going up there to live for the rest o' her life, I would crawl on my knee and beg her not to go. I'd tell her to stay and I'd let her do as she like. I'm not ashame to say it, now. That is how I felt. No lie!

And let me tell you, if that girl had used her common sense, or even humbled herself a wee, I might have been her slave for life. For let me tell you—when your child has you in the kind o' position like Karen had me, you're her slave for life, like that woman I saw today in Duane Reade; and whatever they want to do, they do; and whatever they *don't* want to do, they don't do. And if they turn out good in the end, they'll say it was *in spite* o' you. And if they turn out bad . . . well, of course, it was *because* o' you. Any which way you turn, you lose.

Pops went to bed around 10 o'clock. I heard his brother come in through the front door at 10:30. He said hello to his sister two times. She didn't answer him at all. All the time I could hear her moving through the house. Going to the pantry, the fridge. Then at 11 o'clock, I hear when everything in the living room just one by one shut down.

I called out softly, "Karen?"

She didn't answer, so I called again. This time my voice was louder, but even more loving in tone.

Who says I didn't try? You know what Karen do? She slam the bathroom door. And before she slam the door, I hear some teeth get suck.

I didn't want the boys to know I was crying, so I walk down by the back fence. You want to see me feeling in the dark. For if you move too fast and the clothesline catch you, head gone clean, one time.

So, I feel and feel until I found the stand where we use to bleach the clothes. And I drop my face into my hands and bawl. You'd think somebody dead or I just got a telegram that I lose my job. I don't remember how long I was bawling for, but it was a good amount o' time, and is while I was bawling that she made her big mistake.

At first I didn't hear it. Then I hear it, but I didn't know is what. Then I figure out is what, but I couldn't believe that what it was is what I hear.

My fellow classmates and professor, I could hear it just as you can hear me now. Clear, clear, clear, clear, clear. But let me tell you, when I really decide for true that I was hearing what I hear, I cock my head and listen it good to be more sure again. And when I think of what Karen was doing, and how what she was doing indicate where she was going to go, going end up down the line, a spirit rise inside me and a voice say—and when I say "say," I mean "say," like how I'm saying this to you here now—"You better get off your ass and go in that house and do what you have to do. Otherwise, you going to lose that child. Don't care if she hate you. Don't care if she never talk to you for the rest o' your life. Don't care if she even go as far as change her name so nobody won't know she's your blood—go in there and do what you have to do. You can't make this pass. You can't make this pass. You can't make this pass at all."

You know what the girl was doing? You know what the girl was doing? Who in here this evening can stretch their mind far enough to imagine what this girl was doing now, on top of everything she a'ready did that day?

She was singing in the shower. On the top of her voice. Like is "Prostitute" she name. And you know what she was singing? Guess and tell me. Go into the furthest part of your mind where you pu' down ideas that don't have no use and things that just don't make no sense.

The little wretch was singing, "Born Free."

Wha' kind o' idiot she think I was? Because I never finish school she think that would pass me just so? She think I don't know sarcasm and irony? She think I wouldn't get the point?

Jesus Christ!

As I start to walk up to the house now, leaves crunching under me like gravel and I get a mind to bus' her ass with everything I touch. The pole that hold up the clothesline. A piece o' switch from off a bush. Even down to the little floppy belt on my duster. One time I grab for the rake.

When I step up on the back porch, I turn on the light and see Miss Noddy iron in a corner by the iron board, and a palm it for the cord, but the body was too heavy to maneuver so I put it back. And Jesus Lord, the closer I get—naturally—the louder she sound. And all I can think is, *If I lose her, then the odds is that I'll lose her brothers. For she's the oldest. And all this Rasta foolishness is going round. And if she turn worthless, them going turn worthless too.*

Singing in the shower like a damn prostitute! What? She crazy? Or is bad she think she bad? In truth, that gal did think she bad. Singing in the shower like a damn prostitute! And worse, she was doing it for spite!

It had to be spite. It had to be spite. Because I never ever hear my daughter do a thing like that before. Never in my life. Never in hers. Because she know my rules. But is not only the rules. She know how a thing like that would make me feel—like a mother who don't train her children right!

When I step in off the porch, I kick off my slippers by the door. I didn't want the wretch to hear me coming through the house. Is like I was James Bond or Emma Peel. I go inside the kitchen. Nobody don't hear me make a sound. And I start to search around. How come when you really want a thing you can never just find it yet? It took awhile, but eventually I found the kind of thing I had to use.

I took my time and pass the rooms. Barefoot on the cool gray tiles. Everything turn off except the bathroom light. Sometimes I stop and listen to make sure she didn't hear me, then I walk again. I could hear the boys snoring little bit. Good. They were asleep. It was me and she alone.

When I push the bathroom door, the little bugger was so caught up in herself she never hear me. Nothing register to her at all. No change in light. No new shadow. No little something in the air. How you could be in a small bathroom with hot water running and somebody open the door and you don't sense a little something in the air? You know how? When you feel like nothing can't happen to you because you're the ruler o' the world.

Believe you me, I stood up there with the extension cord in my hand for about five minutes and she didn't see me. It was a old brown one that was suppose to throw away because one end of it was frazzle out. Well, good. Cause now it was my little cat-o'-nine.

I listen to the singing. I watch her shadow through the blue curtain. I could hear the rag *slop-slopping* as she soap up herself, which mean the licks going soak. How she never see me? Perhaps her eyes was closed.

And the more soap she soaping, and the more sing she singing, the more loud she getting loud—no, it wasn't just me—and the more loud she getting louder, the more she start to stress the words.

"Booooooooooorrrrrrrrrrrrrrrrn frrrrrrrrrreeeeeeeeeeeeeeee." Like she was chanting. Then after a while she slow it down, and start to overemphasize each word until it don't sound like a song no more, but like a political speech.

So what a joy it was when I draw the curtain . . . *voom* . . . and she look at me and couldn't talk.

She wanted to scream, but she couldn't scream. She open her mouth and cringe but the scream wouldn't come out, like it frighten too, like it get a glimpse of what going to come.

And I look at her, you know. And I see how she nice and plump and soapy, and I start to imagine all the sounds the strokes going make, and the marks they going leave.

I size up all the juicy parts and then I start to beat.

I brace one foot on the tub, you see. And I grab the shower curtain rail. And when I sure I have a anchor now, I start to put it on. I beat that wretch so much that one time she slip in the tub and I jump in there with her, although the water soaking me and wetting up the floor. And wha' she do? She kick me—she kick me—and use a dirty word and say she hate me. And is that time now I *really* put it on.

The boys hear the noise of course and come to watch. And before she plead with me to stop or she apologize, Karen start to tell the boys to go away.

"Stop watching me. I'm naked. I'm naked. Mummy, they're watching me naked. Tell them I'm too old for them to look at me. Tell them to leave me alone."

And when she say that now, I put it on some more.

As I paint her body red, I look at her and say, "You think you is a woman in this place?" *Whap.* "You think you is woman, eh?" *Spa-DIE.* "What you have to hide?" *Whap.* "You're brother." *Whack.* "And sister." *Vap.* "Same mother." *Zip.* "Same father." *Vam.* "And further . . ." *Whap.* "And further . . ." *Whap.* "And further . . ." *Whap.* "You're a child." *Skish.* "You're a child." *Wha-cka-PIE.* "You're a child." *Pie.* "You're still in school. You're still in school. You're still in school. What you take this for? You think you's a woman in this place?" *Whappa-pappa-pappa-pappa-PIE!*

Finally, she said it: "Sorry, Mummy. Sorry. I won't pass my place again."

I'm going to be honest with you. While I was beating her I began to feel a little guilty, but not too much, because I had the conviction that what I was doing was right. Because I knew—and even she told me, more than once, years later—that I was saving her life.

You know where she'd gone that afternoon when I had to wait for her for an hour outside her school? Not to the shopping plazas. Years later, she confessed. To an apartment with an older guy.

Claudia was fooling with the fellow. I forget his name. He use to own a club in New Kingston, near the Pegasus Hotel, and Claudia inveigle Karen to go with her to meet him on a side street near the school; and up in his apartment she saw him take a spoon he use to wear on a chain around his neck to give Claudia cocaine. I was so naïve about certain things, I didn't even know they had cocaine in Jamaica those times. After Claudia snort it now, the fellow took her in the bedroom and start to use her as a mattress, and poor Karen was so nervous she start to beat down on the door until the fellow open it, and she see Claudia naked on the bed. Is run she run back to school from New Kingston why she was so sweaty. After she left, Claudia make the fellow drive her back to school and she wait for Karen at the front gate to make her promise she wouldn't tell nobody. So that is how I saw them coming 'cross the hockey field same time.

Listen, I don't want to bias you against Claudia deMercardo. Is two sides to every story, but the fact remains she's not alive to give you her own. I don't want to get into the *why* of it. When I ask, I don't get anything straight. All I know is they found her body tie up in a car trunk in Fort Lauderdale with plenty bullet in her head. Rumor had it some people took her hostage and her boyfriend run away and didn't pay. That was maybe 1988.

In conclusion, I would like to say that I apologize for going over time, and I know I maybe didn't do the "how to" aspect very well. But I didn't want to push it, cause I saw that certain details make you cringe.

However, if you can allow me one more minute, I'd like to leave you with a bit of advice—love your children but don't let them use that love to rule you. Harden your heart when you have to, and put it on. They strong, you know. You ever see them on the playground yet? Jumping and rolling and all o' that?

In Jamaica we say that puss and dog don't have the same luck. I can't tell you what will work for you. But I can testify about what work for me.

Listen. Let me tell you something. You think I had any real trouble with Karen after I straighten her out that night?

No sir. You think I had to give her something even close to that again? Not at all. I had to drop a little one slap every now and then, for sure. But nothing big like that.

Children have memory, you know, so whenever I got frustrated with her and the arguing and the stubbornness, I use to make it go and go until it reach a certain point. After that, I just say cool and easy, "Karen, I think you're over-heating. You need to cool off. Go take a shower, nuh."

After that, let me tell you, she see everything my way.

ALL AH WE IS ONE
by *Elizabeth Nunez*

O n a steaming hot day on a Caribbean island that shall not be named, an African American couple, Joseph and Anita Streeter, a husband and wife in their forties, walked into the Paradise Country Club with their teenage daughter, Linda. They paused briefly at the reception desk, but finding no one there, headed straight for the changing rooms next to the swimming pool. Ten minutes later they emerged.

Joseph, his black skin gleaming in the brilliant sun, was wearing light blue swimming trunks, his wife, whose skin was not much lighter, had on a red halter-top bathing suit, and his daughter, neither as dark as her father nor as light as her mother, her hair in braids to her shoulders, wore a white bikini that showed off her perky bosom, slim hips, and long, shapely legs. Joseph climbed the steps to the diving board, and looking to his right and left, apparently to make certain no one was in his way, bounced twice on the board and dove into the water, barely making a splash. His wife and his daughter, who were standing at the edge of the pool looking at him, applauded.

"That was fantastic, Joseph," Anita said when he surfaced.

"Your turn," Joseph countered.

Anita climbed the ladder. When she reached the top, she turned her head to the right and to the left as Joseph had done, and noticed something extraordinary. The pool, which minutes before was crowded when she, her husband, and her daughter had arrived, was now completely empty.

Moira McShine, who was lying on a plastic chaise under the shade of an umbrella, as her mother had advised her, since her skin tended to tan faster and darker than her lighter-skinned friends, had witnessed the retreat from the pool. She had not seen when Joseph Streeter dove into the water, but she was aroused from her daydream by Mrs. Forester's querulous voice as she passed in front of her, dragging her two protesting children: "A big black man like that! He doesn't care who's in his way. He just dived in. Didn't care if the children were there. He could have killed them. That's why we don't want their kind here. Why we have *rules*."

Moira sat up in time to see Anita Streeter poised on the diving board. Below her, mothers and fathers clapped their hands and called to their children to come out of the pool. Barbara and Helen, Moira's best friends, who had invited her to join them at the Paradise Country Club, were sitting at the edge of the pool dangling their feet in the water. When Mrs. Streeter dove in, they got up, wrapped their towels around their waists, and walked toward Moira.

"You see that?" Barbara said, and rolled her eyes.

"What?" Moira asked, genuinely puzzled.

"That big black woman. They always spoil everything."

And the Streeters did spoil everything. Children were whimpering petulantly, some shrieking, as parents pulled them to the changing rooms. Sunbathers grumbled as they slipped on dresses, pants, and shirts over their bathing suits, and teenagers rushed to line up behind the two wall telephones in the foyer to call their parents.

"Coming?"

Barbara had to ask the question twice, for Moira was still entranced by the photograph her eyes had taken of an elegant dark woman in a red bathing suit that showed a figure that her father would describe as "hourglass": an ample bosom, a well-defined waist, hips that flared and tapered into perfect thighs and legs. A woman who in no way could be styled as big. Full-figured, but not *big*. A woman who seemed uncommonly attractive.

Before Moira could turn away, her eyes locked with those of Mrs. Streeter's teenage daughter, who was not in the pool. She was standing next to her father near the diving board, lips curled, eyes filled with more disdain than Moira had encountered in all her sixteen years.

The next morning, the story was plastered all over the daily newspaper. Mr. and Mrs. Streeter were painted as two thoughtless black people, too lazy to take the long drive over the mountains to the public beach, and "boldface too boot," in the words of one eyewitness. Just because they saw "decent people" bathing in the pool, and because the pool could be seen from the street, they figured they could stop their car and take a dip.

"Americans!" a reporter wrote indignantly. "They think they own the world. Those two and their daughter didn't care one cent that they were disturbing the peace and tranquility of our families trying to spend a quiet morning with their children. They just jumped right in the pool without so much as a 'Beg you please,' splashing water all over the little children and frightening them." He quoted one mother who said her daughter was crying so hysterically she had to take her to the doctor. "Tourists," fumed the reporter, "some of them have no respect."

But the reporter could not have been more wrong. By the time he had discovered his mistake, the printing press for the newspaper had shut down and it was too late for the editor to recall the stacks of papers that had already been picked up by the deliverymen for distribution the next morning.

What the editor, a French Creole in his fifties thinking about retirement, was told that evening as he was polishing off a rum punch in the Red Lion Pub, was that Mr. and Mrs. Streeter were not ordinary Americans, not ordinary black people either, not even regular tourists. They were guests of the U.S. Ambassador to the island, now a republic since it had gained its independence from England some twenty-five years ago. They had not found their way accidentally to the swimming pool in the Paradise Country Club. They had not stopped their car because they had noticed people bathing in the pool and decided to take a dip too. They had gone to the club intentionally, at the invitation of the U.S. Ambassador, who had taken the precaution of indicating so in writing on a note that he had given to Mr. and Mrs. Streeter. When the family had entered the club, there was no one at the reception desk, so they had gone directly to the pool, assuming that no problems would arise if they showed the note when asked.

There was more that the editor found out. He found out

that Mr. and Mrs. Streeter were important people in the United States. Mr. Streeter was a well-known and respected Civil Rights lawyer and his wife was a professor at Princeton University, a member of the Ivy League.

The apologies came swiftly and abundantly. The radio blared them on the hour. Before the newspaper arrived at the doorsteps of houses and shops the next morning, everyone on the island had formed an opinion on what had happened at the Paradise Country Club the day before.

"Bet those stupid people thought their black skin was going to dirty the pool," Horace McShine said to his daughter. (Horace McShine was considerably darker than his wife, from whom Moira had inherited her light skin.) "You'd think with Independence, now we own our own island, people would forget all that nonsense about who light and who white. Sometimes I think we harder on our own black people than the English."

But the Americans were not satisfied with apologies. They wanted the truth, plain and unadulterated. They wanted no pretense about frightened little children, or stories about mothers trying to pacify them. They stated their position clearly in the statement they gave to the newspaper: "Those people came out of the pool because we are black. They did not want to be in a pool with black people."

The manager of the Paradise Country Club was foolish enough to be defensive. Interviewed on the early-morning news, he argued that if Mr. Streeter had shown the staff the note from the U.S. Ambassador, there would have been no problem.

"Mr. Streeter said there was no one at the reception

desk," the interviewer countered. "And he had seen other people walk right into the club."

"Of course. They were regulars."

"Mr. Streeter said he waited for the receptionist, but nobody came."

"We plan to fix that. The receptionist will be disciplined. But you just can't walk into a private club and go in someone's pool. I'm sure you can't do that in America. I think Mr. Streeter was projecting."

"Projecting?" asked the interviewer.

"All of us live here together good, good. We are a cosmopolitan people. We have Indian, Chinese, Portuguese, Spanish, French Creole, English, and black people living good, good together here. We don't have all that racial trouble they have in America. I really didn't appreciate Mr. Streeter's insinuations. People were frightened. They thought he was an intruder."

"Like a thief?"

"Well, not exactly like a thief. But how would you like for someone to just come in your house and swim in your swimming pool? We're sorry for the mix-up. I myself would have come out and greeted Mr. Streeter if he had shown us the note from the Ambassador. We're not like the United States," he said again. "You know our slogan. 'All ah we is one.'"

And most of the people on the island agreed. The Streeters should lighten up. "Foreign people take things too serious," was the general consensus of many of the passengers in the dollar taxis on their way to work that morning.

By lunchtime, talk radio had taken over. "Come on,"

said the radio host. "Skin color not like cheap cloth. It don't bleed in the water. You could mix black and white and pink and yellow and they don't stain one another."

His sidekick chuckled. "I tell you, if skin color does bleed in water like cheap red cloth, it have a lot a people go jump in the water hoping that the red color stain out their black."

"Or the white bleach it!" the radio host roared.

The Streeters were incensed. That black people—for they were certain the radio talk show host and his callers were black—would speak so disparagingly of their own kind in public, on the air, enraged and confounded them. They shot back with terse, angry statements that were printed in the press. If they were white, they contended, no one would have left the pool. Yes, perhaps they could have waited longer for the receptionist, but it was a very hot day and they had a note from the Ambassador. It was reasonable for them to conclude that when the receptionist finally arrived, it would be easy enough to show the note. But it was because they were black that the receptionist did not give them the courtesy of inquiring if they had permission to swim in the pool.

Mr. Streeter went on to add that he was certain that many of the white people in the pool that day were foreigners who did not have membership in the club. But the management *presumed, presumed,* without any other evidence except skin color, that because those people were white they belonged in the pool, that they had to be guests of the members. He had no doubt that the receptionist was the one who sent out the alarm for the people to leave the pool.

About the comic banter on the radio, Mr. Streeter said

he was deeply hurt and disappointed in his black brothers and sisters. He expected more from people who had got their independence from the white colonial powers. He said he expected them to be as outraged as he was. He ended his interview with the reporter with a show of erudition. He was not a psychologist, he said, but he was an educated man. He read. And if his black brothers and sisters had read what one of their black brothers from another island had written, they would understand that they were still in prison, in the prison of their colonial minds. Read Franz Fanon's *Black Skin, White Masks*, he said, flinging out the words derisively at the reporter, who recorded them precisely. Try to improve yourselves.

Never judge a book by its cover. Little children learn this adage with their ABCs. The Streeters heard none of the pain and frustration submerged beneath the jokes that criss-crossed the island all day. Had Mr. Streeter limited his criticism to the management of the Paradise Country Club and to the idiots who came out of the pool, the people would have trusted him. Eventually they would have admitted him into their circle, and he would have discovered how they had survived. How, through years of brutal slavery, how, though their island was used as the seasoning station before Africans were shipped to America, they had not merely survived but had excelled.

They would have explained to Mr. Streeter what they meant by seasoning, assuming he would not understand. For they knew that in the big countries, people did not season their food before cooking it. That it was reputed they took raw chicken, just as it was in the package from the store, and cooked it like that without chive and thyme and lime and garlic and so on. So unless they explained seasoning, the Streeters would not understand how you could season a man or woman and change people's smell and their taste so that when they reached America, they would behave just so. They would plant cotton, haul wood, fetch water, and you would only have to add a little salt and black pepper to get them to remember how the red pepper and green onion and lime used to cut through their open wounds.

If the Streeters knew what went on at the seasoning station, they would understand that you had to be strong, you had to be smart, smarter than the seasoners themselves, to outfox them. You had to know how to cover up your own taste and your own smell, so though they rub you down with garlic and shado beni, and on the outside you smelling like you seasoned, on the inside you haven't changed at all. You still the same thing. You still the same original man, the same original woman.

But Mr. Streeter had presumed to know more about them than they knew about themselves. He had taken it upon himself to be their teacher and to give them advice. So they concluded that he was like every other foreigner—never mind he was black—who thought he was better, superior to them, who looked at the sun and sea and reached the same conclusion: This was a playground, home to light-headed men and frivolous women.

And it was true that the island was like a playground. The sun shone brightly almost every day, bathing the trees in flashes of gold. And they never had those hurricanes that devastated the other islands, for the island was situated in the doldrums, neither too far nor too near the equator, between those latitudes where the winds died down and the ocean subsided. A playground indeed: long, white beaches at the base of thick, verdant hills. Sky bluer than the sea and sea blue as the veil on the statue of the Virgin Mary on the side altar of the Roman Catholic Cathedral. Clouds most of the time whiter than the alabaster statues of those white Catholic saints. If God had planned to design a playground where people could relax and be happy, He could have created no better.

But people spoiled it. People from the cold places in the North. First, they killed the fighting Caribs and infected the peaceful Arawaks with their nasty diseases. Next, they dragged the Africans over in chains and seasoned them. When they had used up the Africans, they seduced the Indians and Chinese with promises of land for labor. Then they abused them too. It took two world wars to stop them. After that, there was nothing else for the people to do but to make a callaloo.

All ah we is one. But everybody knew where his place was in that straight line of one.

Things eventually got so out of hand with statements and counterstatements from Mr. Streeter and the management of the Paradise Country Club appearing daily in the newspaper, with the radio waves virtually cackling as hosts and callers tried to outdo each other with their witty remarks, with everyone, even children, seeming to have an opinion, that on the fourth day, when calypsonians began to sing about "the commotion on an island in the ocean" and "black stool in the pool," the Prime Minister was forced to intervene.

Black stool in the pool! It was the last straw for the Streeters. The calypso was a perfect example of self-loathing, Mr. Streeter declared. Those calypsonians were calling themselves shit, for to be sure, their skin was as black as his. So the Prime Minister got together with the U.S. Ambassador to work out a solution. He would put on a good island fête, the Prime Minister said. He would invite African, Indian, Chinese, English, Portuguese, Lebanese, Syrian, French Creole, all kinds of mixed-up people. He would show the Streeters "how well we all get along."

The Prime Minister chose to host his party at 4 in the afternoon and at the home of a friend who lived on the top of a hill, not far from the main city. He decided his residence was too formal and might inhibit the free expression of his guests, causing them not to mingle with each other in the way that would prove to the Americans that on his island, *All ah we is one.* He selected this particular house for many reasons, not the least of which was that to get it, the Streeters would have to pass through a winding road bounded on both sides with new residential developments, some of which were in the beginning stages. He wanted the Streeters to arrive in sufficient daylight so that they would witness firsthand the industry of his people, who were often maliciously castigated as lazy good-for-nothings. He knew that if the Streeters had woken up before dawn and gone into the main town, they would have seen the flurry of activity that took place there every workday morning, a curious pantomime barely lit by the rising sun: men, women, children moving rapidly, with concentrated determination, almost without sound, except for low murmurs and the beat of shoes against the concrete pavement. They would have seen polished-faced children dressed in starched school uniforms, boys in khaki pants, blue shirts, and ties; girls in white blouses, pleated skirts, and socks above blinding-white sneakers. They would have seen workers in their company uniforms, professionals in dark suits, and yes, they would have seen all sorts of people of varying degrees of African ancestry as well as Indians, Chinese, English, Portuguese, Lebanese, Syrians, and French Creoles.

But the Prime Minister did not think it was likely that the Streeters would find themselves at the heart of the city at dawn, so he orchestrated this sampling of his island's population at his fête, and instructed the driver, who was to bring the Streeters to his friend's home, to point out the finished houses along the way and the ones under construction. He wanted the Americans to know that the island had its own architects, engineers, carpenters, electricians, plumbers, and construction workers, and that most of the raw material they used—paint, cement, bricks, slate, corrugated zinc, wrought iron, tiles, nails—were manufactured in local factories.

The Prime Minister wanted the Streeters to know this and to be at the house when the sun came down, for he wanted to see if they would not be awed to silence when the sun spread fire across the sky and bloodied the sea below it. When from the front lawn of his friend's house they would look down on the panorama of his city—roofs descending like scales on fish, one after the other, to a green savannah and afterward the sea, blue stretching lazily across the horizon before the sun turned it red.

"Let me hear what they have to say then," the Prime Minister said to his wife, as he dressed for the redemptive fête.

And his wife reminded him that the house, too, was something to see. It was designed by a brilliant woman, a lawyer, with more talent than she had time, who, between teaching and writing books on the law, studied the architecture of the old Victorian houses that the English colonists had built with alcoves and eaves and fanciful lacy fretwork, and the spreading homes on the plantations of the French Creoles, with their wide verandas and elegant windows that opened to the floor, and the tapia-roofed houses of the Indian farmers, and the wooden structures on stilts the Africans had made. She had incorporated all these designs into her own unique vision so that the house she designed retained the memory of all that had transpired on the island, all that had brought happiness, but suffering too, to this place bathed by the sun.

"Don't forget to tell them it was a black woman who designed the house," the Prime Minister's wife said to him.

And all went well as the Prime Minister had planned it.

On their way to the house, as the Streeters passed the new homes and the ones under construction, they got a lesson on the industry and talent of the islanders. At the house, they found themselves struggling for words to compliment the owners, overwhelmed by the magnificent wide verandas on the top and bottom floors, framed by ornate wrought iron reminiscent of Victorian fretwork; stunned by the lush, round baskets of green ferns hanging down from the ceilings of the verandas and contrasting splendidly with the red clay color of the outer walls of the house. Inside, the designer, the female lawyer, had chosen a palette of tropical hues hinting at the splendor of birds, flowers, and fish to be found on the island. When the sun began to descend and paint the sky in oranges and reds, the Streeters were pulled, like the rest of the party, to the edge of the lawn so they could look down and across, down to where fish scales glinted in the dying flames and across to where the sea surrendered its blues.

Afterward, when the Prime Minister determined the Streeters were sufficiently impressed, he gathered Indian, Chinese, English, Portuguese, Lebanese, Syrian, French Creole, and all the earth tones of African ancestry around the Olympic-size swimming pool at the back of the house. As soon as his aides had quieted the crowd, he began what Mr. and Mrs. Streeter considered an apology, but what their teenage daughter, Linda, flouncing down on their bed that night, still smarting from the insult to her family, described as nothing less than "a vulgar display of West Indian arrogance meant to dazzle our eyes and befuddle our brains into submission."

This is what the Prime Minister said.

"Mango—or from your part of the world—apple," he began, smiling broadly at the Streeters, "don't fall far from the tree, but in your case, I have to say the mango fell and went far beyond the tree."

A loud tittering erupted among the guests, and if Mr. and Mrs. Streeter did not understand the Prime Minister immediately, it was soon clear to them that he was doing his best to compliment their daughter. She was, he said, the most beautiful flower ever to grace the garden of his island.

Having achieved his objective of "lightening up the situation," the Prime Minister then rhapsodized on the colors to be found on his island. He spoke of the hues of the tropical rainbow, the colors of the different birds, big and small, singing birds and birds that never sang a song. When the ibises come home to roost in the Caroni swamp, he boasted, they turn the trees red with their feathers. He dug his hand into his pocket and pulled out the note his wife had given him, and as if he were an expert on tropical horticulture, he reeled off descriptions of the flowers she had written down— poinsettia, hibiscus, chaconia, bougainvillea, anthurium, lily, oleander, ixora, amaryllis, bird of paradise. Finally, with a politician's sixth sense that he was losing his audience, he extended his arms, and spreading them wide open as if to embrace the entire room, pointed out to the Streeters the array of skin colors before him, ending with a line from the island's national anthem: "Here every creed and race find an equal place."

"So, if," he said, "some misguided persons gave the Streeters the impression that on this island we discriminate against our brothers and sisters because their race is different from ours, we apologize. We are truly sorry. For here, as you can see, we have all colors living together in harmony, from black to white, from Indian to Chinese, from English to African, from Portuguese to French Creole, from Syrian and Lebanese to Jew. Yes, Jew," he said. "When the rest of the world refused to take the Jews, though it was common knowledge what Hitler was doing with them in the concentration camps, our island nation took every last one who came to us asking for shelter." Neglecting to clarify that us were the English colonists, the Prime Minister then concluded, "This is the kind of people we are. Yes, Mr. and Mrs. Streeter, you can't find any place in the world where people are less prejudiced. So I say we're sorry, and on behalf of the entire country, I hope you come to visit us again."

Applause. The steel band the Minister of Culture had recommended, following the Prime Minister's lead "to show the Streeters what we can do," and in keeping with the island's unofficial motto "to lighten up the situation," burst into a brisk rendition of the road march from the last year's Carnival.

But the Streeters's daughter, Linda, was not persuaded. At her insistence, her father had arranged for the McShines to be invited to the party. She had observed that Moira was the last person to leave the pool and she wanted a witness at the party. When the Prime Minister ended his speech, she walked over to Moira.

"If," Linda sneered. "If? Well, you were there. You know there are no ifs and buts about what happened."

Moira stammered an apology. "People don't usually behave like that," she said.

Linda smiled grimly. "And do dark-skinned people like me and my parents *usually* come to your pool? Or do they only let in black people with light skin like you. Colorism," she said, before turning away, "is the disease that has infected your island. Come to the U.S. We have discovered the cure."

THE ANGER MERIDIAN
by Kaylie Jones

Saturday, 8:30 a.m.

I never wrote a word in this pretty hand-woven Mexican notebook that Mom gave me last Christmas almost a whole year ago, because I was afraid Stony would find it. Now he's dead.

I'm glad you're dead. There.

Eight years I spent in this marriage. Stony's first marriage lasted six months, and apparently the divorce was quite the scandal in certain Dallas circles (his ex was a cattle baron's daughter) and he intended to make this one work, no matter what.

I'm not from the area and I guess that was a big plus for me in Stony's estimation. We got engaged at Le Cirque in New York City. I was teaching French in a fancy private school in the city, and Stony often had business with Wall Street firms.

When I opened the black box and saw the ring—it looked like a frozen pond, I swear—I thought, *Mom will be so happy*.

"So, will you marry me?" he asked. My mouth opened on an intake of breath, and his cell phone rang. He took it out of his pocket, flipped it open, leaned back, and began to talk in a rapid tone of good humor, as if he were sitting behind his big glass desk in his office in Dallas. I waited patiently while he worked out a deal on a high rise and his eyes turned strangely luminous, a look I associate with the manly activity of closing in on prey. By the time he slapped his phone shut and turned his attention back to me, his eyes had slipped out of focus, as if he'd forgotten where he was.

I'd barely gotten my quiet "Yes, Stony, I'll marry you" out when he laid out his two deal-breakers: one, that he'd never get divorced again as long as he lived no matter how bad it got; two, that if ever he didn't come home in time for dinner, I shouldn't expect him to call because sometimes things got away from him at work, like when he was playing golf with a prospective client. Little did I know that people in Dallas take their golf extremely seriously, and sometimes the golf *talk*, after the golf itself, goes on until the wee hours of the morning.

This is a man who can't take a shower without his cell phone lying within arm's reach, on the black granite slab surrounding the two sinks. A man whose cell phone rings while he's proposing. And he can't call me to tell me he'll be late for dinner?

I should have known. I should have folded up my pretty linen Le Cirque napkin, placed it neatly on the table, and said, "No, thank you," and walked right out. But Mom would've never forgiven me. She'd been waiting for this moment for so long. Imagine me, the *klutz*, landing a millionaire entrepreneur with a law degree from UVA! I couldn't wait to call her.

The first thing she wanted to know was how much the ring cost. I had no idea how much the ring cost, and told her so. This made her angry for some reason. She went all quiet like she does, and that is no fun when you're calling long-distance to San Marcos, Mexico, and the phone is crackling and you think you may have been cut off.

To say adapting to Dallas was hard for me at first would be a gross understatement. I spent my childhood as the daughter of a diplomat, hopping from country to country, all over the world. Most folks in Dallas have never left the state, let alone the country, except perhaps for a little foray to a gated resort in Mexico or the Caribbean.

My daddy taught me never to pass judgment, because people are different in every country and have different values, but honestly, I never met a more self-satisfied bunch than these Dallas Texans. The state as a whole seems to be suffering from post-traumatic stress, presumably inherited from their ancestors who bravely fought at the Alamo, a battle which they seem to firmly believe is continuing to this day.

Stony took me there once, to San Antonio. What a tiny little place the Alamo is! Nothing like you imagine. I told him so and he was offended, which means his jaw muscles pulsed and he went around stamping his feet like a bull and not talking to me for three hours.

This is probably because, as a group, Texans are plagued with gigantomania. In Texas, bigger *is* always better, and theirs is bigger, no matter what you're talking about. (Apropos of large, Stony liked to remind me ad nauseam that in college, in the locker room, his team mates called him "Mandingo.") And my ring. Back to my ring. Stony wouldn't be cajoled into even hinting how much it cost, so my mom talked me into getting it appraised in secret (just in case) and the nice jeweler Mr. Liebenthal at the mall told me that while it is truly a very *big* diamond, it is quite flawed, and only worth twenty thousand dollars. "*Only?*" I repeated, for this did not seem to me an insubstantial sum; however, when I called Mom in San Marcos to inform her of this news, she said over the crackling long distance line, "You've been sold a pig in a poke."

In Dallas, at first I cooked up a storm. Wonderful things from recipes I got off the Internet. The only acquaintances I had were the wives of his friends, so I had all the time in the world. In the beginning, he was late only once in a while, and more often than not, I'd get a "heads up" call. Then suddenly he stopped calling, swaggering in past midnight at least once a week, then twice a week, then three times, until I gave up cooking for him entirely. Thank God I have my little Tenney, beloved angel, who keeps me more than a little occupied. The other mothers at her school say, "You *really* ought to get a nanny. The Mexicans are terrific, and cheap!" What do I want a nanny for? I spend her school hours bored to tears, just waiting for her to get out so we can start our day.

There's this fancy store not too far away that delivers. I call in the evening, around 8 p.m., after Tenney is in bed, and I order the most outrageous things—caviar, stone crabs, chocolate mousse cake, whatever I want—and charge it to his Platinum Visa card. I like to sit out on the terrace when it's warm enough—and it often is—and look at the skyline. It's a beautiful, colorful skyline, a bit like Miami, with the skyscrapers all lit up. The planes flying overhead remind me of all the places I've been and the ones I'd still like to visit with Tenney.

I never said a word about his being late and he never said a word about the charges to his card. Why be angry? It serves no purpose, that's what I've always believed.

Tenney was born two weeks early while Stony was in New York on business. I had what they call a *placental abruption* and practically bled to death in my sleep. I woke up and it was like that scene with the horse in *The Godfather*. I had to be rushed to the hospital by ambulance and have an emergency C-section. I was a mess. Mom couldn't even make it up from San Marcos in time for the delivery.

But that's okay, it wasn't anybody's fault.

The next morning I came to, and there was Tenney, my perfect baby, smiling up at me. *Hello again*, her eyes seemed to say, and I had a strong feeling we already knew each other from a long time ago. Tenney latched onto my breast like a little vampire, as if she'd been practicing for this moment for months.

Awhile later, Mom staggered in from the airport and collapsed into the armchair next to the bed. She lit a Marlboro and said, "How could you do this to me? I thought I was going to have a heart attack." I could smell fresh scotch on her breath from where I was lying on the bed. It was understandable, who wouldn't have a drink or two after a night like that?

"I'm sorry," I said.

"Well, thank God it's not a boy. In a million years you couldn't have talked him out of calling the kid Stonewall Jackson Browne V."

Stony had an ancestor, a lieutenant whose sepia-toned photo graces the entryway, who had been a personal aide to the Great General in, if I'm not mistaken, the 2nd Corps, Army of Northern Virginia. These Southerners just can't seem to let go of that war. I told Stony in no uncertain terms, from the moment I discovered I was pregnant, that there was no way on earth I'd saddle a son of mine with the name of a wife beater. This made him extremely angry (the muscles in his jaw again, the telltale sign), but it was Stony's goal in life to never again break a sweat in a confrontation, except in racquetball or perhaps golf.

"An *alleged* wife beater," Stony countered icily, "if you're talking about Jackson Browne the songwriter. And anyway, the name Stonewall Jackson Browne was in my family long before that whiney fool became a pop star."

We really never fought, and our polite exchanges continued along these lines for the next eight months.

A nurse came in and yelled at Mom, "Are you out of your mind, smoking around a newborn?" I was glad, because I was afraid to ask her to put out her cigarette, she seemed so upset. Mom stuck the lit end into a styrofoam cup of water on the bedside table and it fizzled out, making a horrible smell. The nurse briskly took the cup away, holding it at arm's length as if it contained a sample of the ebola virus.

"Dumb cunt," observed Mom in a haughty murmur, as she watched the nurse retreat in her squeaky shoes. This made me chuckle nervously, and my caesarian incision began to pulsate as if a hot iron were being poked into my lower abdomen.

On the wide windowsill was a tall glass vase wrapped in a huge pink ribbon, with two dozen of the most exquisite long-stemmed pink roses I'd ever seen, and the smell! Mom handed me the card, which said, *With all my love, Stony.*

"Now that was really nice of him," Mom said in a flat tone that I couldn't decide whether she intended as sarcastic, or not. My TMJ must have been acting up because I started to get a dime-sized ache under my left ear, burning hot to match the incision.

Stony's secretary Janine came by during her lunch break and her face simply lit up when she saw the roses. "Oh, my, they're perfect. Stony said to order something nice. I thought, well, you know, pink."

I smiled shakily and asked her if she wanted to hold the baby. Mom chuckled ghoulishly in her chair. The pain in my jaw had spread and the whole left side of my face was aching so wickedly I could no longer feel the caesarian incision. I wanted more morphine and buzzed for the nurse, but she wouldn't come, presumably still miffed at Mom. After a while I started to cry, so Mom went out and started to yell up and down the hall that she was an ambassador's widow and if someone didn't come right now she was going to call the President of the United States (a Texan, with whom our

Democratic family held no clout whatsoever, but they didn't know that).

The nurse came running, and in a few minutes I felt better. After an appropriate interval, during which Janine rocked and cooed at Tenney, I asked them both to excuse me, I was a little tired and needed to get some rest.

Eight years later and here I still am, in this long, high-ceilinged apartment in a tall building on Turtle Creek Road, owned by Guess Who's corporation, with pretentious wide arches connecting the living, dining, and kitchen areas, through which you could put a bowling alley if you wanted to.

This morning, 4:15 a.m. by my beautiful platinum Rolex that never slows down, I was sitting on the terrace, drinking a cup of warm milk in the dark, looking out at the Dallas skyline in my ashes-of-roses silk robe and nightgown from Saks (last year's Christmas present from Stony, chosen no doubt by Janine, with her excellent good taste), when the doorbell rang.

I thought, *Oh well, Stony forgot his keys again*, or, *Stony can't find his keys because he's had a few too many cocktails with a prospective buyer*. But no.

Nick the doorman didn't have time to ring up and warn me before two big uniformed cops were standing in the apartment. One was tall, wide-shouldered, and black, and one was tall, wide-shouldered, and white. They wore dark blue short-sleeved uniforms that exposed their muscular and threatening forearms. They both had the same Texas accent that I still associate with the oxymoronic partnering of ignorance and authority. Their eyes were already old and hard in their flat, smooth, unlined faces. I wanted to cry out, *I didn't do it!* even though I had no idea what it was they were about to accuse me of.

The white one, whose nameplate read *Johnston*, took the initiative and stepped forward. "Mrs. Browne?"

I nodded dumbly.

"Mrs. Browne, your husband's been in a car accident."

I continued to nod, waiting for him to tell me where I should pick him up.

Slowly he uttered, "I'm sorry to have to tell you this, Mrs. Browne, but he didn't make it."

My mouth fell open, but no words were immediately available to me. I wondered how many times in their young lives they'd had to do this. My next thought was, *My God, I'm free.* But I took care not to change the frozen expression of horror on my face.

"Oh, you poor man," I said, placing my hand on his chest for a tiny moment. I realized my hand was shaking. "What a terrible job you have . . ."

"It was a head-on collision," the other policeman, Officer Bales, offered. "He probably didn't feel a thing." He reached out to take my elbow, as my knees were beginning to buckle beneath me. He guided me back to the couch, where my cup of warm milk was waiting for me on the coffee table. He sat me down. The two of them stayed standing, which forced me to crane my neck to see their faces.

Officer Johnston shifted in his boots as if he were standing on uncomfortably hot sand. "You may as well know this now, cause you're gonna find it out anyway—it'll be in the papers. There was a girl in the car—"

Oh my God—Tenney! I thought, and jumped up, obviously not thinking this through, for Tenney had been sleeping, tucked in safely, since 8 o'clock.

"Sit down, Mrs. Browne," said Officer Johnston.

Officer Bales took out a little notebook and read something. "LouKreesha Smalls. L-o-u-K-r-e-e-s-h-a. Do you know this person?"

I knew who she was. A tall, dark, callipygian waitress with dreadlocks at the Blue Bayou, where we used to go sometimes to hear music. I remembered with a sick flip of my stomach how Stony liked to make fun of her name. He and his business partner, Bucky—the Buckingham in *Buckingham and Browne*—kept an ongoing list of names of African-Americans they thought were particularly amusing. At the top of their list was LaPoleon, followed closely by P'are, and in third place, LouKreesha. The condescending way they greeted her whenever she came over to our table with an order, taking such pleasure in turning her name over in their mouths, made me so uncomfortable that one day I finally decided to speak up.

As she sauntered off, swinging her wide ass, I said, "Lucrezia is actually quite an interesting name . . ."

They all turned their faces toward me, their smiles suddenly frozen like ghoulish Mardi Gras masks.

"Wasn't she a Greek goddess or something?" said Martha Buckingham, without losing a beat.

"She was an Italian noblewoman," I countered. "Lucrezia Borgia. The Borgias were a prominent Renaissance family. She was one of the greatest poisoners of all time. Back then you couldn't get divorced, so she poisoned her husbands to get rid of them. There was an opera—"

"I knew that," Stony interrupted quickly, one of his favorite lines. And they all cracked up.

Later, on the way home, he told me it would be best from now on if I kept comments like that to myself. I didn't say anything.

I've been a knee-jerk liberal all of my life and proud of it, and I decided that I'd rather stay home with Tenney than go out with him and his ignorant, racist friends.

"She's . . . LouKreesha's a waitress at the Blue Bayou," I informed the two officers, like a good schoolgirl who's done her homework.

They glanced knowingly at each other.

"What?" I demanded. "What?"

"Well," Officer Johnston sighed deeply, "without getting graphic"—he was blushing now, and I felt suddenly sick—"she was killed too."

"The position they were found in . . ." Officer Bales added, then shook his head as if he were truly sorry for me. "It's gonna be hard to explain, if you know what I mean."

"You mean, like in *The World According to Garp?*"

They stared at me, dumbfounded.

I shook my head and brought my hands to my face to convince them of my confusion and desolation.

It's not even 9 in the morning and already I've received a slew of phone calls. Gossip and horror spread like wildfire, it's incredible. On the very first ring, I picked up because I didn't want to wake Tenney. It was 7 o'clock. Apparently, Martha Buckingham couldn't wait another minute. "Oh, honey. I am so sorry."

I had nothing to say. I waited. She waited. I could hear her breathing fast; she sounded excited. "I told Bucky, I said, 'Bucky, this is just *bad*. A . . . *black* . . . girl.'"

"Yes. A white girl would've been so much better," I shot back, shocked at my own sarcasm, which, as we practice it in New York, is unknown to these good Dallas folk.

"Oh, honey, that's not what I meant and you know it. It was just so . . . inappropriate. A waitress like that. I told Bucky like *months* ago, I said, 'Bucky, you tell him to just *quit* it.'"

Months ago? So. That meant, if Martha Buckingham knew, everyone knew. Everyone except me, the sarcastic New Yorker. "Thank you for calling, Martha," I said woodenly, and hung up on her as she was saying, "I'll stop by later . . . bring you a casserole . . ."

I called the doormen and told them under no circumstances to let anyone up.

Not five minutes later the phone rang again and I let the machine pick up. It was one of the local papers.

Then, just now, Janine in her gentle voice, murmuring into the answering machine, *"Um . . . Petia, pick up, honey. Please. The IRS is here at the office. It's the Criminal Investigation guys."*

I rushed to the phone and grabbed the receiver.

"I'm so sorry," Janine whispered. "They have a warrant to open the safe."

"What safe?" was the only thing I could think to say.

"Well, Stony's safe."

"Do you have a key, or know the combination, or whatever?"

"Yes."

"Then open the safe," I said.

She told me that the IRS agents would be over in a little while to talk to me.

After I hung up, I did what my daddy taught me to do back in 1978 when Idi Amin Dada gave us two hours to get out of Uganda: I took off the ring and the Rolex and hid them in the battery compartment in the back of Tenney's talking blue teddy bear.

I WANT TO DISTURB
MY NEIGHBOR
by Geoffrey Philp

I always hated Friday evenings. Friday evenings meant one thing: Bible study. Now don't get me wrong, I'm not a heathen. Never was, never claimed to be. It's just that every—and I mean every—Friday evening, when all my friends were out partying, drinking, walking down Daisy Avenue with their boyfriends or girlfriends, just having a good time, I had to stay home with my mother, my Aunt Shirley, and a changing cast of guests from their church.

Why? Well come on, the judgment was at hand.

If I had an easy life, it wouldn't be so bad. Let's say if Bible study came after an afternoon of kicking back with a copy of *MAD* magazine or listening to a group of rastas talking about the imminent destruction of the capitalist system and the establishment of a u—no, *i*topia—in which weed would be legal, you could hear reggae on the radio at all hours of the day, pork would be outlawed, having books by Walter Rodney and Malcolm X wouldn't brand you as a trouble-maker or a reprobate, and a man would somehow, without real effort or excitement, find himself blessed with several queens who would all get along—you know, African stylee.

Bible study came after I'd washed the dishes, cleaned my room, and cooked dinner, and it followed a routine. Aunt Shirley or my mother would call me out of my room to meet their guest. I would take my time to come out, wave and mumble a polite enough hello, then shift my weight from leg to leg as my aunt and mother explained that I wasn't yet living in the truth, which would make the guest—every single guest—invite me to bow my head and pray with them. I would then refuse and they would come back with their second offer—to allow them to pray for me. The second they closed their eyes, I'd ease out of the room and lay in bed and listen to bootleg tapes from Jah Love, my favorite sound system, as I twirled my afro into something dread, and handwrote music reviews for *Yout' Talk*, my school newspaper, while they prayed for my soul through the night.

If you have any sense at all, you must be wondering, *Well, why didn't he just go out with his friends while the old folks prayed?*

But hear me nuh: Before you rush to judgment, just thank God or whoever you pray to that you never get one o' my mother lick dem yet. Pass *what* gate? When *who* praying?

Leave room is one thing. Leave house is somep'n else. But leave yard? Baba, is a next t'ing that.

So one Friday now, what a policeman would call "the day in question," things went as I've described them. I was in my room—if you can imagine a prefabricated Jamaican house: louver windows, gauzy yellow curtains, tile floors, dark wood bed with an iron spring, a trunk full o' old clothes, walls festooned with posters of soul singers and Third World revolutionaries, and a dresser with doilies and bottles of Big Wheel, Brut, and Old Spice colognes—when a piece o' bloodclaat bass began to roll through the house like a fog.

"Courtneigh!"

My mother kept calling me but I didn't answer her. What would have been the point? I knew why she was calling me. She knew why she was calling me. She wanted to run off her mouth 'pon me about the music, as if it wasn't coming from somebody else's house.

I knew where it was coming from. She knew where it was coming from. The house behind us, which was owned by a rasta bredrin named Jah Mick. We grew up with Jah Mick. He used to be my older brother's closest friend, and they'd both gotten soccer scholarships to the States. Jah Mick had gone up as Michael, what society people like my mother used to call "a decent boy." But he'd come back six months ago with a new name and a new flex, a beard, and long dreads—a "boogooyagga." You don't need no translation. So it mean is so it sound. Say it, "Boo-goo-yagga. Boo-goo-yagga." It sound bad, eeh?

Now, I knew why Jah Mick had turned up the music like that. He'd started a magazine named *Rootsman Kulcha*—yes, it was just as you've conceived it—and whenever he was short of inspiration, he'd turn up the heat on his old tube amp and the air would be thick and sweet with dub sounds. In the meantime, my mother's temper began its slow burn.

"Courtneigh Clifford Robinson! Come here right now!"

I went into the living room expecting to find a parade of the usual suspects on the big green sofa. But there in all his splendor was my Uncle Tyrone.

My first thought was, *He's saved?* My second was, *Aunt Shirley knows about the go-go at the Stable who produced a little filly on the side.*

"Courts," my mother said, as she flattened the pleats on her stiff blue dress, the one she starched and ironed every Thursday night, "I want you to be a good boy and go over to your *friend's* house and tell him to turn down that god-forsaken music."

"How you know is over there it coming from?"

"Who else plays that kind of music round here?"

"I don't know . . ."

"Look. Don't form fool with me. I have ears. I can hear. Is only Michael alone who plays that kinda boogooyagga music none at all, and is spite him trying spite me why him playing it so high on a Friday night."

"Ma . . ."

She turned to her sister. "Is Satan you know. Is Satan."

"Ma, you can listen to me for a minute? Not that I trying to cause any problems or anything but—"

"Who you shouting at?"

"Ah not shouting, Ma. But I have fo' talk up because you say the music loud."

"So the music doh loud to you?"

"That's beside the point—"

"Doh pass your place with me, y'hear, 'bout *point* and *beside*."

Uncle Tyrone chimed in: "Boy reach fourth form and ready fo' turn man."

"So why you blaming me, Ma?" I said quietly.

"I just can't take it. This is the kinda thing that cause a

place to get run down. Next thing, you start to see people from Stand Pipe start to come round here because they think somebody keeping dance. And when that start to happen, every piece o' clothes you have disappear off the line."

"So, Ma, if the music is such a botheration, why you don't tell him one day when you see him? You know him from him small. Him not goi' bite you."

"No. I can't talk to all him again. Him gone to the dogs. Head boy at St. George's College. Gone to the dogs."

"That's how he is when he's working on a project," I said, as I turned to go back to my room.

"The only project he's working on," she said, "is blaspheming! Talking 'bout Haile Selassie is God! He is a blasphemer! From now on, I'm going to ban you from associating with blasphemers! Don't you ever set foot over there. If you ever set foot over there again, you cannot come back in this house. Boogooyagga music come mash up my Bible study like how ganja mash up that boy's mind. *Stop.*" She held her arms out to the side and cocked her head. "You hear that? Boom-chicki-boom. Boom-chicki-boom. You think I can take this whole night? Boom-chicki-boom. Boom-chicki-boom. And he used to be such a nice, good boy. His mother used to sing at Kingston Parish Church. She was an alto in the choir, until . . ."

I could have said the words for her, *the divorce*. Jah Mick's father had divorced his mother just as Jah Mick was about to go to the States, and this, according to my mother, was the reason for the change—a blast from the past—*a broken home*.

My mother was thinking about divorcing my father and

she was afraid that something dreadful would happen to me, so she spent a lot of time praying for me when she should have been praying for my father to come home.

My father was an accountant, a good one at that. And because of this, he was often called away to audit hotels and sugar estates. Short trips would last three days. It wasn't strange for him to be away for weeks. In that time he'd rarely call. But women would from time to time. My mother took her own accounting. *Boops!* Another outside child.

"Ma," I said, "I have a headache. And my stomach not feeling so well. I can go and lie down?"

"After you go over to the house and tell him to turn down the music."

"I thought I wasn't supposed to go over there. You confusing me now."

"Hurry up and go and come back. I will make some Andrews."

"I don't have a headache, Ma. Nutten not bothering me."

"So is lie you was telling?"

"No, Ma. I just can't take this anymore. Everything ah say is a fight. Everything him do is a fight. The man just playing some music. Is not a crime."

She glanced at Aunt Shirley and Uncle Tyrone, then crossed her arms. Looking at me squarely now, she said, "If you don't go over there and tell him to turn it down, I going to call the police and tell them that he has ganja in the house."

"Ma!!"

"Ma *what*?"

"You'd really do that?"

"No, but that is not the point." She glanced at Aunt Shirley and Uncle Tyrone again. "God forgive me. Tell him that I am very distressed about the music and that I cannot have my Bible study, and that I'm going to call the police and tell them that he has ganja over there if he doesn't do it."

"But you said you wouldn't do it, Ma. So what's the point?"

"I don't care who or what is involved, you have to listen to me."

"I thought I wasn't suppose to tell no lie."

"Nobody not asking you to tell a lie. I'm asking you to tell a lie? I'm giving you a message to give somebody. Who's to tell if I might change my mind. I might call Superintendent Samuels, yes, if him go on like him bad and have hard ears. Sammo wi' know what to do with him. This is a residential area, after all. Nice, cool Friday evening and all you can hear is boom-chicki-boom. The place gone to the dogs, man. Gone to the dogs."

It was time to clutch at straws.

"Aunt Shirley . . ."

"You didn't hear what your mother said?"

"Uncle T—"

"Yuh hair need a trim."

I could have walked through the gate but I jumped over the fence. Talk about flirting with danger. The fence was lined with a prickly hedge. But it wasn't just this. My mother called anyone who jumped a fence a boogooyagga. That's how they come to grab the washing off the line, you know.

Over the fence. Had I ever seen my father jump a fence? No. Any member of his family? No. Any member of hers? No. But yes. Uncle Tyrone one time when him used to screw a woman up the road and her husband came home. Those was the days before the Fosbury Flop. Uncle T. took a Western roll over the top of a big rose bush and a prickle hook him in him pants crotches. In the rush him did forget fo' put on him underpants, and when the pants tear, two guinep and a Chiney banana drop out and a next door neighbor helper bawl, "And him love talk 'bout plantain."

We lived in the middle of a very long block. So I had to walk a quarter-mile or so to the corner before I had to turn, go up, and walk a quarter-mile again. This gave me lots of time to think.

How was I going to tell Jah Mick he had to turn down his music or my mother was going to call the beasts? It was about the threat as much as the lie. The man wasn't doing anything, really, yet she thought it was okay to terrorize him with the name of the police like she was casting out a demon in the name of Jesus. *In the name of Jesus, come out!!!!*

We accept the rastaman today. We see him and his fashion victims all around—the colors, the music, the hair, the food. But in those days in Jamaica, decent people like my mother thought of them as cells of infection that had to be cut out. They were spreading Africa throughout the body politic. Decent girls were being seduced. Decent boys were dreading up their good, good hair and swearing their allegiance to Selassie, taking oaths. The disease was spreading via body fluids. And music was both sperm and blood. They felt they had to stop the flow at any cost.

Trim hair. Comb beard. Crack skull. Kick down. Jump 'pon. Beat up. Lie. These words began to come to me as I listened to the instrumental music coming from my bredrin's house. At first it was stuttered. Then, as I kept saying it, it found its space between the drum beats in the riddim and became a kind of chant.

Trim hair.
Comb beard.
Crack skull.
Kick down.
Jump 'pon.
Beat up . . . llllllllliiiiiiiiiiiiiieeeeeeeee.
How de policeman
Deal wid de rasta.
Trim hair.
Comb beard.
Crack skull.
Kick down.
Jump 'pon.
Beat up . . . llllllllliiiiiiiiiiiiiieeeeeeeee.

When I got to the gate of the man who was teaching me everything about the Jamaica being worked at and wished for by my classmates and friends, I turned around and took two fast steps down the block. Houses that I'd passed in a trance only minutes before became concrete to me. You know what I mean—not concrete like concrete, but real, alive, alive with real meaning. Junior's house. David's house. Paul's house. Gail's house. Jennifer's house. Maxine's. All friends from short pants and marble days till now. None of them were home. They were in the park, either playing football or watching it, before they went to the movies when the sun went down.

I was in a panic now. What if my mother was right? What if all my friends and I were going to die because we didn't believe in her God. All of my friends. Their friends and their friend's friends. People I didn't even know they were friends with. All of them condemned before the final judgment . . . unless, of course, they changed.

If I got home in time, I thought I could avoid it. I could ask them to pray for me. And all I had to do was repent of my ways and I would be saved. All I had to do was play my cards right and I could join my mother, Aunt Shirley, and Uncle Tyrone in the coming paradise on earth.

Marley's "Natty Dread" was playing now. The intro. Those heraldic Eastern-sounding horns.

I would never be a rasta, I told myself. Never. Never. Never. I pumped my arms harder. Never. Never. Never.

At this point I heard his voice: "Yuh warming up?"

It was only then that I fully understood that I was still in front of his house, but off to one side. I'd turned and taken two steps—for sure. But after that it was strictly knee lifts on the spot.

His front door was open but I couldn't see him. I would never be a rasta, I told myself as I opened the gate . . . so . . .

God forgive me till ah reach back home.

Jah Mick had been watching me from the living room. I could tell he was feeling *irie* because he'd taken off his black tracksuit and was sitting cross-legged in front of a speaker.

Vibe-sing out. When I stepped inside off the veranda, he tucked his dreads into his tricolor tam and smiled from deep inside the bush of his beard and moustache. The green carpet felt fat beneath my feet. The room was as it had been when his parents lived there—heavy brown drapes that never opened, Morris chairs, a mahogany breakfront with shelves and shelves of figurines, and framed paintings of sunsets and tropical birds on the walls.

"So little lion," said Jah Mick, "what you defending today?"

I didn't answer. My tongue was in my throat. Eventually I said, "Nutten."

He laughed and said, "You can't defend nutten, little lion. You mus' always defend somep'n. If you don't stand for somep'n, you wi' fall fo' anything."

"So how the magazine coming?" I asked.

He shook his head and said, "Not so good. That's why you see me here trying to hold a vibes. The music kinda loud. Come talk to me in the room."

The room was where he slept and worked, and it had a velvet poster of Haile Selassie on the door. There were lots of soccer posters on the wall—Pelé, Beckenbauer, Eusébio, and Cruyff—and furniture that looked like mine.

The prefab walls had dulled the music to a blobby throb, but the layout on the drafting table buzzed. He kept his books in the other bedrooms. Books that I'd borrowed and read in secret . . . Garvey, Kenyatta, Fanon . . .

"I want to talk to you," I mumbled, as he sat on the edge of the bed.

"You cool?"

"No . . . no. That's why ah need to talk to you."

Fifteen minutes later, after I'd started and stopped many times, he said strongly, "Talk up, man. Talk up. You mother never teach you fo' talk up?"

"My mother," I began, "my mother . . ."

"Yes?"

"My mother . . ."

"Say it."

"My mother say you mus' . . ."

"*Mus'?*"

He stood now and went over to the drafting table. He stood in a way that put his back to me. All of a sudden I could talk.

"My mother say you mus' turn down the music."

Without looking, he asked, "And if I don't?"

"She goi' . . ."

"Goi' wha'?"

"Well, she say . . ."

"Say wha'?"

"She say she goi' call Sammo and tell him you have ganja over here."

He turned to face me now and I turned my back to him.

"I have ganja over here?" he blurted. He sounded like a young head boy who'd been accused of cheating on a test. "I have ganja over here? Your mother say she goi' tell Sammo I have ganja over here?" His voice deepened into anger now. "So wha'? You support that?"

I turned around to face him. "Wha' you t'ink?"

He stepped right up to me and put his hand on my

shoulder, which made me jerk and wince. I woulda under-stand if him did lick me.

"No ganja not here. I doh smoke and I doh allow nobody fo' smoke over here. And you know that. So how you coulda come to me with a message like that?"

"Doh act like you don't know how she stay," I replied with irritation. "You make it seem like is my fault that you turn dread and she turn to the Lord. The two o' oonoo come in like crosses to rass. Just turn down the music, nuh. Just make live easy, nuh. She is an old lady. She can't change. Certain kinda music goi' burn her. And when it burn her, is me she take it out 'pon. Is not you. You is a big man. You live by yourself. Me still live with my mother and she taking your fat and fry me."

"So wha'?" he said pointedly. "Is my fault that your mother is a pagan heart? Miss B. used to be a nice lady, then she make this church thing fly inna her head, and now is like ah living in a prison. Every Friday evening is this singing and praying and talking in me head. Eleven o'clock o' night sometimes and them still going on. Is wha' so, El Paso? Them doh have any consideration? Them only business 'bout themselves?"

Before I could answer, he pressed on.

"And is not me alone complaining 'bout it. Is nuff peo-ple in the area start to complain that people knocking on their gate and when they go out there is somebody want to give them a pamphlet or invite them to a meeting. Bredrin, none o' this was going on before your mother found the Lord, so everybody know is because o' she. Most people round here grow up Anglican and Catholic. They doh too like this Jehovah Witness t'ing." He dropped his voice into a whisper now. "Not that I'm passing judgment . . . but . . . you know, people have it as a cult."

"So what you want me to do?" I asked, then puttered around at the drafting table as if the conversation was done. The layout was in trouble. If he needed music to inspire him, he needed to turn it up some more.

"You know, if the police come here they goi' bring ganja to find . . ." he said matter-of-factly.

"Yes."

"So what you goi' do?"

"I already do it. I tell you what she asked me to tell you, and now is up to you."

"Yes, you do it, but you more than do it. You done it too."

He took a deep breath, and then blew it slowly through his mouth. Our friendship was over and he wanted me to think that it was all my fault.

"Turn off the set when you leaving," he said, and sat down on the bed again.

"You not fair, Jah Mick. You not fair."

"Just turn it off," he said slowly. "Just turn it off. I have to go back to work. And I need peace and quiet for that."

"So is my time to leave?"

"Not saying that. Just saying is my time to work."

Before I closed the door to his bedroom, I said, "So you have me up now, Jah Mick?"

"Shame o' you, man. Shame o' you. Jah love everybody. You know that a'ready. Tonight before I and I go to sleep, I and I goi' pray for you . . . ask Jah fo' protect you in the midst of the heathen. Fret not thyself, little lion. When rev-olution come, all pagan heart goi' get what is theirs." He smiled now and pointed to the hair beneath his tam. "But by dem time deh, you wi' truly know yourself and grow your covenant. So when the judgment come, Jah Jah wi' watch over the I. You let me down still, but I and I overstand. You living under pagan influence daily, so some o' it must rub off. Stand firm till such time though. Stand firm. Vengeance is mine. So Jah say. Vengeance is mine."

I could have said a lot of things before I left. But what would have been the point? After that I didn't pray for a very long time.

A LITTLE EMBARRASSMENT FOR THE SAKE OF OUR LORD

by *Konrad Kirlew*

Your father will be ordained tomorrow," Mrs. Riley announced to her children, during their Friday-night family devotion.

"Why are they ordinating him?" Justin asked.

"Ordaining. The word is *ordaining*. After you've been a minister for a few years and proven yourself, then you get to take more responsibilities in the church."

"Like what?"

"Like baptizing people and marrying people."

"Does this mean that you won't be at my recital next Sunday, Daddy?" Barb asked.

"I wish I could hear you play," Pastor Riley said, "but I have a church board meeting next Sunday."

"Couldn't you have it another time, or start it earlier or something, Daddy?"

"I'm sorry, I can't do that."

"Why not? You're the minister!"

"Listen to me very carefully." His voice rose into boss mode. "You kids don't seem to understand the importance of the Lord's work. I can't make all of your events, okay. And that's just the way it is."

Pastor Riley glared at each of his children to make sure they got the message. Pauline looked as if nothing had happened. Barb screwed up her face. Justin glanced at the cover of the Bible in his hand. Even Freddy, their two-year-old brother, looked sheepish. Sis, their helper, patted Barb on the shoulder as if to say, *Hush, never mind.*

"Let's finish this discussion and not spoil a good worship," the pastor continued.

Mrs. Riley told the kids that they would be going to Montego Bay tomorrow and their father was going to preach, so they had to wake up early for the drive from Black River.

Justin was excited. Tomorrow's trip was going to be important. He could tell this from his parents' voices. As they said their prayers at the end of worship, he prayed for all their friends and relatives, especially his eldest sister, Sheila, who lived in Canada. He also prayed that Jesus would help him to be a good boy, which wasn't always easy, and watch over them while they made their way along the country roads tomorrow, and help Daddy to preach a good sermon tomorrow for the ornamentation.

Pastor Riley sat on the platform of the Montego Bay church, the biggest and most important church of his denomination in that part of Jamaica. It was a concrete block building with an impressive vaulted ceiling, a baby grand piano, a small pipe organ, and stained-glass windows. The church was packed. It was hot, despite the overhead fans and the open windows. Some of the congregation halfheartedly waved paper fans with wooden handles that looked to Justin like giant popsicle sticks. From his seat in the front row Justin could see his father sitting in the big chair reserved for the preacher, directly behind the pulpit. His father was wearing a new black suit, a starched white shirt, and his favorite tie, which was the color of dark wine and had a subtle paisley print.

Justin thought his father seemed a little nervous when he was being introduced. The introduction was made by Pastor Ed Townsend, the president of the western region of the church. Townsend was tall and burly, black as coal. He had a booming voice and what some people called a military bearing. Everyone referred to him as "Uncle Ed" or "The Chief." But never to his face. People were afraid of him. And not just unimportant people. Ministers as well.

"Pastor Riley is a son of the soil," Townsend bellowed, "and the husband of one wife. Sister Riley is an outstanding nurse and the Lord has blessed them with four lovely children." He asked the Riley family to stand.

After they sat down, Justin told his mother softly, "He made a mistake. There are five of us. He didn't count Sheila."

She looked up at the ceiling fans, thought a bit, then scribbled on a piece of paper, *He probably forgot.*

Justin reached for her pen and began to write a question, but his mother took the piece of paper and crushed it. With a quick pat on his leg, she implied that they could talk about it later. But not now. In church.

When Pastor Riley finally approached the mike after the Chief's operatic introduction, Justin wondered what it felt like to be called to speak in front of so many people.

He'd seen his father speak in church many times, of course, but the thought always came to his mind. Whenever his father spoke in church, he seemed to grow somehow. It was as if he changed into a bigger man. His shoulders. His chest. His voice. Barb called it the preacher voice. It was deeper, slower, and had pauses that conveyed a strong effect. Each pause would bring you forward . . . draw you in.

What did it feel like to change that way? thought Justin. The thing that caused the change, were you born with it? Was it a blessing? Do I have that thing inside myself?

When little Freddy heard his father's voice, he shouted, "Daddy! Daddy! Daddy!" broke away from Sis, and ran to the pulpit as fast as his little legs would go.

The congregation sighed and laughed, and Pastor Riley offered, "Was it not our Lord who said, 'Suffer the little children to come unto me and forbid them not, for of such is the kingdom of heaven?'" He stepped away from the pulpit, lifted Freddy, and gave him a big, warm hug, and joked, "This one will be a preacher."

He called Sis to come and get the child, but when she came the child began to fuss and wail. There was an anxious moment there in which the pastor had to choose between being looked at as a man who loved children or a father who knew how to control a child, and he smiled right through it. But when the moment passed without appearing like it was about to end, he took the child away from Sis and set him on the big chair behind the pulpit.

"I want you to be very quiet," he stage-whispered. "Listen carefully and take good notes." Freddy nodded solemnly, quieted down, then quickly fell asleep, giving Pastor Riley more material for a joke.

As Justin watched all this, he thought, I could never get away with that. He was jealous and a bit annoyed. But minutes later, Pastor Riley told a story that annoyed him even more.

"There was once a little boy who had misbehaved, and his mother said, 'When your father gets home, I'm going to tell him.' Now the little boy knew that once his father came home, he would surely get a spanking. When the father arrived and his wife gave him the news about the son, the father called the little boy into his room. Before his father could even remove his belt, the little boy started singing, in a quivering voice, a song his parents had taught him. You may know it."

Pastor Riley started to sing, and not having a very good voice, really sounded like a kid who was in trouble.

> *God can do anything, anything, anything,*
> *God can do anything but fail.*

Justin knew the story. It was one of those family stories parents think are cute and which their children hate. *He* was the little singer boy. He had heard his father tell it before, but never in church.

"Well, when he started singing, the father's heart just melted. There was nothing he could do but smile and put away his belt. That was faith. He had repented, and had faith that God and his parents had forgiven him, and that he could avoid a spanking. Of course, the father pointed out to his son that if he misbehaved again he would be spanked, even if Gabriel himself came down and played the song on his golden trumpet." Everyone laughed. "We can apply faith to every aspect of our lives, even occasionally to get out of the trouble we've put ourselves in. We need the simple trusting faith of a child." He continued, "I won't say who that little boy was, but he's someone I know very well."

Justin felt as though the entire church was staring at him and giggling. His father might as well have stripped him naked and paraded him around the church to show how healthy a child could be on a vegetarian diet, another of his new kicks. *Note the well-formed limbs, the clear eyes, the strong teeth, and the perfection of his circumcised manhood. Vegetarianism: If you're serious about the kingdom of heaven.*

Justin wanted to die, but only after his father had been strangled slowly in painful ways.

Barb hummed the first line of "God Can Do Anything" in Justin's ear. He threw her an elbow. She threw it back. Mrs. Riley gave them one of her don't-you-dare looks and they calmed down. Justin made plans to poison the entire family when they got home.

Finally, church was over. As they were ushered out, Justin kept his head down, refusing to look anyone in the eye. The family stood outside and took pictures and shook hands. "Smile nuh, man," Pastor Riley said at one point to Justin, who was pouting and scowling the entire time.

In the car on the way to Uncle Ed's house for lunch, Pastor Riley said, "What's wrong, Justin? Who trouble you?"

"Did you have to tell that story?" Justin asked. "Everyone knew who it was!"

"Cho, man, I didn't tell the story to embarrass you. You're too big to be worrying about those things. I was trying to make a point. Jesus used examples from his life all the time."

"From his life, but not from other people's lives."

"We know that it was a little embarrassing for you," Mrs. Riley said. "But it shows that you had faith. That's a good thing."

"Well, Jesus isn't around to be teased by His friends," Justin answered. "He's dead. I'm alive."

"Don't look now," Barb said, "but Jesus isn't dead. He's alive!"

"Didn't He die on the cross, Barb? Has anyone seen Him lately?"

"Haven't you heard of the resurrection, stupid?"

"Now if you can't say anything nice," Mrs. Riley said, "don't say anything at all." The older children mockingly mouthed the last phrase together, one of their mother's mantras.

"You can't use other people's stories without permission," Barb continued. "That's a copyright violation. Justin, you should sue him!"

"Enough, Miss Lawyer," Pastor Riley said.

"If you win," Barb said, "don't forget to pay your tithe."

Justin couldn't stop himself from laughing. Here he was, trying to enjoy a good sulk, and Barb was making jokes. Even Mrs. Riley smiled.

Pastor Riley didn't get it, or maybe he didn't want to.

"That's enough. You're too force-ripe. I used the story as an example, not to embarrass you. But you're in good company. Our Lord suffered far more than a little embarrassment on the cross."

"I'm not anybody's blasted example," he muttered. It was only after he'd said it that he knew he'd said it aloud.

"But wait," Pastor Riley said, and shot a look at the rearview mirror to catch Justin's eye. "What did you say?"

Justin didn't answer.

"Boy . . . what . . . did . . . you . . . say?"

Justin kept quiet as he thought of what to do. If he did as he was told and repeated what he'd said, then he'd be "rude and bright 'pon top of it," and if he didn't answer, he'd be "acting like somebody tell him him is *man*."

Justin mumbled something that his father couldn't hear. It was nothing. A kind of baby talk. So he didn't repeat it and he wasn't silent. Two birds. One stone.

"I heard you," Pastor Riley said. "Where did you learn that sort of language?"

"You called Pastor Gordon a blasted fool a few weeks ago," said Justin. His parents had been talking on the porch when he'd overheard it and had quickly changed the subject when Justin came into view.

Mrs. Riley left it all up to her husband now and kept staring at the road ahead.

"That doesn't mean you should repeat it," Pastor Riley said, to break the crust of silence that had quickly built up. "And besides, you had no right to be listening to big people's conversation. You're out of order."

By this time they'd arrived at Uncle Ed's.

"We'll finish this when we get home," Pastor Riley continued. "And I don't want to see that donkey face anymore today. Keep this up, and when you get home I'll give you something to have a long face about."

Barb began to slap away imaginary insects from her legs and arms, teasing Justin in the secret spanking code.

"Sing your way out of this one," she whispered. Justin did his best to tune her out.

Uncle Ed lived on a hill in Reading, just outside of town, in a large white two-story house. As they turned off the main road, Justin noticed the driveway lined with coconut trees and stones, the bottom of the trees and the stones painted white. The lawn was huge, and flat—to Justin, perfect for a football game. When they got out of the car, he could see the ocean in the distance and the city in the foothills down below.

"Does Uncle Ed have children?" Justin asked his mother, as they walked toward the house.

"No, he doesn't."

"So who lives in all these rooms?" He pointed to the trees around them. "Do they eat all this fruit by themselves?"

They went inside and mingled with a few other ministers and their families, some of whom they hadn't seen in a while. Justin could almost predict the comments: Barb had her father's facial features and complexion, Justin had his mother's smile and quiet personality, Pauline was a mixture of her parents, and Freddy had his own look—at which point Pastor Riley would say he looked just like his grandmother. Justin said nothing but the minimum. Just enough to be polite.

They saw Pastor Pointer, who had just returned from England, where he'd been working on a doctorate for many years.

"Riley," he said, "it's been over ten years." He turned to the children. "Your father and I go back a long, long way. Since we were colporteurs selling books to make our way through college in the States." To Pastor Riley now, he said, "Last time I saw you, you were a single man throwing your net into the Sea of Galilee. How many children do you have now? These are all of them?"

"Yes, yes," Pastor Riley said. "Just these four. The Lord has blessed. Seems like every time I even look at my wife, there's another one."

He introduced the kids by name and they all shook Pastor Pointer's hand. When they were finished, Justin asked his mother, "But what about Sheila?" He tried to make eye contact with his mother. "She's our sister."

Mrs. Riley smiled and looked at Pastor Pointer as she laid her hands on Justin's head.

"Mommy," Justin pressed, "Daddy is forgetting about—"

Mrs. Riley pinched him.

"What is the little man saying?" Pastor Pointer asked.

Justin hesitated. His parents glared. "We have a sister named Sheila."

Pastor Riley reached for Justin, pulled him to his side, and said, " I . . . ahh . . . had a daughter years ago, before I was a Christian . . . and ahh . . . she lives abroad with her mother."

"Oh, I see."

"So," said Pastor Riley. Justin felt a tremble rushing through his father's arm, "how was . . . ahh . . . England?"

They left Montego Bay after dark, and the ride home was quiet. All of the children were asleep except Justin.

Pastor Riley drove fast, as he always did. Justin waited tensely for the moment he knew would have to come. They made their way through the narrow roads, the darkness sometimes broken up by lights—electric in the towns and kerosene in the districts where the farmers lived.

Justin tried to take his mind away from the inevitable by taking pleasure in the way his father changed the gears, how he made the engine of the Morris Oxford hum with music, how he dove into the corners with flair, passing overloaded trucks on small roads, the car's roof line just a little lower than the giant wheels.

But it was hard to keep his mind at rest. His parents were discussing all that had happened that day, including the chance that Pastor Riley might be sent to lead another church. They were doing it indirectly, but Justin understood a little of their code. It was mostly "my man" this and "our friend" that, but sometimes they'd use a Bible name like Joshua or Moses or Zaccheus, which he knew referred to little Pastor Daniels, the conference secretary.

Except for the code, they spoke as if no one else was in the car, as if the children in the back did not exist. Justin began to hope as time went on, began to consider the possibility that his father might let things slide because the ordination—he made sure to get it right—had gone well. So what if afterward there'd been an awkward moment? The moment that mattered had gone extremely well, except for the little foolishness with Freddie.

When they got home, Mrs. Riley went into the kitchen to fix supper and Pastor Riley called Justin into his room.

Justin felt prepared because he knew the routine—before

the spanking his father would say, "Do you know why we have to do this?" He would nod yes, then his father would say, "Tell me, so I know you know." At this point Justin would say "It's wrong to tell a lie or take something that isn't mine," or something of the sort, then, depending on his father's mood and the nature of the deed, he'd either hold out his hand to receive the blows in his palms, or try not to resist when his father took his wrists and held them with a single grip above his head and rained down on his bottom with the brown suede belt.

This time, though, nothing was said. Routine was shoved away. Pastor Riley reached for Justin and began to rain down on his bottom with the belt.

And Justin refused to cry. He didn't know what stopped him. It wasn't like he was trying. Or that the beating didn't hurt. It was as if something had hardened up and blocked his throat at the point where the tunnels from his mouth and nose went their separate ways, so neither sound nor snot could come. And without these two, it seemed the tears just wouldn't come. Just wouldn't come, which just made things worse, because his father needed tears as proof of contrition.

Mrs. Riley entered the room without knocking, crossed her arms, and said, "Enough, dear. Enough. He's got enough now. You're going to damage the child."

"He's too facety. Too own-way. I need to beat it out of him. If he can't hear, he must feel."

"Mummy," called Justin. "Mummy." He began to squirm now, as he watched his mother standing only feet away. "Mummy. Mummy."

He got away, but Pastor Riley stretched and caught him and began to rain on him again.

"I hate you!" Justin shouted, as he twisted with his face pressed up tightly on his father's heaving chest. "I hate you. I hate you. I wish you weren't my father."

Mrs. Riley grabbed him from her husband. Pastor Riley continued to swing the belt as she did so, and it almost caught her in the face.

Justin and his mother lay huddled in his bedroom for a very long time, then she sat up on the side of the bed with her elbows on her knees and her face in her hands, and he curled up with his face against the wall.

She lay beside him once again and began to rub his head and neck, then got up to open a window to allow a cooling breeze to come in.

"Why is Daddy so mad?" said Justin when he'd stopped shaking.

"You were rude to him."

"I've been rude before . . ."

"You tried to embarrass him. That wasn't very nice."

"He did the same thing to me."

"Yes. But not on purpose."

Justin thought about that for a few moments. It was true. "Mummy, what's the problem with Sheila?"

Mrs. Riley paused for a few moments, as if to collect her thoughts. "It's not that she's a problem, but it reminds him of a time in his life that wasn't very good for him, before he became a Christian. Have you ever done something that you wish you could forget?"

"So he should see what I mean about telling my stories to the church."

"Perhaps."

"Well, I'm sure if he did something bad Jesus will forgive him."

"I'm sure He has." She paused, seeming to debate whether to go any further. "Don't repeat this to anyone, but some of the men in the conference didn't want him to be ordained, even though it happened years before he was a minister. Your father is very sensitive about it."

"Was Pastor Gordon one of them?"

"I'm not sure who all of them were," she said, "but that's not important."

Justin thought about things for a minute. Then he had a bright idea. "Mommy, can Daddy get another job?"

"What do you mean?"

"I don't want to be a preacher's kid. I just want to be normal."

"You are normal. Your father loves his job, it makes him very happy. It would be bad for him to change that." She paused. "And you can't change your parents. You're the son of a pastor."

"But I'm more than that."

"Of course you are."

"So why do we have to be an example?"

"The people in the church believe your father represents God. If he leads his family well, they think he will be a good leader of the church."

"But that's not fair to us."

"No, it isn't." She paused. "Puss and dog don't have the

same luck."

"Can't Daddy understand that we don't want to be examples?"

Mrs. Riley retreated into another of her silences. To Justin, they all had meanings. Sometimes he felt that his mother could see inside his mind, read his thoughts at the same time as he was thinking them.

"You may not fully understand this now," she said, "but serving God and the church is the most important thing in your father's life. Anything he thinks will help his ministry is good. Anything he thinks will interfere with it is bad. Like it or not, you have to understand that."

She paused and took a deep breath.

"Today you were in the unfortunate position where your father felt he had to choose between you and his ministry." She looked away from Justin and glanced out the window for a moment. "But always remember that your Daddy loves you very much, and he doesn't mean to hurt you."

Yes, Justin thought to himself, but he loves the church even more.

She hugged him for a long time, and he wanted her never to let go. Finally, she said, "It's time for bed, your brother needs to go to sleep," and she left the room.

The night was quiet except for the chirping of crickets and frogs, a strangely soothing sound that Justin used to think came from the power lines. Through the window he could see the sky pinpointed with stars.

Years later, when he had occasion to think about this time, Justin would remember it as the first time that he got an inkling that there were ways in which he and his father would never connect. But on that night, he understood that he hated this part of being a child—having to live by confusing adult rules, not being able to do what he wished. In that moment, childhood felt like a prison.

Before he closed his eyes, he remembered that he hadn't prayed. He was too tired to get up to kneel and so he just lay there, eyes half-closed, and asked God to help him be a good boy who would listen to his father. He closed his eyes, then opened them again. He looked up at the stars and wondered where God was, and if He had really heard.

SUGAR
by Sharon Leach

The girl in the leopard bikini walking along the beach, past the sunbathing tourists, is swinging her hips. As she walks, her bare feet kick up tiny puffs of white sand. Her legs are strong, and brown like mine. Her braids—real braids that have been done at some fancy foreign boutique, perhaps, rather than by one of the local girls here—hang down her back, cascading like a waterfall at midnight, swishing from side to side against her bottom as she walks toward the calling waves. She knows the greasy sunburned white men, eyes hidden behind their smoky sunglasses and thick novels tented atop their huge red bellies that surge over their swim trunks, are watching her. So she sticks out her small chest, like a fashion model walking down a catwalk, her hips swinging in time: *swish, swish, swish.*

The girl in the leopard bikini is slim and fine-featured and alone on vacation here, at the resort. I do not know her name; she has never spoken to me. She perhaps thinks of my station as being too lowly. Or maybe it is because I am a woman. But I can tell that she is not that much older than me. How can she afford a vacation here by herself? I have seen her a few times at night, talking and laughing with those same lobster-red men with the flabby paunches. I like to watch her from a little distance on the nights that I serve drinks beside Ernesto the Cuban at the tiki bar. She has been here at the resort for almost two weeks now. Longer even than Peter and Denise who've been here eight days. Under an ink-black sky with shooting stars falling like rain, she will lean forward to listen to one of the men who says something in her ear over the din of the calypso house band. A breeze ruffles by and I imagine the reflection of the votive candles' flames flickering in her eyes. She tucks a few loose braids behind her ear, and I see an earring. It is a real diamond stud, I know, because of how it glints in the light.

She laughs and her voice is a thin cry. The girl could be me.

But she is not. She is just another rich American—a black one at that—who can take expensive island holidays by herself. At night, her braids tied atop her head, she wears different beaded dinner dresses and smells of expensive cologne. Watching her sip her Absolut and cranberry juice, I imagine a glamorous life that I pretend is my own: fancy designer clothes and shoes, maybe a car, and breezy summer vacations.

"Ah, my Brown Sugar." Peter's voice cuts into my thoughts like a blade striking wood, startling me so that I jump guiltily. Peter and his little blond wife are a couple from Texas, in the faraway land of cowboys and John Wayne. Today I am on housekeeping duty, which is why I am in their room. I spin around sharply to see Peter standing in the doorway beside my cart, hugging Denise, who is a good foot-and-a-half shorter, and who appears to be growing out of his side like an appendage, or a tumor.

"Mr. Peter, Miss Denise," I say, stepping hurriedly away

from the window and dragging at the bed sheets. "I'm sorry, I'm not done yet. I only just got started." It is a lie, because I've been in the room for more than twenty minutes already, but, because of my daydreaming, it is still untidy, with clothes, half-opened suitcases, and glossy magazines strewn all over the floor and across chairs. "I'll be out of y' way soon."

"Sugar."

I can hear the wheels of my custodial cart squeaking and the sound of the door closing and I feel a fist close around my heart. Suddenly Denise is lying on the bed, the sand that was clinging to her body in her tiny bikini shivering onto the half-removed white cotton sheets. "Poor Sugar," she says, a smile in her voice. She has wrinkles in the corners of her eyes when she smiles. "Imagine. Working on your birthday. You know a girl's twenty-first is extra-special."

Denise is pretty, like the white women I've seen in the movies. The ones I've seen here at the resort aren't. They mostly have flabby guts, stretch marks, and bad teeth. Even without makeup, though, I can stare at Denise for hours and feel hypnotized. With her shapely girlish figure, I can hardly believe she's a grandmother; she has told me that they have a daughter who's just had a child of her own. I am surprised she remembers that I told her when my birthday was. No one else has. She pats a space on the bed, her green eyes sparkling like emerald chips telling me that I should sit.

There is a click and the air conditioner groans to life. The room is spacious: one of the larger beachfront ones with bay windows and ceramic-tiled floors that the richer tourists prefer. It is furnished just like the other rooms along this stretch, with rattan chairs, a mahogany chest-of-drawers, and a TV. In the center of the room is a low glass table on which sits an old orange juice carton containing a beautiful bougainvillea bouquet. Each of these rooms comes with an outside terrace and a nice view of the sea. Once, when my younger sister Celine spent the day with me while I did my rounds, we locked ourselves in one of the rooms that was unoccupied. We stripped down to our underwear and laid on the bed, eating insipid leftovers from a plate we had stolen off a tray left outside one of the occupied rooms—watching TV and letting the air conditioner blast us until our skins were ashy. We stared at each other and burst out laughing. We were soon sobbing with laughter. "This is it?" Celine gasped finally, wiping her eyes. "Air-conditioning and TV? Rich people really fool-fool!"

I laughed, but deep down I wanted to be one of those people who could afford silly holidays and hotel rooms. I saw their possessions carelessly lying about when I cleaned their rooms: CD players, video cameras, those little computer gadgets that played music; the things I would never ever be able to afford. And I would do anything for that life.

Now Peter is suddenly in front of Denise and me. He is mostly lean, although he has the beginning of a beer belly. He is tan with limp, thinning hair the color of wet sand, which he keeps always in a ponytail beneath his cowboy hats. Today, he is bareheaded and his wet hair, splayed about his shoulders like octopus tentacles, reveals a balding pink head.

"Mr. Peter," I say quietly, my fingers playing with the hem of my cotton-candy-pink maid's uniform. I can see a fish in his tight swim trunks. I turn my eyes away.

"Su-*gah*," he says in the slow way that I imitate in the

mirror sometimes. He pats his stomach and makes a sucking noise between his teeth. "You're a naughty girl. I told you, it's *Peter* and *Denise*. And we're still waiting for your answer."

I glance over at Denise, who's bobbing her head and looking expectantly at me. "We're offering good money here," Peter continues in the voice that makes the blood sing in my ears. "I know I don't have to tell you how much Uncle Sam means around here."

I remain silent, the pressure in my chest making me feel faint. Through the muffled ebb of crashing waves just beyond the window, I hear my heart pounding. Peter is right: One Yankee dollar is like a nugget of precious gold and can fetch almost one hundred Jamaican dollars on the street. Hotel pay is not good—the rich owners who play hug-up with the government are the ones who reap most of the benefits. Still, it is better than nothing. I think of what the money can do: fix a patch of Ma's leaky roof; buy clothes for the other children. I think of Isaiah in Kingston, the only man I have ever been with, the only man who has ever loved me. The money can take me to him.

I feel Denise drawing little circles on my back with her fingers and the sensation is not unpleasant. She sits up so that she can speak directly into my ear, whose lobe still has the soiled little loop of string that was threaded in when my ears were pierced a few weeks ago. "Yes, Sugar, naughty girl," she says. Her lips are cool against my skin, her voice smoky, hoarse. It reminds me of a trickle of water in a dried-up riverbed. "We'll be going back home day after tomorrow. So? What's the answer gonna be?" She places a damp kiss on my neck, soft as morning dew, before blowing on the small hairs on my face.

I feel goose flesh rising on my arms and I feel sick, as if I am going to puke.

Outside the window, the sun shifts suddenly behind some clouds, then appears again, streaming in through the windows, lighting the room, and their faces, making them seem harsh, unkind. I look out at the sunlight on the water, and in the swell of people my eyes find the girl in the leopard bathing suit doing strong laps in the distance.

I imagine the girl is me.

She smiles at me when I bring her plate to her table. It is already 11 in the morning; the dining hall is deserted. She is sitting alone at a table set for four, her braids spilling down loosely about her shoulders, framing her tiny face. Today, instead of the leopard bathing suit, she's wearing a low-cut, sleeveless white top—under which she isn't wearing a bra—loose-fitting white pants, and white sandals; next to her, my clothes look like they should be in a pile of garbage. Up close, I see that she is even prettier than I'd believed; brown eyes, small nose, sloping cheekbones that accentuate her small mouth. She's ordered the saltfish fritters, calalloo, fried Johnnycakes, and a mug of chocolate tea.

I set the tray down and tell her the food is good, and she seems surprised that I can speak at all.

"You, uh, speak English real good," she says, giving me a small smile before leaning forward to smell the food. "You new here? I've never seen you around, I don't think."

I tell her that my friend Adele, who's supposed to be on dining hall duty today, is out sick so I have to fill in for her. "I'm usually on housekeeping," I say. "Sometimes at night I work in the bar. I've seen you there before—you always take Absolut and cranberry juice."

I stand waiting for her to remember. And what, maybe ask me to sit with her? Already I can imagine us being friends—she will tell me her name and I will tell her that she is the person I would most love to be in this world.

But she immediately seems to forget that I am there and starts to eat. I feel dismissed, useless, like a comma almost.

It is a clear day and the sun is pouring into the dining hall, a large pastel-colored room with a view of the beach and many tables set with white tablecloths, fancy heavy crockery, and gleaming sterling silverware. In a quick movement of her head, there is a flash, a sparkle at her ear through the fall of her braids.

And I cannot move. I know that I should, but I am helpless; my feet are heavy, as if they are stuck to melting tar. My stomach begins to quiver because I want to lay my cheek against that large stud sparkling in her ear, and to feel the smoothness of that jewel against my teeth. Nothing seems as important to me now as getting two real diamonds for my ears—not Ma's roof, not the clothes for the children, nothing.

Not even Isaiah.

Outside, I see a million butterflies flitting about in the golden sunlight. He once told me that there's a place in Kingston where, in butterfly season, you can see them falling out of trees like golden rain. We made plans to marry beneath one of those trees. But those plans, like Isaiah, have all disappeared. Suddenly, an image of Peter and Denise appears before me, the money they have promised me for one night.

It is only for one night.

As I turn and walk away, I wait for the guilt I expect to wash over me, telling me what to do. But it never comes.

In the yard, the younger children are chasing a mother hen and her baby chicks on a scabby patch of grass. They do not notice when I lift the latch of the dilapidated wooden gate and walk in. The smell of chicken poo is strong in my nostrils. Celine is on the front porch talking to a boy from a neighboring district who has ridden his bicycle up to see her. She is the sister that follows me. She is prettier than me, with good hair and a straight nose.

"Sugar," she calls out, waving. From where I stand, I can see her soft breasts bouncing beneath the thin cotton of her blouse.

"Where's Ma?" I ask.

She shrugs with a typical teenager's irrational annoyance and turns back to continue her flirting, to continue listening to that breadfruit-headed fool's silver lies.

My mother is sitting on a three-legged stool, bent over washing clothes in a pan under an old banyan tree at the back of the house. Her hands are busy making the *scrips scrips* sound I liked hearing as a child.

"Ma," I say, approaching slowly, my street shoes covered by a film of dust that came from the mile-and-a-half walk from the hotel. Guilt makes me imagine the odor of sex radiating off my skin, which is raw from scrubbing it clean in the shower I took in the maid's quarters after sneaking out of Peter and Denise's room before daylight.

She looks up wearily after a while. Her body is strained

and old from having too many children too fast. She has an unhappy mouth and eyes that, in the mid-morning haze, are the color of coffee grounds.

A soft breeze ruffles the tree leaves and rains down twigs in my mother's hair. "You get pay?" she asks sharply, spitting on the grass at her feet before curiously eyeing my satchel. Poverty has roughened her once-soft edges, she has forgotten how to say thanks, how to smile.

I look at Celine, who has come around the back, towed on the boy's bike. I can tell she's come to see what Ma and I are doing. I peer at her and wonder if she has allowed the boy to do things with her that he shouldn't. In Plantation, where we live, it is easy for dreams to turn into vapor when you are poor. I remember the previous night with the Americans: the flash of pale skin in the moonlight, and mine barely even discernible in the dark of the room, and how I had sat still, frozen with fear and guilt, when Denise's hands found the front buttons of my uniform and Peter walked naked to the window to pull the curtains, his skinny pink sausage dangling between his legs. How I'd remained rigid when Denise's tongue flicked like a snake's over my nipples and other parts of my body that I am too ashamed to say, and then how, in spite of myself, I had gradually begun to rock my hips as Peter grunted and thrust deeper and deeper inside me.

A lizard, the color of many rainbows, slithers by on the ground. I hand Ma the bulging envelope, from which I have removed a couple of the Yankee hundred-dollar notes for myself that I will hide in a secret place, beneath a loose floorboard in a corner of the dining room. The rest of the money in the envelope will keep my mother and my sisters and brothers fed and clothed for a while.

"I had to work two shifts." I say the lie with a smile. "I made some extra."

She looks suspiciously at me before snatching it away with a soapy hand, tucking it into her bosom. "Just thank God that you get that job over there at the hotel," she says, resuming her washing. "You lucky." She slaps at a mosquito on a varicose-veined leg and begins to hum the melody of a hymn she sings at the clap-hand church she visits on Sunday mornings. She does not say another word to me.

Again, I am dismissed.

I turn and walk toward the crumbling little house, with its leaky roof and rickety floorboards, hearing the words of the hymn trembling in the air.

A mighty fortress is our God . . .

I can see, looming over the roof of the house, the distant hills, brown and parched from the prolonged drought, something that all the Yankee dollars in the world cannot fix. As my mother's off-key humming fills up the morning, I find myself wondering what I would say if tonight, when she crawls onto the spot beside me on the mat we share, she asks me how I really made all that money. What would I say?

I think maybe I would close my eyes and picture myself as the girl on the beach in the leopard bikini with two diamonds in my ear. And, above the sound of crickets chirping outside our window in that vast country night, I would tell my mother what she wanted to hear. There in the dark I would whisper, "Ma, the Lord moves in mysterious ways."

MARLEY'S GHOST
by Kwame Dawes

1.

There is a man in a room with walls lined with old newspapers. That is the most reliable thing that can be said. A small room in a two-bedroom bungalow in a small development called Ensom City, just outside of Spanish Town. A characterless house in a neighborhood where hardworking folk—cement and garment factory workers, policemen, soldiers, chauffeurs, low-level civil servants, and enterprising street vendors—make a basic living. He has abandoned the island, the town, the district, the neighborhood—and the rest of the house—for this room lined with newspapers. They make the place look like a gift cheaply and hastily wrapped on the inside. They are already ochred with age; the colors on the comic sections faded.

The air in this room is old. Nowhere to go, it festers into a stink, the smell of a human being undecided about living or dying and depressed enough not to care about the smell. The moisture from sweat and breath hangs in the air like a despondent fog.

The man has been lying on the single bed in the room, on the same sheets, for days. Sometimes he gets up and walks around, a tall man who carries himself like a person who has suddenly lost a great deal of weight, with the unnecessary expansiveness of someone who has been told that he is smaller than he really is. Perhaps it is the airiness of his clothes or slowness of his movement, but something about him is in contradiction. It would not be surprising to hear him say, "I feel like I am in someone else's body." But he does not say this. What he says is, "She bound to come back . . . the bitch." There is no drama in the way he says this.

He scratches his unkempt hair, wincing at the tenderness of his scalp. Then he runs his hands across his face, his scraggly beard—a peppering of tight curls over his gaunt jaw. His skin has the quality of deep tanned leather stained with dark polish. Hair grows on all parts of his body—long, thick, gleaming strands on his arms, his shoulders, his toes, and his ears. His beauty is the subtlest of things. It arrives long after you have seen him and dismissed him as strange. But when it arrives, it overwhelms you with its certainty—it startles you with the brilliance of an unexpected smile.

He gets up occasionally to hunt down some stale bread from the bottom cupboard of a cracked dresser, or to sip water from a rust-stained porcelain sink in the corner of the room. Sometimes he just stands up and touches everything in the room as if trying to remind himself that he is alive. A peeling chair, the cracked dresser with a large blank wooden frame where a mirror used to be, the sink, an olive-colored military sack, an unsteady bedside table with a massive boom box resting on it—he touches everything. A black telephone glimmers under the bed like a wet frog about to pounce. It has not sounded in days.

The room has one high window just above the bed, a window laddered by brown louvred panels. Little light comes through this window even at the height of the day because the thick foliage of a black mango tree crowds it, its leaves sometimes poking through the open louvres.

Strips of muted light pattern the floor—which is strewn with clothes and a plague of gutted oranges. There are easily sixty or more carcasses scattered around the room, peels curling, some turning brown with decay. Their tart scent complicates the smell of human waste. Tiny fruit flies hover like moving mist over the floor and the occasional green-bottle fly darts around the scattered clothes.

This is his cell. His hiding place. He has been in this cell listening to *Exodus* on auto-replay on the tape deck since his woman left him, his African-American woman who thought she could come to Jamaica and ride her way through difference, through a history that is nothing less than tortuous, through his chronic sense of failure. But she could not. She left. Now she is gone, he has been listening to *Exodus*, trying to consume himself with that inspired merger of politics and love, trying to let himself be lifted by the wisdom of the prophet. Those are the reliable facts. Beyond them nothing is certain. Beyond them hover the edges of his sanity and little is definite in that place.

He is lying on the bed, his face toward the ceiling. Forty years old—that is his age, although lately he has been losing count. These days he wants to start counting from 1945 instead of 1962. This confusion consumes hours of his day. When he can stop thinking of his woman leaving him, he starts to think of the year of his birth. Now it is February 6, 2002. He thinks he should be dead.

Sounds come from outside the room. Sounds of a city determined to pursue its Third World rituals of laughter, dubwise, gunshot, car crash, screwing, hallelujahs, praise, and the telling of stories. The world goes on. A man's woman has left him. She has left him to travel back to America where she came from. He has driven her away. The world outside does not find this narrative especially remarkable. Women come and go. The world outside does not know this man, does not care about this man. The world outside does not care that this man has been in his room for six days eating oranges and trying to decide whether to take his medication or not. His woman has left. She may be pregnant. He is not sure. He wants to follow her but he doesn't know what he would say if he did catch up with her. He could sing a song, ask her if this is love he is feeling. He thinks that if he could sing that song, if he could conjure up the spirit of the man singing the song in his head—a short, skinny man with a head full of flowing natty dreads and a cocky sense of entitlement to the love of a woman; any woman, all women—if he could muster up that fiction, perhaps the people outside would care that he is locked up in a cell trying to decide whether to take his medication or not. But he has stayed in the room, eating oranges and slowly stinking up his cell with his wasting self.

He does, though, dream.

He dreams his story. He is a creature of dreams. To enter his mind would be to enter a world of muted light and dreams. The tumbling of dates—1962, 1945, 1981, 2002—

and the narrative of borrowed histories are the swirl of uncertainties that stir up his dreams. In his mind, he has a narrative that extends beyond that which he can own or even claim as history, as truth.

So this is all that can be called reliable: A man is in a room filled with orange peels and filthy clothes; *Exodus* repeats itself on the boom box; his woman has left him and he is not sure what to do. So he sleeps and dreams and becomes. This much we know.

2.

At dawn—it was always at dawn—he felt that he had died and was now waiting to understand what that meant. At dawn, a dew fresh dawn, he would walk out into the half-light and look at the world. Then the world was not so certain of its separateness from the spirit world. Indeed, on such mornings, he could see beyond the earth, beyond the trees, beyond the sky, see into the mist, see everything in spirit and in truth. At dawn, the world was unconvinced of its mere earthiness. The world seemed completely different and he felt as if he had died at least once before. It was as if, during the night, while he was lying there in his bed, his body had curled into itself as if he needed to make space. He had curled into a tight ball as if he had never left the one-room apartment on First Street where, thirty years before, he had to share the small bed with Spider, his cousin. It was as if he had to make space for another body on the bed.

After stretching, he planted his feet on the cool tiles, then walked out onto the back porch to stare into the hills, trying to remember something, still feeling as if he was sleeping, feeling as if he should be somewhere else.

This is what it had been like since his return to Jamaica. He had been away for eighteen months. It was the first time in a long while that he had been away from home for that long, in one stretch. The travelling had been hard. Cold. He missed the yard, the gathering of men in the yard to kick some ball, to sit down and chat pure foolishness. He missed that. He missed the arguments about nothing. He missed the studio filled with smoke and the echoing of music shaping itself. He missed that. He missed the taste of the air, with its dust, with its stench of dead things. He missed eating an orange, pulling on the tart sweetness, or sucking on guineps, missed the taste of their slippery seeds, the flesh bright in his mouth and the tiny cups of green skin scattered around his feet along with the carefully stripped seeds, white with only the barest hint of pink flesh on them. He missed the sun on his back. The sun on his skin. The way the heat would come on him.

He had looked in the mirror after a few months abroad and had begun to feel white, to feel as if he was losing definition, his sharp edges. He felt as if he was losing himself in the mute gray of Babylon. He hated it. He spent most of his time indoors, in the studio, pretending to be writing songs, making jokes with the musicians who were on tour from Jamaica. But he was in mourning. That is what it felt like.

When they told him that his assassins had been found and that they were to be tried and executed, he did not hesitate. He would go back.

Three men came up to Babylon from Jamaica to get him.

Three men no one would have dreamed could sit on a plane together. Two were serious generals of the street who had shed much blood in their battles against each other. The other, the third, was a longtime hustler, a man who had never sacrificed the independence of his criminal lifestyle for politics. He was very careful about that. He was a gunman, a robber, a t'ief, and he was going to rob whoever came along, and he did not give a rass whether they were Labourites or Socialists. He was a gleeful informer and the only reason he was alive was because of his firepower. But many had tried. Few wanted to associate with him. He was a genuine mafia man. That was who he was.

The three Magi came to the house to tell him that the two men who had come to execute him had been found. Joseph sat with them around a table to talk. The whole thing was a charade. They all knew it. Joseph knew it, but it was a ritual that had to be carried out. They came to tell him that it was now safe for him to go back. Joseph did not know anything about the two men they were holding. He did not know if they had anything to do with the shooting. They asked him, they repeated the names, they described the men. He knew nothing of them. He had not seen their faces as they fired bright sparks of light from the shadows of the mango tree in the yard. He had seen nothing.

But he knew that the Magi had a lot to do with the shooting and if they came to talk peace to him, if they came to tell him that it was safe to come home, then it meant that it was safe for him to come home. If they claimed that these were the ones who did it, then it was enough for him. But the ritual of atonement had to be carried out. The ceremony. The execution. It would take place in Kingston and Joseph was to be there. And Joseph, gong as ever, said he would be there, for peace was all he cared about. Peace and justice.

He returned to Jamaica and watched them hang the two men. He stood and looked the men in the face and watched them hang. Then he left the ghetto in a BMW and drove to his house uptown. He stepped into the dusty yard and sat on a stone under his special hibiscus grotto. He sat there and no one came to say anything to him. There he filled his head with the dizzying relief of smoke that helped him reach for somewhere else. He was home.

Death was familiar.

He had watched the men hang and had seen their spirits leave their bodies. But the spirits looked thoroughly confused. They had no idea where they were supposed to go. Someone was going to bury these bodies, but would this person know to light candle and hold a nine night to tell the spirits where to go? Joseph had been comfortable with the familiar taste of death, but not simply as a physiological truth, but as spiritual truth—something that went beyond the body failing to breathe again. He knew, though, that something integral had died in him as he watched the stinking fear of the two men, and smelled the shit and sweat of their writhing bodies. He had chosen to stand and look. Carried by the tyranny of his reputation and the weight of his responsibility as a tough man, he had chosen to watch. But it was more than that—it was curiosity and a peculiar desire to defy death by staring at it. He watched the men die and imagined his own death. It had been an impossible decision to make, but he had made it. Now, something had expired in him.

So he smoked his pipe in his backyard and then walked into the house to sleep. He slept.

Now morning was upon him. The radio was chattering. He looked out into the slight mist and he felt that he was dead, that he was in another world. He walked onto the porch and looked at the hills. The hills looked back at him. Then he made his way across the lawn in the backyard to the cluster of ficus berry trees at the end of the yard.

The roots coiled and twisted on the ground in a network of loops and crosses. Thick roots, smoothed and worn by rain and sun like the branches of a tree. They tendrilled their way to the thick trunk of the tree. It shot up straight, chunky like the neck of a boxer, and then spread, as if to mirror the net of roots, into a canopy of thickly leafed branches. The spread of the branches was impressive, a full wide stretch making a circle of shelter. The orange berries would fall and roll under the roots, accumulate and form a carpet of orange along the ground. Some rotting, some hard with sunlight, some still freshly crisp.

He sat among the roots and felt his body going back to sleep again. The sun crawled across his skin. He was home. Around him he heard birds and insects, but he could also hear the traffic, the seepage of radios beating out a medley of reggae and the lilt and drop of radio hosts arguing with callers.

They say prophets, true prophets, are able to prophesy their own deaths. They say that God speaks to them and assures them that their time is coming. Sometimes they argue, but always, always, true prophets know.

Joseph had seen the way those two men had died, and

while he did not know of the cancer multiplying itself from his toe to his bones, to his blood, to his brain, even as he lay there staring at the sky, he knew the weightlessness of being weary of the world—the hollowness of having spoken all that was burning inside his belly. He felt dry, spent. When prophets grow silent it means they have served their purpose.

He could not see the future—that he would be leaving Jamaica again in three months to go on tour, flying late at night to New York to fill Central Park with skanking white folks, to then collapse, pale and trembling, his skin pallid like dead flesh. He could not speak of the journeys from doctors to doctors to herbalists to visionaries, or of the long, bone-aching flight to that small village in Germany. He could not know that women would soon be his keepers.

He had slept out in the open for several nights and he was beginning to lose track of the days. The sun came up and went down.

He moved among the trees as if in a dream.

3.

In the middle of the night he wakes up expecting to see a wide-open sky with the dusty scattering of stars framed by the dark shadow of mountains. But all he sees is a blank grayness of walls around him. No. He was in a room, but this room is so small, with walls so close to him he cannot breathe. He wonders how he has gotten here, gotten to this place with walls covered with newspapers, a room that does not smell like the disinfectant-neat room of sunlight and white sheets where he had fallen asleep. Instead the place smells of an unwashed body, the funk of rotten flesh and the heavy musk of human waste, and the peculiar tart scent of rotten oranges. He opens his eyes and begins to feel meaning crawling toward him—the hint of a narrative that he knows to be an explanation for what he is seeing and smelling.

The logic creeps nearer, the way a dream fades away and waking insinuates itself on the mind. The meaning of the smells comes in small spurts of revelation—first the pressing need to get up, to take a shower, to call his aunt and ask her for money, to ask where his woman has gone and if she will come back. And the memory of his woman—whose name he sometimes forgets because it is too painful to call it—hits him hard. It fills him with such a terrible sense of panic that he turns away from the thought and tries to bury himself in another flight, another memory. He can tell in those brief moments that he is running. He can tell, too, that he is dying an inglorious death. He knows that if he were to simply get up, walk over to the cracked wood cabinet, open the dark brown plastic bottle, and pour out three pills, if he were to take those pills and sit on the edge of the bed waiting for them to slow everything down, waiting for them to bring him back to the gloom of his reality, he would probably understand everything happening in him and around him.

But he does not want to move.

He wants to die.

But he wants to die in a narrative of his own making. He understands that the narrative given to him is empty. In that narrative he would die for a woman. He would die because he cannot convince her to overlook his madness, overlook his cruelty, overlook his inertia, overlook his history, and simply love him. He is dying the kind of death that will warrant a brief note in the newspapers—nothing dramatic. *Forty-year-old man found dead in Ensom City home.* He does not want that kind of death.

Stretched out on the bed, allowing the delirium of his hunger to carry his mind far from this place, letting the sound of reggae blanket him—*Exodus* playing again and again—he will find better meaning for himself, for his path. He will travel into his own myth. Willing himself to dream his own narrative is becoming painful but necessary. Yet he can also tell that what he is dreaming is not entirely myth. He is remembering, too. Remembering the twisted way in which his life is changing into a legend. He expects to wake up at the end of this, at the end of staying in this room full of voices, memories, colors, textures, tastes, smells, with enough in him to make his passing a wonderfully meaningful thing. He closes his eyes.

He was born in 1962. The year the nation was born. When he was born, ska was jumping around the city. In that year, someone said that he was a child of the future. An old man touched his forehead and said, "As your fortune go, so go the nation." He would be told this so many times that he was sure he had heard the words of the old man himself—and he would live his life wondering whether he was guiding the fate of the nation or whether he was simply reflecting a nation bent on its own self-destruction.

His journey passed through the fearful, hopeful millenarian years of the 1970s, the years when everyone knew that some dread apocalypse was to come. Then he entered the chaos and sexual wildness of those 1980s, when he discovered that women loved him, when he walked from woman to woman, searching for meaning deep in their flesh. In the 1990s, he was trying to beat back the gruff voice of Capleton, chanting another apocalypse, but this time with blood in his eyes. With it came the frenzy of cars crashing, bodies mutilated, flesh exposed—the coked-up madness of a city coming of age, hungry to remind itself of its own strength. This was a country in trauma as it struggled to show that it still had possibilities, a country caught up in a midlife crisis, looking back at the hopeful years, the years of promise and prophecy and asking, *What is left, what is left, what do I have to show for it all? Am I still sharp looking? Do women dem still go for me?*

Every narrative that enters his mind is a narrative in search of meaning. He is not sleeping when he concludes that were he to travel into the soul of Bob Marley, he would find his true self.

They were both born on February 6. But one day, in 1981, when Bob Marley expired, one sunny day in May when he breathed out his last, something left that emaciated body and travelled across the Caribbean Sea and found its way into him in Kingston. It was the morning he stepped out of the Psychiatric Ward of the University Hospital into a brilliant day. His body, after the discarding of its fat, was a taut muscular thing, his eyes finally clear and his mind ticking with the promise of better days ahead. He had a paper bag filled with pills and, though no one was waiting for him, he was unperturbed. He was going to go up to Papine, catch a bus down to Half Way Tree, and then another that would take him to Ensom City, where he would clean his small house and begin to live again. In that moment, still standing out on the concrete walkway, having shaken the hand of the doctor on duty who kept asking, "Yuh sure you alright? Yuh don' wan' me call anyone?"; after smiling wryly at his favorite nurse, the one who kept saying to him, as if to convince herself that she was not mad to have had an affair with an inmate, "You are different. You so intelligent. We gwine to hear about you. Don't forget me, yuh hear?"; after waving to her and smiling at the gap in her teeth, and the bigness of her muscular body that contrasted with the delicate fragility of her pale skin: After doing all this, he stood alone, breathed deeply, and was about to walk, when it came upon him.

It came not like wind or tongues of fire, but like a blanket. A heavy blanket that gathered around him and kept wrapping about his face, making it hard for him to breathe. He was gasping and wrestling, trying to fight it off. But the more he fought, the more the cloud spoke, the more the cloud carried into him the words of all the Bob Marley songs he knew. More than that, it carried the words of a man asking, *Oh Jah, oh Jah, why has thou abandoned I and I to the four winds—I's Ethiopia, I wan' res'. Why yuh bring me back to Babylon?*

He knew that it was the spirit of Bob Marley consuming him. So he breathed. As he breathed deeply, he began to feel the cloud coming into him. When it did so, he began to cry, to weep uncontrollably. He felt his body fall to the ground. Then he felt the strong hand of his nurse around him.

"I tell you, him not ready yet . . . The man not ready yet . . . Jesus . . ."

"Is the heat, man. Jus' the heat. Him discharge already. Steady him there . . ."

"Take him inside. Help me . . ."

"No, him alright. The doctor sign him out."

"Why unoo so wicked. The man need to come back inside . . ."

"See. See, him look better already. Hey, bossy, bossy, yuh alright?"

By then he was standing on his own again—and he felt stronger. He felt parts of himself taking on new shapes. He did not have to ask any questions about what had happened. In his head two different languages spoke, two different memories. They were wrestling with each other, trying to find meaning. Then, quite suddenly, sadness filled his chest again. He turned to the light-skinned nurse with her long eyelashes and her freckled face, her dark brown eyebrows wrinkled with worry, and he spoke as if to comfort her.

"Bob dead," he said.

"Who?" she asked, as she touched his wet face.

"Bob, Bob Marley dead . . ."

"Yes," she said. "It just come on de radio . . ."

He had calmed down. He was not crying. He felt his face tightening into a scowl, that familiar brooding scowl. When he spoke again, it felt like his voice was coming from somewhere else.

"Bob cyaan dead, dawta. Nuh fret." He touched her hand. She seemed to know he was fine. He walked away from the clinic, and as he passed a rusty garbage drum, he tossed the bag of pills into it.

That was twenty years ago. Twenty years of dreams, of memories, of trying to chart a path that a living Bob would take. Twenty years of realizing that he is going to die without any glory or fanfare. Twenty years later, he realizes that a woman has brought him down—not some cancer, not some diabolic sickness, but a woman. It has taken twenty years for him to find out that he cannot be Bob Marley with this woman, cannot call her one of many queens, cannot adopt the tough inviolable pose, twenty years to know that he wants her to mother him. And in this interim, he is trying to dream himself to a meaningful death.

The fact is, his world is crumbling around him. Everything is falling apart. Everything is uncertain.

4.

He felt the pressure in his head grow. The plane rose steeply. His head pressed hard against the back of the seat; the lumps of his locks hurt his scalp now. He could feel the slow decay of the sores in his scalp despite the ointment that smelled of mint and aloe. His eyes were closed. Nausea filled his mouth with a bitter taste. He counted in his head, then began to mouth Psalm 91, his fingers tapping the rhythm on the seat handle. The climb continued, and he felt the weight of pressure on his body. For the first time he began to think of the pleasures of death.

He leaned his head toward Rhea, who stared in front of her until she felt his eyes on her. She looked at him, her face still smooth with the dark St. Thomas soil, the brown loam of ancient volcanoes that fed the banana trees rioting through that parish. The African wrap on her head was sky-blue. She would wrap yards of cloth around her head to give the suggestion of locks. Few people knew that Rhea did not have locks. Her hair was thick and he was always laughing at her, telling her that she would not have to do anything to have locks—serious locks. She had thick Maroon hair, black, so dense with fertility that it shone.

Each night, when they lived in the one-room shack on the hills of St. Ann, she would sit there and rub sweet-smelling blue hair oil into her scalp, and then she would yank at the hair until her comb could run through it without hindrance. She didn't cut it, but it never seemed to grow long, it just got denser and denser, the curls tightening with each inch added. He teased her a lot. She was still the church girl he had met on a dusty street in Jones Town, walking to the missionary congregation with her Bible in hand, her white dress stretched tightly around her hips. Her knees knocked slightly and he could not take his eyes off the way the strange stutter of her stride made her bottom roll. She had remained serious about her God. She spoke of Jesus as a friend. No, not a friend, but like a spirit child, someone she had birthed from her own womb. There was something so deeply intimate about their friendship. He had no reason to doubt her Jesus' existence and he accepted him in the same way that he accepted that she had brothers and sisters—they were part of who she was and he understood that. She spoke of all of them in the same way—Jesus, too—as people in her life.

Now her eyes stretched Chinese-like in her face, the black depth of her irises stark against the surrounding white-ness. She was worried about him, but tried to smile. He saw too a sense of triumph in her look, and he found comfort in it. She had won. He was comfortable with that. At last, he did not have to think, he did not have to consider, to read into the motives of the people around them. He simply relaxed and let her take over. It was as simple as that. It was part of his acceptance of something larger—he knew he was going die. This was now quite clear. Jamaica was far away. He had told her that Jamaica was where he wanted to go. But she said she had other plans—they would go to Jamaica after he felt better. First they would go to Miami. There was a specialist there who would help him. Then he would go to Jamaica to recover. He would be incognito. They would stay in St. Ann, far from the madness of Kingston. It would be like those years they had spent as farmers eking a modest living from the fertile soil of those mountains.

They would then spend a year getting his strength back. He would work in the small studio that she was going to set up in the house, and they would have easy access to Miami for medical checkups. The next tour would be to the Far East. First there would be a triumphant week performing in Jamaica—a stadium concert—then another Babylon by Bus through major U.S. cities, including a major show in New York's Irving Plaza where he collapsed and the nightmare began; then the Far East, then Ethiopia, where they would settle.

That is what he wanted, she said. He nodded, but felt deep fatigue hearing it all again—the concerts, the touring, the hangers-on, the band, trying to hold it together, trying to keep the discipline, trying to deal with the weakness he felt.

But he knew what was really coming, so he relaxed, stopped fighting. She would be in charge. He would let her do what had to be done. There she was, sitting beside him as she always did eventually. Even after her face wailed with the imprint of his flat palm, she still ran her fingers through his locks, massaged his scalp until he fell asleep with her. When he had fought with one of his other women, she was always there, her room smelling of sweet hair oil, always there to comfort him. It was her duty. She accepted it. He used to feel guilty about putting her through it, but her stoic acceptance left him incapable of even that. This was what they were. Now she was rescuing him again.

Germany had been a painful time. He had never walked so much. For the first time ever, he liked the cold, the way it seemed to clear the dizziness and clamminess from the fevers. They warned him about going out, but he would walk into the streets, limp his way through the crowds, breathe in the cold air, feel his body coming back to him, feel the sickness of an ague crawling through his system, while enjoying the pleasure of sudden freedom. He walked along the streets staring at faces. He kept his head covered, not in a tam, but with the hood of a jacket; he wore dark glasses and he walked with his head down. He could feel the heat leaving his body through his bare scalp. He started to stuff the hood with rags to keep the heat in. Sometimes he felt as if his life was seeping out the top of his skull. He felt his songs were leaving his brain and floating uselessly in the German air.

Nobody recognized him. Not in that small town. He was just another black man, another alien coming to take people's jobs. The way he walked, the way his body seemed not to understand itself, assured them that he was just another confused, mixed-race drug addict.

He took in the town like a travel book—the quaint cobblestones, the fairy-tale facades, the snow-topped mountains, the tidily cropped trees, everything in order, in careful symmetry. The German talk he heard bounced off him like all the other sounds—alien, strange, and surreal. He knew that he was on the surface of things here, but what was below he did not want to think about. He had enough to contend with.

He walked through the town for days. In the room, he was always thinking that the next dose of medication, the next concoction he had to force down his throat, would break the hold this disease had on him—and if not that, then the compresses, the incense, the diet, the crystals, the shark cartilage, the chanting of dreads in the room—or even the constant piping of "Three Little Birds," his most positive song, the doctor said, according to karmic scrutiny. He let it all happen because he wanted to live. He could not die. Joseph cyaan dead inna Babylon. He believed this with such force, such total conviction, that it made everyone around him believe, too.

The moments of clarity came in the streets. There he thought about dying, thought about the end of it all. Thirty-five years old, and he was watching time slipping by. How could it be? No. T'ings not going to be alright. His skin still bloomed with sores, his blood staggered through his veins; he could feel the poison running through him. The thing was destroying him, making him weak, making him talk foolish all the time. But he also knew that he was a dread and that in his heart he could conquer all things.

This was before Rhea came. The chaos was a buffer of faith. The order she brought killed hope.

Rhea came from Jamaica and saw what chaos he was living in. She looked at him lying in bed with a haze of incense around him. She looked at him and began to cry. He had not even glanced in the mirror in weeks and suddenly saw in her face what he must look like. He saw in her eyes what a pathetic sight he must seem. He knew at once how she would appear at his funeral, knew what her eyes would say. Her shock and pain lasted no more than a few seconds, but it was enough. She smiled at him, and then exploded in anger at everyone else. She opened the windows, grabbed the waste-paper basket, and threw candles, incense, pills, needles, crystals, concoctions, and various warming cauldrons into it.

She would have picked him up and carried him down to the waiting car by herself, but she had help. She had brought with her three other women, friends of hers he instantly recognized. These three women came in distinct shades. There was Bessie, a deep and mellow woman, her black skin regal in its unequivocal purity. She always wore red and seemed always to be smiling, even when you could see flame in her eyes. Blossom was sepia-colored, her hair limp, seemingly wanting for life. She carried herself with the aloof diffidence of light-skinned people in a dark-skinned world. Her kerchief was blue—the color of the sea. The third, Barbara, appeared chameleon-like, matching always the mercurial patterns of her personality to the seeming changes in the shade of her skin. Everybody liked her, but no one could figure her out. They assumed it had to do with a beauty that was constructed from the contradictory qualities of symmetry and ambivalence. She was the spokesperson in times of conflict. She was able to calm things. Her color was pale green. These women were consistent about their colors—combs, scarves, broaches, bracelets, and necklaces—always something in their color.

They all lived in England, big-bosomed Jamaican women who thought very little of what he did, what she did, but they were old friends, her sisters, and they would be her sisters for life. They worked as nurses in London and were the only people she could depend on. They had the stern pragmatism of nurses, women who understood what it was like to help people who hated them, to clean up the shit and piss of people who could not stand them because of their skin color. These women were the ones who came to help her move him out. They looked disgusted as they walked through the rooms. They shook their heads and moaned deep inside their chests as if they had just witnessed the most tragic of moments.

He wanted to tell them to get the hell out of the place, wanted to call them whores of Babylon, heathens. He wanted to tell them not to look down on him and his locks and his Rasta truth. He wanted to cuss them, turn them out, bring down fire and brimstone on them. He knew their type. He knew the way they looked at him. He could feel their condemnation, their righteous sense of triumph. Not just because it was clear that his Jah was not doing much for him now, but because Rhea was the one rescuing him. She was the one they had comforted during all those years when he was showing little regard for her; she was the one who had suffered and complained to them about him; she was the one whom they had told to leave his wutliss self and move on to something better. She had left the church and turned to this Rasta foolishness because of him, over this reggae music. Now Rhea was going to rescue him.

They carried themselves with the stoic pride of women who could take anything, take everything, and then be there to punish their wayward men by loving them, by feeding them in their time of weakness. For some, it was their final and only revenge, their one moment of power. Rhea was enacting this power and they were there to help her. It had nothing to do with love. They knew that Rhea loved this man. They too loved their men. They loved the men who had done them wrong, who had left them saddled with children, who had left them for other women. That was never an issue. Their power was not in their capacity to love but in their capacity to be needed, in their capacity to forgive these men with the weight of their ancient memories, their ability to hold each detail, each betrayal, each abuse, each act of brutality, to hold it as an investment, a kind of loan to be paid back in full. This was the rite they arrived in Germany to enact with Rhea. They paid their own fares. They did not ask her to pay even though she could. They did not argue with her. They did not like the man, but they knew what had to be done.

They cleaned him and carried him down the stairs shrouded in blankets. They laid him in the car, patting him softly like a puppy, as the one in red drove them for five hours through country roads and small villages, until they reached Munich. They carried him into another hotel, with a larger suite of several rooms, a kitchenette, and a view over a lake.

They sterilized the room with steaming white towels and buckets of warm disinfectant. They dressed his sores and gave him painkillers, while Rhea made plans on the phone for all of them to travel to Miami in a few days time. They sang hymns, said nothing.

The hymns carried him back. They took him back to Jamaica, and he was too weak to fight the way they carried him to familiar places of comfort and possibility. They sang with the thick, round harmonies that could consume a room with their force, their weight. They kept guard on the door, and when the doctor came the next day to see him, they blocked him from entering. They told the doctor that Joseph was already out of the country.

The doctor left, but he was followed by Joseph's disgruntled entourage who had been camped out in his room, in the hallway, scattered around the hotel—fucking women, smoking weed, lingering as if someone had already declared a wake. They came to the new hotel, some brandishing vulturous knives. The women stood firm. "Stab me den, nuh. Stab me," the green woman said calmly. The men walked away. The women let Russell, Joseph's cook, come in. Joseph would not eat from anyone else. Not even Rhea. Russell was the only one who expressed relief at Rhea's arrival. He had felt helpless obeying the doctor's twisted instructions about food for the dread. "If 'im gwine dead, den 'im might as well enjoy a good livity while 'im 'ave life." Rhea agreed without agreeing. She told him to cook the food that Joseph liked. He served up mounds of mashed yams islanded in thick callaloo and okra stew, spiced with various herbs and coconut oil. Joseph ate gratefully. He trusted Russell.

Rhea told Joseph the plan. He listened. He could feel his body slipping from him. His scalp was hurting him more than ever. He knew that the sores were now all over his head. He imagined that their seepage inwards was touching his brain.

He picked up his guitar one morning and began to sing. Soon he forgot the words. He started to cry. He sat there, staring at the brown high-rise buildings and the misty skyline, and his mind was blank. He could not remember the words.

Russell sat in a chair behind him. He realized what had happened to Joseph and quickly began to recite Psalm 139. As the words came out of Russell's mouth, Joseph began to sing with him. His fingers worked their way around the fret board and he found melodies to carry the psalm. The two continued like this, a song breaking out in the room, the sweet taste of holiness. Russell's face had the wooden toughness of a sun-hardened sea jetty. His locks were virtually red and clumped in disarray around his head, just like the heads of his fellow bredren who fished the waters of Bull Bay on the rugged south coast of the island. His face was a lumped mass of muscle and overgrown pimples. Few recognizable expressions passed through that face. But sitting there, looking at the back of Joseph's head, his face softened into strange liquid textures. He was crying as he spoke.

The song carried through the room, around and around in circles. The women did not look at each other. Their eyes were filled.

Lord, you have searched I and known I,
You know my sitting down and my rising up;

You understand my thoughts from a far off.
You comprehend my path and my lying down,
And are acquainted with all my ways.
For there is not a word on my tongue
But behold, O LORD, You know it altogether.
You have hedged I behind and before
And laid your hand upon I.
Such knowledge is too wonderful for I;
It is high, I cannot attain it,
It is high, I cannot attain it,
It is high, I cannot attain it.
Where can I and I go from your spirit
Or where can I and I flee from your presence?
If I and I ascend to heaven you are there;
If I and I make my bed in hell, behold, you are there.
If I and I take the wings of the morning
And dwell in the uttermost parts of the sea,
Even there your hand shall lead I,
And your right hand shall hold I.

Line after line Russell spoke, and line after line Joseph transformed into a melody. His fingers feathered the frets as his right hand brushed the strings to create a wash of harmonics. He was just barely managing to bar the chords to create clean notes. He chanted, coaxing his clumsy fingers to speak in the familiar sharp slash of the reggae chop—bright, fresh, yet always behind everything. Russell's voice was a steady bass line making spaces and filling them, making spaces and filling them. Outside the gray of the town seemed insignificant.

"We leaving tomorrow," Rhea said quietly. "We going home."

Joseph nodded. He was ready.

5.

He wakes up and knows that it is night by the sound of the crickets; their sluggish noises echo in the small room. For a moment, he is sure that a cricket is in the room with him. He panics, his heart pounding at the imposition, and then his situation comes back to him like an old sick smell—he is not trying to live. A cricket, a scorpion, a lizard, a snake, what would any of those matter to him now? The tape seems to have stopped. He reaches for it, when a sudden click reminds him that it is simply turning over. Soon "Natural Mystic" grows like a web of whispers around him.

Joseph knows he has been dreaming about dying. He knows the end of the dream and yet he wants to finish the dream. He prefers to call it a dream even though he knows that he is not really sleeping. What he is doing is thinking. He is thinking so deeply that it feels like a dream. His thinking is like a prayer—a way of making some order out of his life. Or maybe it is not order he wants, perhaps he wants to recreate it.

There is a tendency to helplessness that has haunted him for years. It made him sit dumbly in the room while Melanie, his woman, virtually begged him to say, "Please stay," by prolonging her departure, by the way her body seemed to soften despite the harshness of her words, by the wetness in her eyes. He sat there helplessly saying nothing to her. So she left.

For him, to have acted then would have been utter hypocrisy. His life has been shaped by this incapacity to act.

He sees.

He sees the brutish way of this country of his. He knows personally many of the high-ranking politicians and business folk whose cynicism has led them to engage in the crude violence of the society. He knows that the stories of violent death, corruption, terror, and fear are rooted in something quite simple—people taking advantage of centuries of abuse. He says nothing about any of this. He does not complain, he does not accuse; he sees. He cannot imagine a way out of this morass. He has tried to write songs about it, thinking that perhaps were he to turn away from those friends, turn from the system that birthed him, turn to the myths of reggae, he would find a way to fight, to resist. But it does not happen. He is still himself, still consumed by the rituals of his privilege and unable to speak the language of radical action. It is a failure of the imagination, he knows.

How to reconcile the two worlds he thinks are his? Melanie helped him to feel, at least for a moment, that there was a true path for him—a man who could look at his country with new eyes, her eyes—and find a music to speak to that country. Now she has gone. She has gone because he was not there to protect her when she was attacked. She has gone because he could not step away from his anger at her goading him to act, to shake off the inertia of entitlement that he wore, her way of making friends with everyone she saw regardless of their class, their color, their age. She has gone because he told her that she was a true Jezebel—a bloodsucking woman who had tricked him into bringing her to

Jamaica. He told her this and never took it back. So she has gone because she was an alien in an alien world and it was hard for her to sleep at night not knowing what he would do. She left because she no longer believed his promise to be her guide, to lead her along the paths to the place where the berries are, the soft place of noises, sounds, and sweet airs that he had described so well to her as he seduced her outside a club in a forgettable southern American town.

She left because he would not take the medication. She did not know who she would meet hovering over her late at night, and he could not tell her anything to reassure her.

Somewhere at the back of his mind he is waiting to hear her slipping the key into the lock, and then to see her peering into the room with that smile on her face. "Hey, baby," the way she would say it that would make his skin prick, his groin tickle instinctively.

He is listening over the sound of the music. All he hears are the crickets.

6.

The God, tall, light-skinned, and strangely anemic in a baggy navy-blue sweat suit, strolled through the lobby toward them, his locks bobbing behind, his eyes flaming. He had the presence, the kind of confidence that forced people to pay attention to him. The muted sunlight from the wide windows looking out into the cluttered tarmac caught his chains, an array of crudely crafted chunky gold pendants that dangled around his neck.

Behind him hurried Bobo, a short, round man who insisted on wearing clothes that were decidedly too tight, who insisted, despite his copious stomach, on tucking his shirt into his tight black leather trousers. Bobo was out of breath. He wore a pair of dark glasses that wrapped around his face. He would have looked sinister if the rest of his body had not seemed so comical. He could barely keep up with the steady, assured stride of The God.

Joseph looked down when he saw them approaching. He had hoped that they would announce the flight before this confrontation.

Rhea and the three women stood up and moved toward The God and Bobo. Bobo was pointing. The God stared hard, not at Rhea or the women, but at Joseph. Joseph caught his eye and looked down quickly. He did not want to look up. He stared at the ground, then he looked into the sky. He was trying to disappear, to throw himself as far away from this moment as possible.

He was tired. The drive to the airport had worn him out completely and he was not looking forward to the flight. It was going to be painful. The sores on his back and his bottom were weeping that morning, and when one of the women had rubbed them gently with some anti-bacterial ointment, he could hear her muttering at the tragic ugliness of it all. "Why, why, why them let this happen, eh?" She was not expecting an answer. In fact, for the three days they had been in the same room, these women had not spoken to Joseph except to give him simple commands like "Lean back" or "Sip" or "Lift up." They were working for Rhea, no one else. They simply worked, gave comfort as no one else could.

But that morning, one of them, Barbara, could not help herself. She wondered why anyone would allow this man to go through this, this man with sense, with money, with a name around the world, why they would let him go through this kind of foolishness. She wondered aloud, as if Joseph was not there.

Now, at the airport, Barbara was standing slightly ahead of Rhea, looking at this tall, lanky dread striding toward them. Joseph knew then that it was possible that he would not be on the flight out of Germany. He knew that his broken body might be taken back to another room in the city, another smoke-filled place, for someone else to rescue him, but he did not care anymore. He wanted to have his guitar with him, his Bible, and the Miles Davis tape he had been playing over and over again for weeks. He would go wherever he was taken. It was already over.

The God could bring no magic with him, just the assured look of someone who was born to be in charge. The God would come and argue that they went back too far for him to let this woman come and take over his life. The God would say that he would be better off with friends, real friends, with the bredren. The God would say that he could not die. That Rasta could not die. Rhea would never say that. Rhea knew, like Joseph, that he could die. The God would say that Joseph was a bonafide dread, and a bonafide dread could never die, it was impossible. The God would tell him that all he needed to do was humble himself and look to Jah and he would get a chance to travel to Ethiopia. There he would find the nice plot of land that they had both picked out those many years ago, that spot where Joseph planned to retire, put up his foot and plant, plant, plant, and watch Jah give the increase. The God would remind him of the dream.

The God would tell him what to do and how to do it. The God would remind him that he has been with Joseph forever and that Joseph could not turn away from a true bredrin. The God would point out that Rhea was a *succubus*, a blood-sucking bitch who was looking for revenge on Joseph; that she was a woman, and woman is never to be trusted over a bredrin. The God would say all this and convince Joseph that he should stay.

Joseph would be too feeble to say anything. Joseph would look at Russell and Russell would look back with the dazed eyes of a man in a perpetually "red" state—the look of a dog assuring its master that it will go anywhere the master desires. Russell would have no answers. Russell would feed Joseph no matter what. He would feed Joseph until Joseph could feed no more. Joseph would get no answers from Russell. Joseph would look at The God and say, "God, yuh right." But Joseph would not be able to move. It would have to be between The God and Rhea and the women.

He watched the confrontation. The God carried himself with the same sly danger that he had brought to the football field. There was nothing physically overbearing about him. He was slight. Fit but slight. His self-assurance lay elsewhere. What he had was a quality of danger, a capacity to believe in his invincibility, in his ability to dramatically change the direction of a game. He always wanted the ball, and when he got the ball things happened. His gift was simple: He was a dreamer with the capacity to dream impossible things and, more importantly, to execute them through his body's remarkable flexibility. He had found a way to respond phys-ically to the unique rhythms that moved in his head. What onlookers saw was a man with the ability to caress a football, to toy with the intelligence of his opponents, to outthink them to the point of bafflement. This, combined with his total fearlessness, made him a dangerous man.

When he stood beside Pelé in the National Stadium, The God still felt that his title was deserved. Pelé was good, but Pelé was a man like any other. Pelé was from Brazil and he, The God, was from a tiny island with no history of football to talk of, but he was The God, and he could take on any man, any man. And he did. He took on Pelé as if Pelé was a local player, and Pelé smiled at the sheer audacity of the seventeen-year-old. From the earliest days it was his way.

Now here, standing in front of Rhea, he had come to get Joseph. On the surface of things, this was a done thing.

"Bobo, tek Joseph bag and come. Russell, help me wid Joseph." He brushed past Rhea and pushed his face into Joseph's face and stared intently into his eyes.

"God," Joseph said, smiling crookedly and weakly.

"Come, bredrin." He reached round to gather Joseph up. Rhea dragged him away and he let himself be pulled from Joseph. He was not going to fight. He had come for the dread and that was the bottom line. The ritual was fine. He would play it.

Joseph closed his eyes and tried to listen to the argument. He could not follow anything. His mind was slipping away again. He was drifting beyond this airport, to Ethiopia, the brown and burnt-sienna of the landscape and the rich dark green of the vegetation, to the small plot of land in St. Ann where he found himself hoeing, getting it ready to plant tomatoes and carrots—Rhea was singing hymns in the shack—to a blazing afternoon in New York, the park over-flowing with people dressed in red, gold, and green, prancing to the sound.

He stood there feeling the strange weight of his Gibson. His feet felt like clay, locked to the ground, while his head spun as if the weed had twisted itself on him. Everything was floating and his body felt lighter. The trees turned upside down as his voice tried to reach for a sound, a faraway sound. He wanted to shout something to that Yankee guitarist and his frantic stage antics, kneeling, lifting the head of his guitar in the air, prancing about the stage with a most un-reggae rhythm. Joseph felt both irritation and a deep fear that something was out of his control. Then he felt his body giving way. He was on the ground. The bass was rumbling. He was unconscious, but he could still hear the music in his head, could still see the light blue of the sky, could still feel the way his body was lifted and the music sounding like a reverb, going on and on.

7.

The man wakes and it is still dark. He knows that something has woken him, but he is not sure what. The pain in his stomach comes on him gradually but relentlessly. It is as if he is forcing his way up from deep water, his breath held and all his thoughts focused on the strain in his lungs. He feels the strain to come up for breath—the rush of bubbles, the cool of the water, and the blinding glow of the approaching light. Then he bursts through the surface, his lungs opening to take in air, his body opening to be fed by the food it desperately needs.

In the aftermath, in the calm after knowing he has survived, after finding breath again, his body begins to remind him of the brute beating it has undergone. Then comes the pain, the pain in his head, the pain in his limbs, the pain deep inside his stomach. It is the pain that has awoken him.

He lies there breathing hard, trying to work out the source of the pain and its meaning. His head is still stuck in the dream of Melanie standing there arguing with The God. The name won't leave him. The God. He knows these people. He expects to look up and see them standing in front of him, arguing in the shadows of the room.

As he lies there, the pain creeping across his ribs, filling his head with an intense pulsing, he begins to think hard about flying away from everything, about going somewhere else. He is willing his mind to focus on the story he wants to take shape in his head. Two people arguing over him, over his body, over his future. Two people. One of them he knows well. It is Melanie. Yet in this incarnation she loves him, she is there for him. He wants to believe in this incarnation.

8.

Joseph could see a pattern. There he was, thirty-five, and he could see a pattern. He was young, but he had been around long enough to know a pattern. He had been married for almost twenty years—they had married at seventeen. Now, nearly twenty years later, he was dying. He understood a pattern when he saw one. The pattern was always the same. Rhea was there when things were going wrong. Rhea was the constant in his life. He did not like Rhea. He needed Rhea. He did not love Rhea. Love had fallen away too long ago.

But Rhea was constant. The more things began to explode around him, the more Rhea was the constant that he depended upon. There was going to be no death without Rhea. There was going to be no crisis without Rhea. She was like his *chi*, a force inside him, sometimes dammed or diverted, but immovably there until he died. He would travel all over, screw all around, fall in love, let his body fall into the softness of other women, but they all understood that Rhea was the one he would go to when he was hungry, when he began to suspect that one of his women was trapping him with *obeah*. Joseph trusted Rhea because he knew that she would never harm him—she needed him. And so he needed her. He spent his life waiting for the inevitable pattern to repeat itself. Rhea was there to make sure that it happened.

Now they were airborne, the plane heading toward Miami. He thought about how quickly The God had given up. There was that look The God gave him, a look of deep regret. He put up a good front. He argued, he cursed Rhea, he even threatened to have her beaten up. But Joseph could tell that he was going through the motions. He was tired of Joseph now. He, too, had given up. It was clear that Joseph was sick. It was clear that the doctor's shark cartilage remedy was not going to work. Money wasted, time wasted, deprivations wasted, hope wasted. Joseph was dying. The God had looked defeated. He stared at Joseph, had assured him, "I gwine come a Miami fe you, Joseph. Don' fret. This bitch naah go control tings," but Joseph knew that he was saying goodbye when he leaned toward him and touched his head. Joseph stared back. He wanted to say something, but he felt a terrible weight on his mind, on his brain. He had nothing to say. He resorted to a stock phrase, a phrase of deep hope-lessness. It made The God's face crumble. Joseph could tell that The God could not cope with him in this state. All through their time in Germany, Joseph had managed to maintain his brash, stoic front. The front of an orphan child.

The God had first met this front when they ran into each other on a bottle-strewn street in Trench Town where The God had organized a football match. Joseph watched on the side while The God toyed with the men who sweated around him. He never scored. He always passed the ball with careful precision. But passing was not his most cherished activity. The God was always intent on demonstrating that he was never alone on the field, for when you approached him, there were three spirits with him. They were the ones carry-ing the ball—he simply stood around while they bounced the ball around from one to the other. They were impish *duppies*, giggling at each expression of bewilderment that appeared on the faces of the men who came at The God. Joseph could see them, the three spirits. They twisted and turned and leapt up and down. Their task was never to let The God touch the ball himself. The God accepted their role and he merely followed them around. Joseph started to laugh out loud at the spectacle. He could see these things. He had always been able to see into things. He was born, his mother had told him, with an opaque *caul* over his face. The midwife declared him a dreamer and a visionary. But he understood himself to be something else, a strange boy who was never bothered by the apparitions that clotted the air in rural St. Ann where he was born and where he grew up.

The God was wearing a yellow and blue shirt with the

Brazilian globe emblazoned in the middle. He wore track-suit bottoms and a pair of sandals. His arms moved as if he was trying to fly—fluid, stretched out, his body pivoting this way and that, his eyes always looking somewhere other than at the ball. Most of the time he was staring into the faces of his opponents with an annoyingly defiant expression in his eyes. They would try and look away, but they would be caught. Their eyes tried to read his eyes, tried to anticipate his next move, but they were always wrong; the spirits were always going somewhere else.

Joseph pulled the bottom of his T-shirt over his head so that it wrapped around the back of his neck, leaving his chest bare. A fat shirtless player was sitting despondently to the side, trying to get his breath back, his body dripping sweat. Joseph nodded at the fat man and then trotted onto the pavement to take his place.

The God, who did not have the ball at that point, nodded at Joseph. Joseph nodded back and scowled. The God grinned. He liked this small man, with a body like a tightly wound machine. Joseph's head was too big for his body, even without the locks. He made this even more apparent by the way he held his head up, his neck stiff, a proud strut in everything that he did. He trotted with the big-chested assurance of a star baller.

But Joseph was not a star baller, he just liked to kick ball on the streets and, as with everything else, he had learned to do it with a street savvy and aggression that usually took him far. Someone pushed the ball toward The God. Joseph ped-alled backwards to face him. He made the mistake of look-ing at The God's eyes. The God was smiling. Then Joseph quickly looked away—but too late. In a blur he saw one of the spirits tapping the ball over his head. As Joseph turned, another spirit had gently received the ball and was trotting beside The God toward the two stones laid a couple of feet apart in the middle of the road. The few people looking on were laughing and chanting, "Pile, pile."

Joseph was angry. The God was grinning. He was moving swiftly toward the goal, and Joseph was at his back, sprinting and determined to make a major statement with this tackle. He raised his left leg and threw it in front of The God, going after the ball, maybe, but definitely going after The God's shin. The God was airborne, arms now flapping like wings. He landed evenly, though, the ball still in front of him. He placed a foot on the ball, stopping the play. Then he turned to face Joseph, who was now stretched clumsily on the ground. Then, without saying anything else, The God turned and tapped the ball between the two stones. Joseph was up already. He was furious with himself. The spirits were giggling and running rings around him. The God came toward Joseph and rested an arm on his shoulder.

"Sorry, yout'. Sorry," he said. His mockery was palpable. Then he trotted back toward his end of the street, the spirits now leapfrogging and somersaulting all around him.

Joseph hurried toward a tall, leathery-skinned, gray-haired dread who was looking to make a pass out of defense. With a small gesture and a stare Joseph communicated that he wanted the ball. With it he started to trot toward The God, who was looking away. Joseph could see the spirits coming before he noticed that The God was casually walking toward him, as if to tell him something insignificant like "hello." Joseph did not repeat his mistake. He kept watching the spirits, dribbling around them, avoiding their playful attempts to get the ball—though they were not restricted by the rules of the game. These spirits used their hands, tugged on garments, and tripped people blatantly, making them look like total buffoons as they appeared to trip over themselves. But Joseph worked his way around them, and before he realized it, he was already past The God and standing face to face with a burly man called Blacka.

Blacka made quick work of Joseph, running into him with terrible ferocity, but not before Joseph tapped the ball toward the two stones behind him. The ball rolled in. Joseph crumbled on the ground, wincing with the sharp pain of asphalt scraping the skin off his knees. He was up and moving toward Blacka, who was walking slowly back to get the ball, his shoulders shaking with his chuckling. The confrontation was too quick to draw any attention until it was over. Joseph picked up a brick from the roadside and smashed it against the side of Blacka's head. Blacka went down slowly and stayed down. He was bleeding. Joseph tossed the brick aside and pulled his T-shirt back over his chest and walked down the street.

He walked quickly without looking back. He could hear footsteps behind him, but he did not turn. He calculated that if the person planned to shoot him or throw a rock at him he would have done it already. At the end of the street he turned and was able to look back without seeming to be doing so out of anxiety, though his heart was pounding. It was The God, walking toward Joseph with the three spirits sprinting around him like dervishes. Joseph slowed. The God caught up.

"Yuh eat *ital?*" he asked.

Joseph nodded. He did not eat *ital*, but he knew that eating *ital* was cool.

"Come, mek we eat some *ital* patty, seen?" The God said.

"Cool," Joseph replied.

"Blacka alright," The God assured. "'Im head well tough."

"Yeah." Joseph looked down at the spirits. They were staring up at him like children.

"Dem soon go home. Is football dem come fe play, nutting else," The God said casually.

"Oh," Joseph said. It all seemed to make sense to him. And as they walked, the spirits lingered behind until they had so faded that Joseph could no longer see them.

The two walked silently for a few minutes. Then The God spoke. "Dem call me The God." It was not a joke, but Joseph laughed. The God laughed too.

They never discussed the incident or Joseph's capacity to see the spirits running around The God. It was understood as something strange that they shared. It was enough to make their friendship happen fast. Its foundation, though, was manly trust, their shared code of manhood, the very basic notion that man-friendship was different from woman-friendship. Man-friendship was quick to forgive, even if volatile. Man-friendship was uncomplicated. Man-friendship understood that women would do anything to conspire against the order of manhood. Man-friendship assumed that women did not truly know themselves. And yet, at a deep, unvoiced level, man-friendship understood that woman-friendship would win in the end. Man-friendship was a charade, really, a vain railing against the inevitability of woman-power, because, at the end of the day, man could not resist the power of woman.

9.

It was late afternoon in Miami. There was a wheelchair waiting from him in the jet way. They bundled him in blankets. He felt too hot but he did not know what to say. He was fatigued by his own fatigue. He knew he was in pain, but now there was nothing but pain. He was no longer able to imagine painlessness. It was becoming harder to call this condition painful. His stomach, he imagined, was a perforated bag of sores. The pain was thorough: muscular, relentless. His head throbbed.

The sun dropped slowly, created shadows on the pink and tangerine walls of the houses tucked in beneath the freeway. The city looked painted, the palm trees opened out sensually in the waning light.

When he first came to Miami years ago, he expected to find America and found, instead, the Caribbean. This was nothing like the metal and glossy brick of New York, nothing like the decay and aged order of Detroit. When things rotted in Miami, they smelled like the earth, they stunk like the sea. They did not have the restrained smell of colder places. Everything was tangible here. The heat clung to the body, made sweat, the people were alive, open, naked; they had skins and they spoke.

There were stretches of this city that reminded him of

Kingston—avenues that led to overpasses with side guards that were crumbling, roadsides where stones, stretches of sand, and craggy grass infested the modernity of the place. Sometimes he would stand outside and breathe the warmth of the city and smell the stench of the ocean—not just salty, but funky, with the peculiar mugginess of humid sodium. It was like Jamaica.

Once he had watched crows circling overhead. They were scattered through the open sky with its untidy puffs of clouds moving casually and independently through the blue. He could tell that something had died not too far away. Now, in Miami again, he felt for the connection to home.

The Ford van that took them through the city was comfortable enough. Rhea sat in the front. Joseph was lying across the backseats with his legs propped up in Russell's lap. Russell stared out. He was thinking of his village in St. Elizabeth on the south coast of Jamaica. He wanted to return to the familiar musky smell of the sea, the dry red dirt, the scent of rotting oranges in his yard, the graves of so many generations of his family. He had the feeling that taking Joseph to that familiar place, taking him out before the sun came up so he could sit on the edge of the sea and allow the salt to heal his body, would make him better, would change him. He imagined that the sight of the hills rising untidily behind the coast would revive Joseph, take him back to a place where things were simple as a birdcall or the taste of a mango. For all its heat, Miami still seemed like an alien place, and Russell wanted to take Joseph far away. But he knew that he would have to stay with his friend, try and feed him with food that could transport him. *A man musn' dead which part the ancestors' spirit not living—a man must return to him navel string,* Russell thought as the city rushed past— the wide streets, the cluttered houses, and the glint of cars speeding in sharp colors across the world.

The three women were in the seat in front of them. No one spoke. Joseph looked out of the side window into the sky. He could see the way the sunset was coloring the evening. He felt nauseous. He thought about dying again. He wanted to be back in Jamaica. Back in Kingston, back in the rugged mountain village in St. Ann.

They arrived at the massive house near the sea at dusk. The streets were empty. No one had announced that the great hero Joseph was passing through. He asked the women to let him walk into the house. It had never been so empty, so orderly, so lacking in life. During the five years he had owned it, he rarely stayed there. Rhea had stayed there for the past two years, after they moved their business due to the problems in Jamaica. He came there to rest in between tours. The house was always full then. It was as if a perpetual party was taking place. People were always stopping there to spend the night, to work in the studio, to just sit in his presence, to come and check out the pretty women who happened to adorn his poolside night and day. The best weed in Miami was available. It was a place of confusion, fights, gun-toting, and deep reasoning about the meaning of Babylon and the dream of returning to Ethiopia. Where the Jamaican house remained rustic, close to the roots, and smelled always of poor people's dinners, this house revealed the pimper's paradise of Rasta success. And Joseph would come there, lament the decay of all that was righteous in the world, but be too weary to do a thing about it.

Now it was empty. The halls were silent. He walked through the wide living area, the orange glow of sunset spilling light on the hardwood floors. Everything was immaculately arranged. He felt as if he was walking into his own mausoleum. He made his way to the room he always used, a small white room in the back of the house that opened out into a bush backyard. From there he could see the sea brimming with color. He imagined Jamaica not too far from there. Sometimes he imagined he could see Jamaica. He opened the French doors and lay on the white sheets, breathing heavily, his body weak with the exertion of this walk.

The voices of the women moving around him, preparing the room, encouraging him to put both feet on the bed, commenting on the hair he was losing, making plans for meals, all came in a wash of muted sounds. He was drifting again. Travelling.

10.

Joseph had seen death. He had seen people killed. He was always startled by the simplicity of death. Not that it was easy to kill people. Killing was painful and it took a great deal of effort. The body wanted to live. The body fought to live all the time. Like chickens beheaded. They ran sprinting around the yard, gurgling blood, spilling blood, their muscles flexing, their whole posture erect and almost dainty. People described it as a maddened run, but it was no madder than the average live and head-intact chicken's wide-eyed sprint. The circling movements, the lifting of the knees and every muscular action were the same, despite the brain being taken away.

The body did not like to die. The body fought death. He had seen it. In films people took bullets and collapsed, as if accepting death calmly and according to a script. In life he had seen people take bullets and curse about the most insignificant things. Death did not bring profound wisdom. He had watched a friend moan and groan about the pain of a bullet lodged in his head, about the headache he was feeling. He watched his friend grow very angry, saw him get up, about to hit out at somebody who was trying to help him by staunching the blood with a towel. He was not out of his mind. This was how he normally behaved. He was angry and he wanted to do something about it. Just as suddenly, he lost consciousness, fell silent, and never woke up. No last statements, no thoughts about a loved one, nothing like that. All Joseph could remember was his friend's annoyance at the guy who was trying to help him.

The death of others was the most normal thing in the world. It was the afterdeath that was extraordinary. He found the missing of people exceptionally difficult. Missing the person, looking out for the person, hoping to see the person in the street, then realizing that the person would not be around again. Gone forever. Thinking that after five years the person would not suddenly return. That after thirty years the person would be thirty years gone. Thirty years out of circulation. Thirty years out of memory. Thirty years faded into something tiny, something insignificant—a moment, a look, a gesture. That would be thirty years of absence. He found this extraordinary.

So he stopped going to funerals. He stopped lingering around the places of the dead. He never carried a coffin, never drove behind a hearse, never went into a church to give last rites to the dead.

11.

A sick man is in a studio playing his guitar. This narrative is more than a fiction, it is a dream that Joseph has had for years. It is a dream that has consumed him ever since he felt he could fly. When he felt the pressure of his sickness coming on him, he found comfort in the willingness of his mind to dream. And with each dream he would add to the story. The plot was familiar to him. It was a legend. The legend came to be his own narrative. It was a narrative that usurped his history every time.

He would allow his mind to travel on airplanes, to drive through quaint German villages, to mingle with the ganja smoke and roots talk of great Rasta singers and players of instruments. He would sit on his porch and look out into the open sky and find himself thinking about what dying would mean. In this way death slipped into his body.

The story was the same every time. He would make that great song, that stunning song, and the whole gathering would weep when he played it, and as they did, his hair would start to fall out in clumps. His locks would fall to the ground. And all the characters that had crowded his head would come crawling out to see the tragedy of his passing. They would hold his body, lift him, carry him to a bed, and he would rest his head on the lap of Rhea and say to her, "I am going," and she would sing "Fly Away Home." And in that moment his arms would fall away, and the three women would come and hover over him and pray for him and plant more dreams of home in his head, and slowly, ever so slowly, he would fade away. It was heroic, in full color, and gloriously holy.

12.

He has lived in this state long enough to know that he has been away too long. For years, the thoughts of home have been a physical thing to him. They have a smell, a taste, the feel of a landscape, the scent of a moment. In the mornings he would feel that strange nausea of excitement and unease that he used to feel before facing the day. But now it was a comforting feeling—the feeling of home with all its strange anxieties.

His mother had been absent. He had not understood this then, for he had never stopped regarding her as a victim of his father's strange silences, his father's capacity to withdraw into the inscrutable density of his books or his cigarettes, sucked on with a sweet passion that was hard to describe. His mother would walk through the house singing of how much she had lost. And she had lost much. His mother had one day come into the living room with the stoic, dull quality of a woman unfamiliar with the ritual histrionics of self-pity, she had come into the living room and said with such sincerity, such pained honesty: "You don't even touch me. It has been months since you have touched me."

This is the same face he saw when Melanie came to ask him, "Why don't you talk to me, tell me what is going on?"

The same pitiful look. "You don't even touch me. Why has it been months since you have touched me?"

He had found this American woman, loved her and lost her. She connected always in his mind with home. He missed home. He missed the rituals of being a hero. He did not think he could give it up so easily. Yet he was sure that after the withdrawal of his illness, after the falling away of his locks in clumps, after the anticlimax of his survival, and after his plans for exile to Ethiopia had ended with the defeat of that land, the death of utopia, even after coming to settle in this simple town, a place completely unsuited to his own sense of reality; he was sure that, after all this, he would find peace, find some quiet, and learn resignation to his new existence.

But it has not worked.

Here, lying in this room, the tape player repeating *Exodus* until the lyrics become one song, he is still alive and she is still gone. He is washing himself with music that will purge the memory of blues and country music that the woman brought into his house, the music she heard all her childhood. Lying there, he wonders how he will get to touch her again, how he will get her to come back, where he will find her—*if* he can find her—before everything falls apart. He feels as if he is going to have to make decisions.

He is tasting, again, the metaphor of home. Jamaica was what he needed, he knows that. He knows he had to come home to live, just as many travellers know they have to come home to die, even though he feared it, feared the violence, the madness on the streets. In the months since he has been back he has felt the fear fading. He can feel his body shaping itself around the comforts of the familiar.

He had wanted to find a woman in Jamaica, someone who would understand him after his years away, someone who he could be with, someone who would want to be with him, want to make love with him, to make certain that if it was anyone, he would be the one to say no. It would be the woman, a Jamaican woman, who would be saying to him, as his mother had said to his father, "You don't touch me—you have not touched me in months. I want you to touch me." Such a woman would feed him, would wait for him, would make him feel like a man—a woman who understood the way a man's body needs to be touched. A woman who spoke his language. A woman who understood that in his silences there is some dignity—some quest for dignity. That is what he missed.

He had planned to come back to Jamaica to find this, but instead he brought an American woman home with him, a woman who made each morning seem like an unknown space. She made his tongue feel heavy with its inability to make sense, to make her understand.

Now she has left him, walked away from him, and here he is, trying to think of whether he should go and find her, or whether he should stay in this room and let his dreams consume him.

The country is as old as he is. He has grown up with the country, and now he knows just how that island feels. He feels like the island. He had promise, but now he feels old. He feels used up. When he contemplates the forty years that he will have lived, when he contemplates what he will do at the stroke of midnight on the fortieth year of his life, he has a sense of what people in Jamaica must be feeling right now.

They are waiting to see if something, someone will come and rescue the country, but are wondering if death will come before that rescue. He looks at the forty years of his life with sadness, a strange weariness. It depresses him.

13.

Coming out of sleep, it takes awhile for Joseph to understand that his weakness may have had something to do with his hunger. The tape is still going. The world outside is defined by the radio. Voices chattering, images of faces looming over him. Then they disappear. He keeps returning to his dream that is no longer a dream but a narrative with sequence and meaning. He has to return to it because it gives him a sense of grounding. But the narrative is being interrupted by voices, by the sound of the telephone that has been ringing for a while now, after a long silence.

Joseph is hungry. He feels the hollow inside him. It no longer hurts. It is a dull pain. He is not dry. He has been drinking water from the tap, walking to the toilet, cupping his hand under the tap, and drinking until his stomach hurts with the pain. Then he goes back and lies down and waits.

He is dreaming of Melanie. Melanie is lying on a table, her legs apart, and a man in a mask, a man with tendril hands that look uncannily like the hands of The God, is leaning down between her open legs and doing something to her. Joseph can tell that the man is feeling deep inside her for something, and when he seems to have it in hand, he is grimacing with the effort of moving it, pulling at it. Melanie is in pain, howling, twisting. There is blood underneath her, spreading. The light in the room is blue.

Joseph opens his eyes. Perhaps she has had an abortion. He struggles to grasp the idea. He closes his eyes again.

Like the fragmented samplings of a surreal dub track, the voices of the world, the sounds of the radio enter Joseph's mind and slip out again, bubbling behind his dreams and over them. The distant sounds of an argument down the street between a man and a woman, the yell of the kisko and ice cream seller on his scooter, the tinkle of the postman's bell, the dogs' sharp bark, the twisted paths of his dreams, all gather in his head.

"This country gwine to hell, Mr. Brown. It gwine to hell . . ."

Movement of Jah people!

"Why yuh say that, sir?"

Rest on your conscience, oh yeah, oh yeah!

"We selling the land, selling the land to tourist, to white people."

And move your window curtain . . .

"It's a old habit, my friend, but what to do?

Good, good, good loving . . .

"Revolution, Mr. Brown . . ."

This could be the first trumpet, might as well be the last . . .

"You mean political revolution?"

Cause every lickle t'ing . . .

"Yes, Mr. Brown."

"My God, my good man. I think somebody should get your address and put you in a museum. You're a relic, man. Don't tell me, sir, but are you a Marxist?"

Open your eyes . . .

"Yes, Mr. Brown. Revolution is what we need. We want

to nationalize everything, Mr. Brown. And we execute all corrupt officials . . . and t'iefs and robbers must be whipped in public."

Woe to the downpressors . . .

"My friend, I am afraid you're mad. You must have fallen asleep twenty years ago, man. Manley is not Prime Minister again, you know, fellow? The Berlin Wall is history."

Let's get together and feel alright!

"Yes, an' damn fool people like you will burn too. Yes. You t'ink I don't know how much coffee land you own up in dem hills? You t'ink the people don't know what a capitalist exploiter . . ."

Exodus!

"Sorry, got to go. Next. People's Voice, what's on your mind?"

Exodus!

"Mr. Brown?"

Yeah, yeah, yeah!

"Yes, ma'am, you are on the air."

Rule equality . . .

"Mr. Brown, I believe is oral sex killing our nation today . . ."

Set, set, set, set, set!

The voices come in and out. His mind catches a phrase and follows its meandering way into chaos, then everything slips away. The music blankets him, and he wakes to the sound of voices, the litany of blood, the litany of corruption, the litany of scandal, the litany of fear.

When he opens his eyes he is on the stage, sees the silver glare of the lights above him. He sees the fluttering of the canvas cover that is stretched over the stage, sees the labyrinth of scaffolding, sees two white boys dangling from the scaffolding, staring down at him in shock, then he sees Melanie's face. He sees the fear in her eyes. Then he closes his eyes again as he feels them lifting him.

Someone was arguing with his woman, Melanie, the American woman, the one who left him. She used to be Rhea. But Rhea does not have her swampy, low-country Southern accent. This is Melanie. This is the woman who wrapped herself around him in their small bed, the woman he screamed at, told her she was so typically Yankee, so bloody self-righteous, and no different from the pigs from that country. The woman whose face crumbled with sadness at the flash of his words, at the fact that there was no way he could take them back. This is the woman who left him. Packed her bags and left him. The one who, when he asked her, "Are you going to leave me here to die?" had said, "You would be happier dead. You know that." And she had left with that. Left on a plane and gone far away.

She laughs and throws herself against him, embraces him, touches him like she has not touched him in a long time. All around them, people are leaving. They are going away from them—going away from the dream. She is laughing and asking him if he wants something to drink, some iced tea or lemonade; offers him rum in a white and blue enamel cup. She asks him if he has taken his medication. She asks him if he needs a bath—a warm bath to cleanse his soul. He has dreamt this before. He can tell that he's going to keep dreaming this as long as no one comes for him, comes to rescue him.

14.

He wakes to find himself where he has always been, in his apartment in Ensom City, sweating and frightened by the dream. Yet the dream is not complete. It is never complete. These vivid snippets are all he can remember—the laughter, the feel of her body against his, the sense that she is somewhere waiting, the heavy ganja-tinged presence of the roots man in his skin, and the hurtling departures of all the people he knows.

15.

No one comes to rescue him. Time is no longer clear. Perhaps days have passed. Perhaps some hours, but long enough for the room to smell like a tomb—a tomb with a freshly buried body. The rot is thick in his nostrils. He wants to fly. He wants to fly so much. But he is anchored. The anchor holds him in the room, in the heat, in the smell of his body decaying.

But he does manage to climb through the thick citrus grove, long neglected and cluttered with intense brush and the tangle of twigs and limbs from the prickly trees. As he walks, he makes a song for the names of home in his head. The heat is steady, though a soft breeze dances around him. He breathes. He keeps wiping the sweat from his hand, switching the brown paper bag from one hand to the other. He tastes the salt dripping from his moustache into his mouth.

He finds her sitting beneath a flowering poui tree at the far end of the pimento barbecue. The wash of orange light from the fading sun and the spread of petals on the floor

around her make her white dress golden, tender, and grace-
ful. Her face is lined with the markings of her years—her
cheeks sharp, her lips still full but wrinkled. Her head is ban-
dannaed and her white scarf moves with the leaves' shadows.
Her feet are bare, resting on the soft petals.

But he knows it is she. Years later, beyond forty, beyond
fifty. He has lived to see her and he recognizes her.

He catches her eyes. They brighten. He waves and lifts
the bag up to her. The brown bag weighted with his offering.

The last fifty yards fill his head with the pounding of
blood, the wheeze of his chest, the grunt of each effort to
move, to reach her.

He feels love seeing her there, feels tenderness for the
woman who smiles at him. When she speaks, the rich
earthiness of piedmont soil falls from her lips. Her voice
carries him to swamps that seem to belong to another
country—somewhere hot and dense, somewhere gummy
with its humidity. The trees there are alien things,
grotesque, bearded, dark green trees that give off smells as
intoxicating as liquor.

He lays the bag in her lap, and she opens it while looking at him.

"Are you taking medication?" she asks, or seems to ask,
but it is like wind. The voice does not stay long. It leaves her
face, and her mouth does not move. She is smiling a simple
closed-lip smile as the voice fades.

"You sure you alright?" the voice says.

He can see a tangerine-colored face looking back at him,
but that too fades. Then it is Melanie sitting there patiently,
her stomach distended, her dark mahogany arms roped with

muscles, her hair dangling in long tight braids down her face, and her eyes glowing with recognition—those black eyes, those deep black eyes.

She bends over the bag and opens it slowly. Her hand reaches in and extracts the damp balls of rolled tamarind flesh spotted with the sparkle of brown sugar. She nibbles the fruit with her lips and holds her body as the flare shivers through her. She holds the sticky fruit out to him and he bites into the gummy flesh, the crunch of sugar against his teeth.

The music keeps coming back to him through the haze. What he wants is the woman who has left him. And maybe this is what love means: the capacity to imagine love far into the future. An impossible place where the paths are not charted and are cluttered with prickly bramble.

"It is my birthday," he says to her.

"How old are you, baby?" she asks.

"Forty," he says.

"Forty? But you died at thirty-six." She is sucking the tamarind balls.

"No, I didn't," he says. "I . . ."

He cannot speak anymore. The music fills the room and then suddenly stops.

He wakes to hear the tape player clicking. The tape has stuck. He is forty. He is not thirty-six.

He reaches to touch her. She is not there. She has gone.

He sits up and stares at the walls—the newspapers. He feels the dust under his feet. He is not dead. He is forty. It occurs to him that were he to stand, were he to walk to the door, were he to step into the streets, were he to travel the miles, he would come to this swampland and find something like love. And he will find a new name, and perhaps he will work out another dream, another legend of love. It comes to him quietly like a memory.

He stands.

The room spins slowly. He takes a step forward and feels the lurching of his insides. The tape clicks on, the sound growing louder until it fills the room with its echoing.

ABOUT THE CONTRIBUTORS

ALWIN BULLY began writing poetry, plays, and short stories in his homeland of Dominica, the Nature Island of the Caribbean. He is a graphic artist, set and costume designer, theater director, and composer. A graduate of the University of the West Indies, he now lives in Kingston, Jamaica, where he manages the UNESCO regional program for culture. He is a student in the Calabash Writer's Workshop.

COLIN CHANNER is an assistant professor of English and the Coordinator of the Creative Writing Program at Medgar Evers College in Brooklyn, New York. He is the author of two novels, a novella, and a collection of stories. His first novel, *Waiting in Vain* (One World/Ballantine), was selected as a 1998 Critic's Choice by the *Washington Post Book World.* His most recent work is the story collection *Passing Through* (One World/Ballantine, 2004), which Junot Díaz described as "a splendid collection by one of the Caribbean Diaspora's finest writers." Channer is the Houston International Festival's first Artistic Director for Literature and the Founder and Artistic Director of the Calabash International Literacy Festival Trust. For more info visit colinchanner.com.

KWAME DAWES is an award-winning Ghanian-born Jamaican author of twenty books of poetry, plays, nonfiction, and fiction. He teaches at the University of South Carolina, where he is Distinguished Poet in Residence and Director of both the USC Arts Institute and the South

Carolina Poetry Initiative. Dawes is the programmer for the Calabash International Literary Festival.

MARLON JAMES was born in Kingston, Jamaica in 1970. He graduated from the University of the West Indies in 1991 with a degree in Literature. His debut novel, *John Crow's Devil,* was an Editor's Choice in the *New York Times Book Review* and a finalist for both the Commonwealth Writers' Prize and the *Los Angeles Times* Book Prize. He lives in Kingston.

KAYLIE JONES was born in Paris, France. She is the author of five novels, including *Speak Now, Celeste Ascending,* and *A Soldier's Daughter Never Cries*, which was released as a Merchant Ivory film in 1998. Jones has been a Writer in Residence in the New York City public schools through Teachers & Writers Collaborative. She teaches at Wilkes University's Masters Program in Professional Writing, and chairs the $10,000 James Jones Literary Society First Novel Fellowship. She has led Calabash Writer's Workshops, and she read from her own work at the Calabash Literary Festival in 2004. Jones lives in New York City with her husband and daughter. "The Anger Meridian" is an excerpt from her next novel.

KONRAD KIRLEW was born in the parish of Trelawny in Jamaica, and lived in the United States for twenty-five years. He now resides and practices radiology in Montego Bay, Jamaica. He was a student in the first Calabash Fiction Workshop.

SHARON LEACH was born in Kingston, Jamaica, where she lives and works as a columnist and freelance feature writer for the *Jamaica Observer*. She has been anthologized in *Kunapipi,* the *Journal of Postcolonial Writing,* the *Jamaica Journal,* and *Blue Latitudes: An Anthology of Caribbean Women Fiction Writers.* Her essays have also appeared in Air Jamaica's *Skywritings* magazine and the *Caribbean Voice* newspaper. She was one of the first beneficiaries of a scholarship to the Calabash Writer's Workshop in 2003.

ELIZABETH NUNEZ was born in Trinidad. She is the author of six novels, including *Prospero's Daughter, Grace,* and *Bruised Hibiscus;* and is the coeditor, along with Jennifer Sparrow, of *Stories from Blue Latitudes: Caribbean Women Writers at Home and Abroad.* A former fellow at the Yaddo and MacDowell writers' colonies, and cofounder of the National Black Writers Conference, she is the Executive Producer of the PBS television series *Black Writers in America.* Ms. Nunez has led Calabash Writer's Workshops, and she performed her own work at the Calabash Literary Festival in 2002.

GEOFFREY PHILP, author of the novel, *Benjamin, My Son,* was born in Kingston, Jamaica and has worked with the Calabash Literary Festival since its inception conducting poetry workshops. His poems and short stories have appeared in *Small Axe, The Oxford Book of Caribbean Short Stories,* and *The Oxford Book of Caribbean Verse.* He lives in Miami, Florida.

A-DZIKO SIMBA is an award-winning poet and short story writer whose work has appeared in a number of anthologies. Born in England to a Jamaican mother and Nigerian father, she has lived in the Caribbean since 1992 and currently resides in St. Mary, Jamaica. She was a student in the first Calabash Writer's Workshop, and performed poetry at the Calabash Literary Festival in 2003.

RUDOLPH WALLACE studied Economics at the University of the West Indies and earned an MBA from the University of Toronto. He has written for radio, television, and the Jamaican theater for over twenty-five years. His stories have won gold and silver medals in the annual Creative Writing Competition sponsored by the Jamaica Cultural Development Commission. He was awarded a scholarship to the Calabash Writer's Workshop in 2002, and was a featured author at Calabash Literary Festival in 2004.

Also from AKASHIC BOOKS

JOHN CROW'S DEVIL by Marlon James
232 pages, hardcover, $19.95

"A powerful first novel . . . Writing with assurance and control, James uses his small-town drama to suggest the larger anguish of a postcolonial Jamaican society struggling for its own identity."
—*New York Times*

"*Pile them up,* a Marlon James character says repeatedly and Marlon does just that. Pile them up: language, imagery, technique, imagination. All fresh, all exciting. This is a good book and a writer to watch out for."
—Chris Abani

SPEAK NOW by Kaylie Jones
300 pages, trade paperback, $14.95

"Perceptive, gritty, and compelling, this is an absorbing book that dives headfirst into issues facing recovering addicts . . . Beautifully written and richly detailed, it is highly recommended."
—*Library Journal*

BECOMING ABIGAIL by Chris Abani
128 pages, trade paperback, $11.95

"Compelling and gorgeously written, this is a coming-of-age novella like no other. Chris Abani explores the depths of loss and exploitation with what can only be described as a knowing tenderness. An extraordinary, necessary book."
—Cristina Garcia, author of *Dreaming in Cuban*